Looking for
Mary Gabriel

CAROLE LAWRENCE

Looking for

Mary

Gabriel

THOMAS DUNNE BOOKS
ST. MARTIN'S PRESS
✠ NEW YORK

THOMAS DUNNE BOOKS.
An imprint of St. Martin's Press.

Design by Kathryn Parise

A chapter of this novel originally appeared in the *Warren Wilson Review*,
Spring 1990.

The lyrics from *H.M.S. Pinafore* by Gilbert and Sullivan are used by kind
permission of the D'Oyly Carte Opera Company.

ISBN 0-312-28541-8

Printed in the U.S.A.

For Bob, who altered my fate,
and in memory of ML

Acknowledgments

I would like to thank the Vermont Studio Center for a fellowship that provided time and a place to work on the early chapters of this novel; Steven Rosenblatt, M.D., and J. Taylor Rooks, attorney-at-law, for answering my questions concerning their respective professions; Alan Rinzler, who provided valuable editorial assistance; and Stephen Parham, Ph.D., who listened. Thanks to Anne G. Shirley for reading and commenting on the early manuscript and to Ursula B. Carmena for sharing her childhood memories and her knowledge of Catholic traditions. My agent Linda Allen's belief in me and her work on my behalf have earned my utmost gratitude, and I am grateful, also, to my editor, Marcia Markland, for her guidance. My husband, Bob, and our son, Will, both gave me their ideas and unfailing support.

The Louisiana State Capitol Building is twenty-seven stories tall. The thirty-fifth floor exists only in my imagination, as do any publications and employees I have attributed to the State Department of Agriculture. I have borrowed some of the streets of Baton Rouge, but the houses and the characters who inhabit them are my own invention. While I have received advice and information from many people, all errors of fact are my own.

Looking for Mary Gabriel

O spare me, that I may recover strength, before I go hence, and be no more.

—PSALMS 39:13

Chapter One

October 1995

The pamphlet was called "Oranges." It was small and slender, no bigger than a prayer book. I had designed it to fit in a shirt pocket or to be carried comfortably in the palm of the hand. The cover was a glossy photograph of a pair of plump oranges, vivid against a dark background of intensely glowing green leaves. The fifty pages within contained a brief history of the fruit, guidelines for its cultivation by home gardeners, and several dozen recipes. The printer had just delivered nineteen boxes of them; I was holding one when the telephone rang.

"May I speak to Bonita Jane Gabriel?" an unfamiliar male voice said.

I hadn't gone by my first name in years. Hearing it again was an unpleasant surprise. "Who's calling, please?"

From my office window in Baton Rouge, on the thirty-fifth floor of the Louisiana State Capitol, built on the bank above the Mississippi River, I watched a matchbox freighter heading out for the Gulf down the playlike river. I loved my view: ribbon roads, doll people, with me high, high above it.

"My name is Dr. Steven Scott. I'm trying to locate the elder daughter of Dr. John Edward Gabriel. Are you Bonita Gabriel?"

I held so hard to the new booklet that it curved in my hand. "Yes," I said.

"This is the East Baton Rouge Parish coroner's office," the man said. "Do you know how long I've been looking for you?"

"Why?" I said. "Why are you looking for me?" He sounded young. He sounded pissed off and very young.

"Your father died Friday morning," he said. "I know it was right before the weekend, and that makes a big difference, but I have been trying to reach a member of the family for over seventy-two hours." He paused, then said, "Do you know what day it is?"

There was a brief silence. He answered himself before I could gather my wits to even recall what month we occupied, much less what day it was. "This is Tuesday afternoon."

I let "Oranges" fall to my desk, felt behind me for my chair, and sank down onto it.

"A neighbor of your father's, a Mrs. Moak, the one who found him and called the ambulance when he fell, told us—"

"He fell?"

"Yes, ma'am."

"Where was he?"

"He was at home. He fell down the back steps of his home and died of head injuries several hours later at Our Lady of the Lake Hospital," Dr. Scott said. "No one knew where you were. Mrs. Moak thought you might be in New Orleans, or maybe in Shreveport, but I couldn't find you listed in either place. I couldn't find you in any telephone book in the state, and directory assistance never heard of you."

"I don't have a telephone at home," I said.

"So I found out," he said. "And then I couldn't find out anything from the Department of Public Safety because you don't even own a car."

I owned a car, but not under any name he was likely to find. I waited. I heard papers rustling.

"You have a sister," he said finally. "Mary Dollier Gabriel." He spoke slowly, pausing between each of Mary's names. His voice faded and returned, as if he had leaned away from the telephone to look down and read from his notes and then come back. "Mary Gabriel is five years your junior? That would make her approximately forty-seven?"

I closed my eyes.

"Is that correct?" he said.

"Yes, that's correct," I said.

"I finally located her at an institution in Livingston Parish, but the nurse in charge wasn't very helpful. She wouldn't let me speak to your sister. She said she had no intention of letting me upset one of her babies with bad news. She was very unhappy about the fact that no one knew where you were," he said. "She said I should get busy and find you. I hate to think what she's going to say when she finds out you've been right under our noses all the time. She said . . ." Here his voice died away.

"Yes," I said. "What else did she say?"

Dr. Scott cleared his throat. "She said . . . these words are not coming from me, now," he said. "I want you to understand that."

"I understand," I said.

"She said, and I quote, 'You track down Mary's big sister and put this monkey on her back. It's high time she got her . . .'" He stopped, then tried again. " 'It's high time she got her . . .'"

I touched each corner of the booklet to my desk.

His impatience was gone and his voice was softer when he continued. "The nurse said, 'It's high time she got herself out here.'"

It was my guess that those were not her exact words. I tossed "Oranges" back into the open cardboard box.

"Ma'am?" the young man said. "Are you still there?"

"Yes, I'm still here," I said.

"Would it be less painful for you, Ms. Gabriel, if I discussed these things with someone else? A colleague, perhaps? Is there someone you trust that I could talk to while you recover from the shock of this news?"

"Of course not," I said. "I am fine. I have no problem with this information."

I thought, as I waited for him to respond, that yes, my life in the Department of Agriculture was in perfect order: I never drew attention to myself; my clothing at work was understated and impeccable; I participated in no interoffice quarrels; I was never absent; I scheduled my vacation a year in advance, always went alone, and never brought back souvenirs or passed around pictures. I had created a life for myself in which I was as close to being invisible as I could get without totally disappearing, and I intended it to stay that way.

"As you wish," Dr. Scott said. "I had to enter the house and go through your father's things. I apologize to you for that, Ms. Gabriel. When I talked to the police about finding you, one of the officers, Captain Gerard Winborn, volunteered to go in with me. He said he knew you. He said you were childhood friends. He can verify that I left everything just like it was."

"How did you find me?" I asked.

"After we came across all of those fruit books written by Jane Mitchell and put out by the Department of Agriculture, we called their office. They gave us your extension," Dr. Scott said.

I stood up. "My father had those pamphlets?" I said.

"Yes, ma'am," he said. "They were in a folder with the name 'Bonita Gabriel' on it, so I just made a guess that you wrote them under a pseudonym."

Jane Mitchell was not a pen name; it was my legal name. I dropped Bonita when I married Leon Mitchell, a peach farmer from Lincoln Parish, in 1966. The marriage was brief; it lasted just long enough for me to rid myself of the name Gabriel. But I said nothing of this to Dr. Scott.

"I found four of them in his desk," Dr. Scott said.

"Oranges" was the newest one. "Persimmons," "Strawberries," "Peaches," "Figs," and "Blackberries" stood on my desk between two terra-cotta bookends in the shape of the state of Louisiana; bookends I had made in occupational therapy at a hospital in New Orleans, which, forty-one years ago, had been run by the Sisters of Saint Vincent de Paul.

"They're real pretty little books," he said. "I enjoyed looking at them. If you ever do another one, I wouldn't mind having a copy, if it's not too much trouble."

"Thank you very much," I said. "The new ones just came in. I'll see that you get one. I'm so glad you liked them."

At this absurdity, as if we had met in a bar and he had praised my jewelry—rhinestone earrings that danced as they dangled or a sterling silver bracelet that glinted in the tavern's faint, false light—we both fell silent.

Finally I said, "What should I do?"

"Okay," Dr. Scott said. He sounded relieved to have somebody to boss. "What you'll need to do is this—you might want to write this down."

Dutifully, I took a pen and pad from my desk drawer.

"The first thing is to get in touch with one of the funeral homes," he said.

I wrote a number one on the pad, but as the young man spoke, my attention fluttered away and lit on an image of my father lying crumpled at the base of the steps. I called my thoughts back; wrote, "Contact funeral parlor."

"You should make an appointment with the director to discuss plans for the funeral."

I wrote a number two. I imagined my father lying naked on a metal table next to the young doctor, so close the young man could have smoothed my father's fair hair or stroked his cheek.

"If you'll tell me which funeral home you want to use, I will be happy to get in touch with the administrator for you," he said.

"Choose a reputable one for me, if you would, please. Any of the mortuaries you have had experience with and trust to handle my father's body will do," I said. "Except for Wellman's. I don't want to go to Wellman's."

I did not want to go back to the place that had conducted the services for my mother thirty years ago. If I had to bury my father, I would do it in a place I had never been before. I couldn't take all of those sweet flowers again. And I definitely didn't want a chapel full of mourners staring at Mary and me.

As I talked, I reached for one of the state-shaped bookends. Absently, I ran my fingers over the baked clay, seeking the roughness of the red crystal bead I had used to signify Baton Rouge, the city of my birth. When I was eleven years old, almost twelve, Daddy came to New Orleans to visit me in DePaul Hospital. My mother could not come, he said, because she had to stay with my sister, but she sent me her red crystal bracelet. The next day, in the little craft house under the oaks, behind the building called Rosary where I stayed, after I punched and pounded and formed the wet clay, I broke my mother's gift, mashed a piece of the faceted glass into each bookend to mark Baton Rouge, watched the clay go into the kiln, and then, accompanied by a nun on my daily walk to the levee, I threw the rest of the bracelet into the Mississippi River. Now I felt only a small hollow where the bead should have been. Catching the receiver between my head and shoulder, I felt all about the surface of my desk with both hands.

"I'll need you to release—"

"Hold on for a minute, please." I left the receiver dangling. I lifted "Strawberries" by a corner of the cover and shook it. When nothing dropped out, I pitched it to the floor. I did this with each booklet. Nothing. I retrieved "Oranges" from its box and shook it, finding that it, too, was empty, I threw it to the floor with the others. I brushed aside all of the papers on my desk and ran both hands over the entire surface. My heart raced. The sudden, furious rush of blood to my head dizzied me. With the litter from my desk all about me, I sank down onto the floor and covered my head with my arms.

"Ma'am? Ma'am?" The coroner's tiny voice sputtered from the telephone.

It took some seconds, but when I lifted the receiver again, I was calm.

"Ms. Gabriel, are you all right?"

"Yes," I said, and I gave Dr. Scott my permission to release my father's body to the funeral home of his choice. He said he would call me back.

I took off my silver snakeskin high heels and removed the jacket of my gunmetal-gray linen suit. On my hands and knees, careless of my smoke-colored stockings, I pushed the chair aside to crawl into the hollow of my desk and search along the baseboard for the missing blood-colored crystal. I had not found it when the telephone rang again. Still on my hands and knees, I backed out from under my desk, reached up, and lifted the receiver. "Yes?" I said.

"Ms. Gabriel, I made an appointment for you at Singleton and Son's funeral home, at two o'clock tomorrow afternoon. It's on Florida Boulevard, just past Airline Highway, on the left-hand side of the street."

"Thank you very much," I said.

"There is one other thing you'll need to do right away," he said.

"What is that?" I said.

"Mr. Singleton suggested that you write a brief notice of your father's death for the newspaper. This should include a few details about his life—where he was born, his age—things like that. Then you might name his remaining relatives."

"There are no remaining relatives," I said. "Only my sister and me."

"Say that, then, and give the times for both the viewing of the body and the funeral service," he said. "Mr. Singleton will help you with that and submit it to the *Advocate* for you, if you'll call him before five o'clock."

"I see no reason to make all of this public," I said. No one at work knew I had grown up in Baton Rouge. They knew me only by my changed name. Nor did they know I had a sister. I could not bear to think of our lives coming under public scrutiny again.

"Surely you and your sister know people who will want to pay their respects. And your father's friends need to be told of his death."

I cared nothing for his friends. And Mary and I—I could not permit myself to think about that yet. Aloud, I said, "Of course. Thank you for your help, Dr. Scott. You've been very kind. And patient."

"Ms. Gabriel," the man said, his tone grave. He sounded older now and more confident. "May I offer you a bit of advice?"

"Yes," I said. "You may."

"Call someone to come and stay with you. Maybe a friend could drive you home. You can expect to be somewhat distracted. Grief will make events seem magnified, even distorted, for a while. It's helpful to have someone with you who is not quite so affected by your father's death."

"Dr. Scott, my father and I have not been close for a long time. I don't think grief is going to be a big problem for me," I said.

"Perhaps not, Ms. Gabriel. But grief can surprise us. Sometimes it's on us and we don't even recognize it. I'd feel better if I knew you had someone to go through this with you. Surely there's someone you can call?"

"No. No one," I said, abruptly.

"Then forgive me for intruding," Dr. Scott said. "This is really none of my business."

I thought, No, it's not one bit of your business. It concerns you not at all, but I said only, "I appreciate your professional interest."

"Please accept my condolences on your loss," Dr. Scott said. He sounded stiff now. Distant.

"Thank you," I said as coldly as I could. I was returning the receiver to its cradle on my desk when I had to abandon my dignity. I cried, "Wait!"

"What is it?" Dr. Scott said. He, too, had dropped his formal manner. He sounded alarmed.

"Where is she?"

"What?"

"Where is Mary? Where is my sister?"

Chapter Two

August 1953

Forty-two years earlier, when Bonita was ten years old, her sister, Mary, only five, and their parents young and still happy, they all lived together in an old house on Oleander Avenue. The Gabriel house had been in the country when Bonita's grandfather built it early in the century, but Baton Rouge had crept up on it. The fields surrounding the house were divided into lots and houses built, streets cut, sidewalks poured. The names of the old roads were thrown away and all of the new streets unwittingly named for poisonous flowers.

Near dusk in late summer the children of Oleander Avenue were waiting for the night watchman in the Gabriels' front yard. They had seen him for the first time early in the summer as they played statues just before nightfall. That night a car drove slowly along their street, a black Plymouth whose doors bore a silver badge in the center of a white oval. Circling this symbol, stenciled in silver, were the words CAPITOL SECURITY. The driver had a thin face, and he wore a hat of the same design that the children's fathers wore to church on Sunday or to work on Third Street. But this hat was tipped forward. Their fathers wore their hats straight on their heads. The man in the car had on a khaki shirt with the sleeves rolled. In the fading light, an unlit cigarette made a bleached gash in his mouth.

The game of statues was under way. Except for Mary, the children had all been thrown and frozen. When the strange car appeared, they watched it, sliding their eyes from right to left in their rigid faces. Bonita saw the man turn his head and look at them. She knew what he saw: a shadowy yard full of children with pale, outstretched limbs.

Bonita, who had been hurled in the game all the way to the neutral ground, a grassy patch between the sidewalk and the street, took the full brunt of his gaze. She had been frozen with her right arm flung out above her forehead as if to make a sighting in the sky, and stood on one bare foot with the other extended behind her. The man slowed the car until it seemed to hover next to her. Transfixed, Bonita looked and looked into his pale eyes.

Mary, a milky smudge in her white playsuit, ran in front of Bonita, and the car picked up speed as it moved away. When it reached the corner, the children broke their studied shapes and ran in one body to the end of the street to watch the car go out of sight. There they whirled and twirled and leaped into the air.

All through the summer they waited for their protector every night, would not go inside when called until they had seen him. And every night, after they witnessed his arrival, the children ran to the corner, danced up and down and called out to the starry night sky.

One warm August evening, they played hide-and-seek while they waited. Bonita was It, and she had tagged Gracie Davis, Adrienne Fish, Frankie St. Germain, and Adam Moak; she had found everyone but Mary. Before Bonita could behold the appearance of the watchman, she had to find her sister.

"There she goes," Adam said as they saw a flash of white behind the persimmon tree.

In the backyard, Mary disappeared under the house. Bonita knelt on the grass next to the steep back steps and peered into the shadows. "Maaaaa-ry," she called.

The Gabriel house was raised to get the breeze and to escape rising water when Ward's Creek overflowed. It stood on square redbrick columns almost five feet tall. Until Bonita was six, she could stand under the house, but now that she was ten and tall, she had to get on her hands and knees to go under it. Adam knelt beside her.

It was the day after Mary's fifth birthday party, and she had not calmed down from it. Except for a few cries and calls and a language of her own invention, Mary never spoke. She had begun to use words at a normal age but, after a few months, abandoned speech. The Gabriel family was waiting for Mary to speak again, though it had been almost three years.

"I'm going around front to watch out for him," Adam said, already fidgety and impatient.

Bonita called and called until she realized she would have to go into the dark under the house and get Mary.

Bonita crawled along the lumpy dirt until she got to the pipes that came down from the kitchen sink. She heard water gurgling down, heard her mother and father thumping about. Bonita leaned forward, straining for a glimpse of light from her sister's white playsuit. "I want you to stay under here until it gets good and dark, Mary," she said. The air smelled of mildew and of water trapped in wood. "I don't care if you stay here all night!" None of these fibs drew Mary out; she remained hidden beneath the house.

A large black cockroach scuttled across Bonita's right hand. She shook it off and tried to stand. Her head hit the beams. She sank down on the moist dirt, which dampened her white shorts and bare legs, and rubbed her scalp. "This isn't fun, Mary. I'm scared of what might be under here."

Bonita heard Mary giggle and saw something move near the floor furnace under the center of the house, the area of deepest shadow.

The tin shell that enclosed the heater rippled. Gravel pinged against its sides. A small shape silhouetted against the remains of the evening light scurried away. In the darkness beneath the concrete steps that went up to the front porch, white highlights from Mary's playsuit twinkled. Bonita plunged into the shadows.

Rocks mixed into the dirt scratched her knees. Chunks of crumbling mortar, broken away from the old brick columns, bruised her hands. Cobwebs, unseen until their gray nets snared her face, clung to her mouth and eyes. Bonita fell forward. A sound between a gasp and a cry bubbled up out of her mouth. She panicked. Her impulse was to flail about, but she was unable to move. Her face was flat against the ground. The thought came to her that she was going to suffocate beneath her own house.

Adam stuck his head under the front of the house. "Mary's out! She's getting away!"

Bonita tried to lift her head.

Adam's shrill voice came again. "He's coming, Bonita!"

With all her strength, Bonita pulled her head up.

"He's here, Bonita!" Adam cried.

As if his words were light, Bonita scrambled toward them and broke out into the gloaming. Trembling, she stood up. She wiped her mouth with her fingers, brushed the gravel from her knees and the seat of her pants. Stars she had not yet seen that evening had appeared in the inky sky. Bonita threw back her head and, turning, turning, looked up in wonder at every glittering star.

"Here he is!" Adam cried.

The black car came slowly down the street. In the pair of white beams that shot out from it, Bonita saw Mary fleeing around the corner, out of sight. Bonita ran along the sidewalk after her. The headlights of the car bounced along the street beside her, picking out sheeny spots on the asphalt. Briefly, the car was next to her, and then it pulled over and stopped. The lights made a silver cloud of the mimosa that bloomed in the St. Germains' front yard.

Bonita ceased running. The man got out of the car. He took the cigarette from his mouth with his right thumb and forefinger and turned it into the shelter of his hand so that it became invisible. "Who's that you're chasing down?" he said.

"My little sister, Mary." Bonita pointed past his car. "She ran off around that corner."

"Jump in," the man said. "We'll catch up with her." He stuck the unlit cigarette into his mouth and got back into the car.

Bonita did as she was told. The chrome handle of the car door was cool to her touch. She felt it on her palm for a long time. Inside, she pulled the door closed with both hands. In the brief time that the overhead light illuminated the inside of the car, she saw that the gray interior was completely bare, the floor mats clean, and not one gum wrapper, cigarette pack, or crumpled tissue gave any clue to the kind of person who drove it. As the man slammed his door and leaned forward to turn the ignition key, Bonita saw the glinting circle of one half of a pair of metal handcuffs hanging from his back pocket.

Bonita sat up close to the dashboard, peering out. At the corner the security guard stopped, looked to her. Bonita pointed left. "That way," she said.

He turned, and they watched the sidewalks on each side of the street. Sometimes fat shrubs blocked their view, and Bonita looked backward at them as they passed, searching for telltale glimmers from Mary's clothing.

"If we don't catch her, she might get kidnapped," Bonita said.

The man looked at her. "Is that so?"

Solemn, Bonita nodded.

When they reached the alley that ran behind the houses, Bonita said, "She might have taken off through there." As the man made the turn into the narrow, pitch-dark passage, they both saw Mary's bobbing blond head. Mary looked behind her into the headlights and veered off into a nearby backyard.

The man stopped the car. He leaned over toward Bonita in the dark. She shrank away into the seat. "I've got to get in there," he said, reaching over to pop open the glove compartment. When the door sprang down, a bulb flashed on, and after he removed a long-handled flashlight, she could see, resting in the white light, a black revolver.

Bonita made a deep-throated humming that resembled the sound a person might make on sitting down to a table before a bowl of steaming soup and a loaf of warm brown bread. "You have a gun."

The man glanced at her as he slammed the compartment shut, but said nothing. "Come on," he said.

Bonita got down out of the car. The rough gravel in the alley hurt her bare feet, so she carefully picked her way on tiptoe behind him as he strode forward, flashing the light between the garbage cans and into the yards of the houses. "There she goes," he said. "Wait here."

Bonita watched him catch Mary in the beam. Mary climbed onto the wooden gate of a white picket fence. "No!" the watchman said. Unhurried but intent, he moved toward Mary. "Come here," he said. He put out his hand. Bonita watched, astonished, as her sister came down from the gate and surrendered to him, let herself be lifted to his shoulders, laughed out loud as he walked back with her: Mary, who permitted no one to touch her, who screamed when her clothes had to be changed. Bonita held out her arms to take her as they approached.

"No," Mary said. She put her hands together and laid them over her eyes, peering at Bonita through laced fingers as she bounced past. "No," she said. "No, no, no, no, no."

Bonita's astonishment increased as Mary spoke. It was a recognizable word!

The man opened the car door, deposited Mary on the backseat, and closed her in. Bonita crawled up onto the front seat but continued to steal incredulous looks at her sister, who calmly smiled at her.

"We've been waiting for that a long time," Bonita said.

"Waiting for what?" the man said.

"Waiting for Mary to talk again so somebody could understand her. Mostly she just jabbers," Bonita said.

The man looked sideways at her. "Is that a fact?"

Bonita nodded.

"How about them apples?" he said.

Bonita giggled.

When they stopped in front of the Gabriel house, Bonita got out and opened the door for Mary. She tried to take Mary's hand. "No," Mary said and pulled away. Bonita took hold of Mary by the crossed white straps on the back of her playsuit. "Wait right here," Bonita said to the man. "I'll be back."

Bonita pulled Mary along, dragged her up the steep steps and into the house.

"Mimi! Mimi!" Bonita cried.

In moments of great excitement, Bonita still called her mother Mimi. When Lottie had been a senior at Sophie Newcomb College, she sang the role of Mimi in a student production of *La Bohème*. John Gabriel, a New Orleans medical student in the audience, fell in love and arranged a meeting before Lottie left to study voice at Juilliard. Within a year, she yielded to his repeated proposals and returned to marry him. "Your mother could have had fortune, fame, and glory," Bonita's father was fond of saying. "But I took her away from all of that."

Until Mary was born, Lottie sang Mimi's great aria so often that "Mimi" was the first word Bonita ever spoke. She thought it was her mother's name. Once, when Bonita was barely three, her parents took her with them to a performance of *La Bohème* in New Orleans, and the manager stopped them as they were about to take their seats. He said crossly, "Is this child going to disturb everyone with her crying?" To which Dr. Gabriel replied—and this was the part Bonita loved best—"Only when Mimi dies."

But everything changed after Mary was born. Lottie's voice was silenced. Bonita and Lottie no longer sang and danced about the house all day as they dusted the furniture and folded the clothes. The most painful change for Bonita came when Mary started to talk and then stopped: Bonita was told by her father then that she was no longer to call Lottie "Mimi." It was confusing to Mary, he said. Bonita was to call Lottie "Mother" instead.

"Mary talked!" Bonita leaned into the swinging door between the kitchen and the dining room until it opened, and pulled Mary around in front of her as she turned so that they were both facing their parents, John and Lottie, who sat at one crescent of the big round mahogany table playing honeymoon bridge.

Their mother looked up. "What did you say, sweetheart?" Lottie wore a soft black and white cotton sundress. A pair of white sandals lay on the floor beneath her chair. Lottie's feet were perfectly formed and looked best bare. All of her limbs were long, slender, and tanned. Her fingernails and toenails were short and rounded and painted the same shade of red she wore on her lips. Without looking up from the card her husband had just placed on the table, Lottie absently lifted the dark curls from the back of her head. "Come help me, Bonita," she said. "You're so good at cards." A bracelet of red crystal beads fell forward on Lottie's wrist as she fanned the back of her neck with her bridge hand, thinking.

Bonita's father moved his fingers back and forth over the faint stubble on his chin as he watched his wife. John Gabriel's hair was fair and wavy. His eyes were a dark, sharp blue. Sometimes, at the end of his long day at work, he went straight to the bathroom to change his shirt and shave a second time. Bonita sensed already that her father loved her mother more than he could easily tolerate.

They were all wild about Lottie. They loved the way she looked and the way she laughed. Even Mary loved her. Bonita was used to watching Mary, and she could read all of Mary's signs. Privately, Bonita thought Mary had stopped talking just to try and get Lottie to notice her more. After Mary was born, Bonita often felt as if Lottie had something else on her mind besides the three of them who loved her so much.

"Mary said a real word! Listen!" Bonita said. She pushed Mary forward. "Do it."

"No!" Mary said and pulled away.

Bonita released her hold on her sister's clothes. Mary marched around the table, slapping the dark, glossy wood with her open palm. "No! No! No! No! No!" She stopped, turned, looked at them, and laughed. "Come here," she said. "Come here."

Bonita saw her own amazement reflected on her parents' faces. They both stood up.

"That's wonderful!" Lottie said. She scooped up Mary, who for the first time didn't yell to be put down. "We knew you could do it!"

John Gabriel put an arm about his wife. He ruffled Mary's blond hair and kissed her cheek. Then he said to Bonita, who still watched from the doorway, "Good work, Bonita! You got your sister to talk! Didn't I tell you, Lottie? All we had to do was wait! I knew she would talk someday."

"How on earth did you accomplish this miracle?" Lottie said.

"I don't know how I did it," Bonita said. She put her hands out palms up and raised her shoulders. "It just happened. That man talked to her when he went and got her, and it just happened."

"What man?" her mother said.

"That man in the car," Bonita said. "The one who rides around. Mary ran off and we had to go catch her."

Lottie turned to her husband. "What man is she talking about, John?" She turned back to look at Bonita and frowned. "You didn't get in the car with a stranger, did you, sweetheart?"

"He's not a stranger," Bonita said. "We see him all the time."

"John, who is she talking about?" Lottie said.

John Gabriel took Mary from Lottie and set her down on the floor. "She's talking about the watchman, Duplantis. The man we hired to patrol the neighborhood early this summer." He put his hand on

Lottie's arm and lowered his voice. "You remember, Lottie," he said. He turned his wife slightly away from their children. "I got Paul Fish and Roland Moak and all the other fellows on the block together here one night last spring, and we decided to sign up for that new security service."

Bonita watched her mother turn her head away and close her eyes. Bonita had learned to guess what her mother felt by the way she moved her hands or the way she pressed her lips together, particularly when it concerned Mary. Now Bonita guessed by the slow way Lottie closed her eyes that her mother did remember that there was a man patrolling their street, but that she really didn't want to think about why. Bonita watched, distressed, as all of the light left Lottie's face.

"How about them apples!" Bonita said.

Lottie turned to look at her. "How about them apples?" she echoed. "Bonita, where in the world did you get that absolutely vulgar expression?" Then she laughed. She laughed and laughed in the old way they all loved, and Bonita was so happy to hear her mother laugh again that she threw her arms up in the air and whirled herself around.

Lottie put her hand on her husband's arm as Mary, let loose, went back to circling the table. "John, did you hear what your daughter just said?"

John Gabriel hugged his wife. "I heard it. I do believe that must have come from your side of the family, my precious. No one in my family ever said a thing like that."

"It did not," Lottie said, laughing as her husband nuzzled her neck.

Bonita turned and raced into the kitchen. She pulled a white wooden chair over to the enameled stove. She climbed up, stood on the seat, felt around with one hand on a shelf, and finally took down a glass jigger that held kitchen matches.

Her mother followed her. "What are you looking for, sweetheart?"

"I need something," Bonita said.

"You know you mustn't play with matches."

"It's not for playing."

Bonita climbed off the chair, ran out the door and down the steps before her mother could stop her.

Outside, the man sat sideways in the front seat of his car with the door open, cleaning his fingernails with a pocketknife. His left leg was extended. His right leg was bent, the heel of his shoe caught on the edge of the open door. He had removed his hat, and the light from the roof of the car poured down on his head. He looked up when Bonita returned, clicked the knife shut and put it in his pocket, jingling the handcuffs as he did so. As he leaned backward, Bonita saw that his name, Orlando Duplantis, was stitched in red script on the pocket of his khaki shirt.

Bonita held out her hand. A red-tipped kitchen match lay in her open palm. "For your cigarette," she said.

The man shook his head. "I never light 'em."

Bonita closed her hand over the match.

"Wait," he said. "What's your name?"

"Bonita Jane Gabriel."

The man reached out and, with the hand that had held the knife, took her closed fist. With his other hand, he lifted her fingers one by one. When he took the match from her hand and his rough fingertips grazed her palm, something between Bonita's narrow hips melted.

"Just in case," he said.

Bonita turned and fled. As she ran, a nursery rhyme flew with her in the dark, a remembered rhyme about someone crying all the way home.

Chapter Three

October 1995

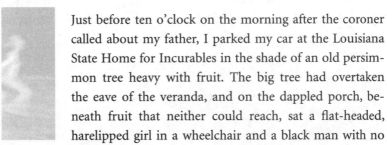 Just before ten o'clock on the morning after the coroner called about my father, I parked my car at the Louisiana State Home for Incurables in the shade of an old persimmon tree heavy with fruit. The big tree had overtaken the eave of the veranda, and on the dappled porch, beneath fruit that neither could reach, sat a flat-headed, harelipped girl in a wheelchair and a black man with no arms and no legs propped between two fluffy white pillows in a wooden rocker. I got out, took off my mink jacket, turned it inside out, folded it, and put it in the trunk. Walking carefully through the persimmons wasting on the ground, I gave the two residents a bright "Hi!" and a counterfeit smile to go with it. They watched me with flat blank eyes as I went by but sat silent beneath the drooping branches.

I shivered. My black silk suit was too light for late October. I switched the bag of presents from my right hand to my left, pulled open the heavy glass door, and entered the building. The walls were lined with patients seated in chairs. Most stared straight ahead, but some watched me come in with excitement. One woman, who was tied into a wheelchair with canvas straps, motioned for me to come over to her and then pointed to her bonds. A man called me "Mama" many times, and another, younger man begged me, "Please! Please, get me a Coke!"

I stood clutching the handles of the bag emblazoned on each side with a picture of a golden cornucopia spilling ears of corn, nuts, and pumpkins onto a background of autumn leaves. I looked in vain for someone with authority. The door to the nurse's station stood open, but there was no one in it. To my left was a long hall. On the right I saw a dining room with tables neatly set for a meal. A curious cry came from the occupant of one of the chairs near that door. At this signal, a young black girl in a white jumpsuit came tearing around the corner of the dining hall and skidded up to me.

"Who you huntin'?" the girl said. Pinned to her shoulder was a black cat with her name, Johnella, written in orange ink across its stomach.

"Do you work here?" I asked.

"Sure do," she said.

"I'm looking for Mary Gabriel. I'm her sister."

"You Bonita?"

I haven't been Bonita for a long time, I thought, but I nodded.

Johnella snapped fingers on both hands. "Lordy, we been wondering if we'd ever lay our eyes on you. Five years! Five years we been waiting to see you."

She stepped back to study me. "Uh-huh," she said, nodding. "I'd a known who you was anywhere. If I had passed you on the street, I'd have stopped you and said, 'Hey, girl! Are you Mary's sister?' You are the spittin' image of your mother. She was some beautiful. But you still look good. You must not love food like I do,'cause you skinny as a rail. What are you? Fifty?"

I gave a little laugh. This woman was making me extremely nervous. "Fifty-two," I said out loud, but I was thinking, If that's any of your damned business.

"Mary keep a picture of her mama and daddy right by her bed, and it turned out just like I thought it would—you look like your mama, and Mary look exactly like her daddy," Johnella said. She pointed to the hall before us. "She down there. Come on, I'll take you."

"Thank you," I said.

"Mary talk about you all the time," Johnella said over her shoulder. "Nobody knew where you was. Where'd they find you?"

I fought the impulse to lie. "I live in Baton Rouge," I said.

Johnella looked at me suspiciously. "How long you been living in Baton Rouge?"

"Awhile," I said.

"Just how long a while?" she said.

"A long while."

"Shit, you been here all the time?" she said. "Why you want to go and do that?"

I shrugged. "Now you can put that monkey on my back," I said. "Now that I got my ass out here." I had meant for the words to come out lightly, but they sounded mean.

"That man tole you I said that?"

"Not exactly," I said.

Johnella laughed. It didn't seem to bother her.

The hall ahead of us was blocked by a large crib occupied by a senseless man curled up in a fetal position. Johnella put both hands on the slats and turned to look at me, her laughter gone. "We're all real sorry about your daddy. He was a nice man. And he was some good to your sister. He bring her stuff all the time: satsumas as soon as they come in season, cigarettes—he give her a carton a week—and clothes. We can't keep Mary in clothes. Fast as he bring them out here, Mary give them all away. And if Mary don't give them away, Aura Lee take 'em and hide 'em in her box."

Johnella pushed the bed against the wall. She put a hand on my forearm. "Mary don't know he gone. We been waitin' for them to find you. We thought you might want to be the one to tell it."

I swallowed, looked away, and nodded. Johnella gave me a pat on the arm before she removed her hand and walked briskly to the door of the last room on the left. "She in here," Johnella said.

My steps slowed. I forced myself to look down the hall where Johnella stood waiting with a hand pressed against a door. I faltered. Johnella came back and placed her hand on my shoulder.

My teeth were clenched. I could feel a muscle in my jaw jumping. I dug my freshly buffed and polished nails into my palms.

"You have a hard time making yourself see Mary, don't you?" Johnella said. "That's why you been hiding out?"

I looked away, unwilling to attempt an answer. The warmth of Johnella's touch made my eyelids heavy. I longed for rest, wished to go down into darkness under that soothing touch, wanted never to wake, never to have to pass over the threshold into Mary's room.

"Mary a forgiving person," Johnella said. "She love you anyway."

I was silent.

"Look here, you go on back to the dining room and get yourself a cup of hot coffee and I'll march in there and tell Mary myself," Johnella said.

I put my fingers to my mouth. The touch of my own cold hand roused me. "No," I said. "I'll do it. It's my place to do it."

Johnella peered into my face. "You sure?"

I could see the spotted amber iris of Johnella's eyes, could see the uneven brown pigment in her cheeks and smell the sweet scent of toothpaste on her breath. "Yes, I'm sure," I said. "But I'd like to take her somewhere else to do it. Go to some familiar place."

Johnella frowned. She took her hand from my shoulder. "It take a whole army of people to keep up with Mary. You don't know what you're getting into."

"Oh, yes I do," I said. I made a fist and touched my breastbone with it. "Believe me, I know exactly what I'm getting into. I have looked for Mary on almost every street there is in Baton Rouge. I have looked for Mary in just about every place a person might go. I've looked for Mary in parks, on buses, downtown, on the levee . . ." I stopped, finally aware that I was hitting myself as I spoke.

Johnella waited patiently to see if I would continue, but I was too tired. "Don't get me started," I said.

She patted my arm. "I guess you do know what you're getting into," she said.

"We'll have to be gone for several hours. I'd like for Mary to go with me to choose a casket. I have an appointment with the director of the funeral home at one o'clock," I said.

"I wish you had called me first," Johnella said. "I'll have to rustle up something decent for her to wear."

I raised the bag I carried. "I brought some clothes—a skirt and blouse for today, and a black dress for the funeral."

"You'll have to watch her sharp," Johnella said. "It took us awhile, but we got her used to staying in this building with no locks. Mary believe she married to Dan Rather. She wrote him so many letters the TV station sent somebody out here to see if she be dangerous. Every night she say he tell her on the news to come to New York to be with him. But so far she never tried to run and do it. Last summer she got all the way to the Stop-N-Go before we noticed she was gone. They called us up and said she was there wanting a strawberry ICEE without no money to pay for it and was it okay to give her one. But even that time she promised me she wasn't trying to get to New York. She was just thirsty for something red and sweet. I sure would hate to see her get a taste of the world and end up in one of them back wards under lock and key again."

"I'll watch her," I said.

"You'll have to see to it that she gets her noon medicines. I'll fix them up and send them with you."

"I'll make sure she takes it," I said. "Does she need to take it before or after lunch?"

"It might be best to do it during lunch. Some of these medicines be bitter, and I usually give a little applesauce to take the bad taste away." Johnella rubbed her forehead and looked toward the door of the room. "Mary sure would enjoy a ride in a car. She don't never get to go nowhere."

"I thought we could stop and get a hot dog. Can she eat things like that?"

"Ain't nothing wrong with her stomach," Johnella said. She turned abruptly, pushed the door to Mary's room wide open, and walked in. "Look here who's come to see you, baby girl!"

I went in the room behind Johnella. Mary lay in a black metal bed with her eyes closed and her hands folded on her chest as if she were a corpse in a coffin. Her bare feet were pressed together, anklebone to anklebone, painted red toenails pointed right at me.

"You'd better open those eyes and sit up to take a look," Johnella said, pinching Mary's right big toe between her thumb and forefinger and wiggling it back and forth. "Somebody here you been wanting to see for a long time."

Mary's eyelids flickered but remained closed. "I heard. She heard. We heard," Mary said, though she still feigned sleep.

Johnella motioned for me to come closer to the bed. I took another two steps. One wall of the room was a bank of windows that overlooked the wooded lawn. A flicker of movement outside caught my eye. I turned my head just in time to catch sight of a large gray squirrel, with a much smaller squirrel in hot pursuit, running down the trunk of an oak tree and across the grass. I leaned forward to follow the chase, but they ran out of my sight, and when I turned back, Mary had risen in the bed before me.

Mary's once blond hair had faded to a dull sandy color. She had painted her cheeks and lips scarlet and drawn her eyebrows into a pair of immense arches with purple eyeliner. I looked from Mary to the picture of our parents beside her bed: she did, indeed, resemble our father, but only in the most whacked-out, crazy way. She was Daddy gone berserk.

"Long time no see," Mary said.

"Long time no be here," I said.

"Mary, that stuff go over your eye, not on your eyebrows," Johnella said. "You look like you on your way to Mardi Gras."

"I like it like this," Mary said. "Bonita? Bonita? Don't you like it like this?"

"It's certainly unusual," I said. "You might set a whole new style. If the folks in New York City get a look at you like that, all the women in the country could have eyebrows like yours before Christmas."

Johnella frowned, shot me a hard look, and said, "What happened to your shoes, Miss Mary? I put them right here by your bed not fifteen minutes ago."

"I could set a whole new style, Johnella, Johnella," Mary said, swinging thin, hairy legs over the side of the bed and feeling around on the floor for her shoes. She looked overmedicated; her movements seemed both languid and frantic. I turned to look back out the window for the squirrels, but they were gone.

Mary slid off the bed and stood up. She wore a brown dress pockmarked with cigarette burns. She was barefoot, the search for her shoes fruitless. On a table next to the bed was a small color television with the sound turned down. I watched a blue number two with yellow hands and yellow feet tap-dance across a stage. In the audience the letters of the alphabet applauded with hot-pink hands. When the blue number two came to the end of his solo, he was joined by a blue number one. They began a new dance in which they alternately formed the numbers twelve and twenty-one.

"How you been doing, Mr. Sister?" Mary said.

I looked away from the television screen. I considered each word carefully. "Fine," I said slowly. "How have you been doing?" My words sounded stiff and false. Long, long ago, I learned that when I was near my sister, a sleeping demon awoke in me and spat words from my mouth.

"Hunky-dory," Mary said. Briefly, her eyes met mine. Beneath the purple eyebrows, Mary's eyes were sharp and watchful. But soon her gaze slid away from mine and rose to search the ceiling. "Maybe Aura Lee got my shoes into heaven," she said.

"Most likely they be in her box," Johnella said, who was on her hands and knees, looking under the bed. "Where's that blue dress I brought you from home? That dress you got on full of holes. Your sister gon' take you out and I can't even find you a decent dress."

"Where are we going?" Mary said.

"Somewhere to get some lunch," I said.

"Can we go to Jumping Jack's?" she said.

"Sure."

Johnella stood up, dusted herself off, and said, "Who you give that dress to, Mary?"

"Aura Lee took it," Mary said.

"Took it, nothing. You give that dress to somebody. I bring you one of my very own still-good dresses one day and it's gone the next. I could just scream," Johnella said.

"I scream. You scream," Mary said.

"We all scream for ice cream," I said.

"Say what?" Johnella said.

"That's what Daddy always said every time Mother served home-made ice cream," I said.

Mary put her hands together as if in prayer and closed her eyes. "Daddy always said. Daddy always read. Daddy always dead."

Johnella looked at Mary and started to speak, but I hastily lifted the bag I carried. "I brought you some new clothes."

"Oh, good. I need some new clothes." Mary pulled off the brown dress over her head, tossed it on the floor, and stood naked before us.

"What you need is to stop giving away perfectly good clothes," Johnella said. "And please cover yourself."

From the bag I pulled a navy blue skirt and a white blouse with blue flowers embroidered on the pocket and collar.

Mary reached for them. "Brand-new clothes," she said. "I called the Salvation Army to come pick up all of those old clothes."

I looked down at the floor and tried not to laugh.

"So they could give them to the needy," Mary said.

I looked up and caught Mary's eye. We grinned at each other. "The needy need your clothes," I said.

"Right," Mary said. "The needy need my clothes. The needy need my shoes. The needy need . . ."

"That's enough of that," Johnella said. "You always got to do too much of a good thing. It was funny once, but it's not funny three times." She took the new blouse from Mary and unbuttoned it. "Try this shirt on. It look too little to me."

Mary struggled into the blouse. It didn't completely cover her breasts.

"Just what I thought," Johnella said. "You still think Mary's your baby sister. She long gone growed up. You be living in the past." She handed it to me. "Where'd you get these clothes?"

"In that big discount store outside town."

"King Dollar?"

"Yes, I think that's it," I said.

"Why don't you take all those clothes back and change them for some in a bigger size? I don't suppose you happen to have any underwear hiding in that bag," she said to me. "We haven't seen hide nor hair of a bra, a slip, or underpants for over a week. Mrs. Gottrocks here give 'em all to the poor, I guess."

"I gave them to the poor," Mary said. "I gave them to the unfortunate poor."

"You gave them to the poor unfortunate poor," I said.

"I gave them to the poor, poor, poor, unfortunate . . ."

"Stop that," Johnella said. "Mary, your sister's bad as you are. You both bad." But she was grinning.

"Here's a bra," I said. "And a slip and some underwear."

Johnella examined them. "This look a little bigger. It might be a tight fit, but I think she can squeeze in." She bit through the threads of the tags on the underwear and gave it to Mary. She put a hand on Mary's shoulder and turned her in the direction of the bathroom. "Now, put this stuff on and go wash that purple stuff off your face while I find your shoes and that dress I brought you."

Mary shook Johnella's arm off. "No! No! No! No! No!"

I stepped back, alarmed.

"Just see if I bring you any more cosmetician supplies, Miss Priss," Johnella said, and she bent to pick up the discarded brown dress.

"I like it like this," Mary said.

I walked up close to my sister. "Mary, it usually goes like this," I said, and I rubbed the thin skin over my eye with my index finger.

"Don't I have a constitutional right to express myself?" Mary said.

Before I could answer, a woman in a lime-green polyester pantsuit strode into the room.

Mary pointed to me. "That's my big sister." She pointed to the woman. "That's Aura Lee. That's my roommate."

Aura Lee's eyes lit up. She had stiff gray hair that had been cut short, like a man's. And, like a man, dark hair grew over her upper lip. Beneath her puffy, damp lips, several strands of the same wiry gray hair that graced her head grew on her chin.

Aura Lee smiled. She walked quickly across the room, took my right hand in both of her hands, and pumped it up and down, saying all the while, "Hey, Mary's sister who never, never, never comes to see her. How you doing?" Droplets of saliva filled the air as Aura Lee spoke. Because of an impediment, this speech came out of her huge wet lips with some difficulty. When the words finally appeared after knocking about inside Aura Lee's mouth, they seemed moist. In my mind's eye, the "never, never, never" dripped with spit.

Aura Lee leaned forward. With her right hand she continued to shake my hand. With her left she touched my cheek. "She's so sweet."

Nodding, Aura Lee looked around at Johnella. "Isn't she sweet? Mary's sister looks exactly like Mary's mother."

"She do have a sweet face. Now let go of her and tell me what you did with that dress I brought from home, and where Mary's shoes is."

Aura Lee stroked the collar of my silk suit. "And smooth. Her clothes are so smooth." She turned to Johnella. "Feel how smooth."

"I don't have time to feel how smooth," Johnella said. "Mary has to get ready to go."

Aura Lee picked up a lock of my hair. "And look how soft her hair is," she said, nodding again and again to Johnella. "Come see how soft it is."

"I can't come see how soft, Aura Lee," Johnella said. "I've got to find Mary's shoes." She opened the closet door.

Still holding a lock of my hair and turning it first one way and then another in the sunlight that poured in through the window, Aura Lee said, in a voice that had changed tone, "And see how dark it is."

I stood very still.

"Dark. Dark," Aura Lee said, tightening her grip on my hand.

I held my breath.

"Dark. Dark. Dark," Aura Lee said, letting my hair fall. She grasped my left shoulder with strong fingers. She put her face close to mine and breathed her sour, heavy breath into my face. "Dark as the sins laid on Christ's back," she said, her grip still frighteningly firm, her words unnaturally soft.

I shrank away.

Aura Lee moved closer. "I know what you did," she said. Still holding tightly to my shoulder, she grasped my right hand. "Your immortal soul is in deadly peril," she whispered.

I tried to pull my hand away, but Aura Lee held fast. I looked around for Johnella, waited for her to put a stop to Aura Lee's attentions, but she was standing on tiptoe feeling along the top closet shelf, still looking for Mary's shoes.

Aura Lee put her lips to my ear. "Are you sincerely sorry for your sin?" she said.

Unbidden and unwelcome, the old words came to me. Bless me, Father, for I have sinned. My last confession was forty-one years ago—

"Confess to me," Aura Lee whispered.

I looked at Mary. My sister watched us intently as she stepped into a pink slip.

Why the hell won't Johnella make this woman stop? I thought. It occurred to me that Johnella was letting this happen on purpose, that she was punishing me for living all this time in Baton Rouge without coming to see Mary.

Gently, Aura Lee took my chin in her cupped hand and looked into my eyes. I was startled to see how kindly she regarded me. She raised her left hand and gently stroked my face. "Confess to me and I will intercede for you," she said and kissed me on the cheek.

It was a moist kiss. When Aura Lee finally let go of me and drew back, my hands were trembling. The outline of the kiss remained and did not evaporate for a long time.

Johnella backed out of the closet, dusted off her hands, and said, "Now that you've saved this nice lady from the fires of hell, would you please tell me what happened to that dress I brought from home and Mary's shoes?" She crossed to Aura Lee's side of the room. "They wouldn't happen to be in your box, would they?"

Aura Lee quickly put herself between Johnella and her bed. "No," she said.

Johnella advanced. "Au-ra-lee."

"No!" Aura Lee screamed.

Johnella went to the door of the room. "Lincoln!" she bawled down the hall.

Aura Lee put both hands flat on the top of a wooden box with a hinged top and a rusted metal clasp that stood on a metal table next to her bed. Behind her, the two squirrels ran back up the trunk of the oak tree. This time the larger squirrel was in pursuit. The blue numbers on the television now made up the audience, and the letters of the alphabet had become the performers. A, B, and C were making their way onto the stage, carrying black top hats and canes.

"Lincoln!" Johnella hollered again.

A young black man in white pants, a red T-shirt with the Marine insignia on it, a Walkman attached to his waist, and a cord leading to headphones over his ears boogied into the room. At the sight of him, Aura Lee knelt and, with her forehead pressed against the wood and her hands clinging helplessly to the lid, wept over her box. The young man, moving rhythmically to music only he could hear, bopped over and gently lifted the old woman to her feet.

"Aura-Lee," he sang. "Aura-Lee. We gots to get in your box." He led her to the bathroom.

Johnella opened the box, reached inside, and drew out a pair of black shoes with gold plastic buckles.

"Look," Mary said. "There are my shoes."

"I thought so," Johnella said as she removed a blue dress. "Here is that dress I brought you from home just yesterday."

Johnella pulled the dress over Mary's head and knelt down to put her shoes on. Still shaky from Aura Lee's assault, I walked over and peered into her box. Inside I saw a folded sheet. On it rested a coiled piece of rope, a dried orange peel, and a black rosary. A tiny Christ lay on the cross and stared up at me. I closed the box. On the top was a handwritten sign taped to the wood. DO NOT OPEN WITHOUT AURA LEE PERMISSION AT NO TIME, it read. Aura Lee's cries hit the bathroom door.

Johnella stood up, gave the waistband of the blue dress a tug to the right, buttoned the collar at the neck, and stepped back. "You don't look too bad," she said. "If you'd get that mess off your eyebrows, your sister wouldn't mind being seen on the street with you."

Mary went to her closet and took out a black purse. Into it she put the contents of the drawer in the bedside table: a lipstick, a purple eye pencil, a round red blusher with a clear plastic cover, and a handful of coupons clipped from the newspaper. "I'm ready," she said.

"Mary, we're not going one step until you take that purple eyeliner off your eyebrows," I said. "Either express yourself and stay here, or take it off and go in the car with me."

Sullenly, Mary pulled a tissue from a box and handed it to Johnella, who licked a finger and wiped until all of the color had been smoothed away. When Johnella finished, Mary's good spirits had returned. She knocked on the bathroom door. "Aura Lee, you can come out now. I've got my shoes." Mary tucked her purse under her arm, waved good-bye to the dancing letters on the television screen, and led us all out into the hall.

"Don't go running off until I get your medicine. And don't let your sister forget to give it to you," Johnella said.

"I won't forget," Mary said.

At the nurse's station, Johnella put a multicolored assortment of pills into a small fluted paper cup. Covering the pills with another cup, she handed it to me. I put it in the zippered pocket of my purse.

Mary went around the lobby and kissed every patient. In the doorway, she turned and surveyed the entire foyer. "Good-bye," she said.

Johnella watched anxiously from the doorway of the nurse's station. "You behave yourself out there, Mary Gabriel," she said.

Mary turned in the doorway. "Mary Rather," she corrected Johnella. "My name is Mrs. Dan Rather, and I'm on my way to New York to see my husband."

Johnella started forward with a look of alarm, but I raised a hand to stop her. "I'll take care of it," I said.

On the veranda, Mary kissed the black man with no arms and no legs. "Good-bye, Leonard. I'm leaving forever." Then she kissed the flat-headed harelipped girl. "Good-bye, Rhonda. I'll never see you again. But I'll call you from New York."

I unlocked the car door on the passenger side. "Let's get one thing straight, Mary. You are not married to Dan Rather, and we are not on our way to New York. We're going to exchange these clothes, eat some lunch, and then we're going to Baton Rouge."

"That's not all we're going to do, is it?" Mary said.

I opened the car door. "No, there's something else."

"I thought so," Mary said as I pulled down the seat belt and buckled her into the seat.

I went around the car and got in. "We'll go to Jumping Jack's if you'll promise me there'll be no more of this 'Mary Rather' business."

Mary shrugged. "If you say so."

But as I drove toward the gates of the institution, I glanced over and saw Mary's lips moving, silently mouthing the name of the person she really wanted to be. When I reached the stop sign at the entrance to the highway, I paused no longer than it takes to draw a breath, then darted in front of a blue pickup truck, pressed the accelerator to the floor, and finally wiped away the remains of Aura Lee's kiss.

Chapter Four

Spring 1954

One Saturday morning in early April, many months after the watchman helped Bonita find Mary, a new family came to live on Oleander Avenue. Bonita sat in a white wooden rocker on her front porch and read aloud from Longfellow's *Evangeline* to Adam, Frankie, Adrienne, and Gracie. As she passed the book around so everyone could see the pictures, a moving van arrived. The sound of cracking twigs and rustling leaves accompanied the large yellow truck's slow progress. When it finally came to a stop in front of the old Garner house, it filled the entire street. Word had gone around the previous week that a new family was moving in. And there was a child! *Evangeline* was thrown to the floor. Bonita's audience scrambled to their feet. "They're here!"

Gracie and Adrienne clasped hands and swung each other around and around. Adam and Frankie leaned over the porch railing to watch. Mary, whose vocabulary had grown to several dozen words and who now spoke sentences of moderate complexity, sat on the stoop scribbling with a crayon in a book of fairy tales. She did not look up. Bonita slowly stood.

A maroon Cadillac drove over the sidewalk and onto the Moaks' grass as it made its way around the truck and into the driveway of the vacant house. A heavy rain the previous day had left the ground soft, and the car left deep tire tracks in the Moaks' front lawn.

"Look what they did to your grass, Adam," Gracie said. "Your mom's going to be plenty mad."

The doors of the car opened. The first person to get out was a little girl.

"Look! I'll bet she's the same age as Mary!" Adam said.

The child did seem to be about the same size as Mary, but to Bonita, the new girl appeared more graceful and, unlike Mary, extremely alert.

"French braids," Adrienne whispered. She had repeatedly told everyone how she longed for them, but her mother refused to take the time for the task.

A man got out of the driver's side. He was not as tall as Bonita's father, but to Bonita there seemed more of him. This man was not only fuller in his body, he had a brown beard that filled his face. He took the little girl by the hand, and they went to the other side of the car and spoke to someone in the passenger seat. It seemed to Bonita that the person was reluctant to get out. Bonita leaned forward, trying to make out a face. She stared with such intensity that the girl turned around to look at her.

Bonita and the new girl looked straight at each other, and Bonita saw something that surprised her. This graceful child, so different from her sister, with hair like that which Adrienne longed for and a sturdy father to hold her hand, gave Bonita a look that made her feel sad. It brought to her mind the faces of children in newsreels who were caught by the camera watching their houses burn or standing near an old well down which a baby brother had disappeared.

All of the children on Bonita's porch immediately turned their backs on the new arrivals and pretended to be doing something else.

Gracie leaned over to whisper to Mary, "Nobody wants that old book. You can tear it to shreds."

Mary immediately threw the book at Gracie, jumped off the step, and ran around the side of the house.

"Ha, ha, fooled you!" Gracie yelled after her. She handed it to Bonita. "Here, hide it before she comes back."

Bonita opened the front door, put both books back in her father's bookcase, and returned to the porch. Finally, a woman wearing sunglasses and a scarf covering her hair got out of the car, supported by the man Bonita assumed was her husband. As the two adults went slowly to the house, the new girl turned and walked along the sidewalk until she was right across the street from them.

"I'm not playing with her." Gracie held her nose. "She stinks. I can smell her from here."

"She doesn't stink to me," Adrienne said. "That white lace pinafore is exactly like the one I wanted my mama to make me for Easter."

"She looks like a freak to me," Adam said.

Bonita went down the steps of the front porch and walked to the end of the sidewalk. She was accustomed to the power that came with being the oldest child on the block. Adam Moak was ten also, but not until thirteen days after Bonita. "What's your name?" Bonita said.

"Laurel Marie Landry," the new girl said.

"Where are you from?"

"New Orleans, Louisiana."

"Can you cross the street?" Bonita said.

The narrow street might as well have been the Mississippi River, so forbidden had it been for Bonita to cross without permission until she started first grade. Mary paid no attention to such restrictions; she ran back and forth across the street whenever she pleased and never even looked both ways for cars.

Laurel Landry shook her head. The blue gingham bows tied to the end of each braid swayed back and forth. "I can when I'm six," she said.

Laurel's face was very round. The taut braids made her fair cheeks and forehead seem exceptionally smooth. This smoothness, and the hint of an appeal to Bonita, seemed to invite questions.

"When will that be?" Bonita said.

"In three months and four days," Laurel said.

One by one the other children joined Bonita.

"Are you going to have a party?" Adam said.

Laurel nodded. "My mother promised me a western party with a real Shetland pony to ride on."

By this time everyone but Mary was standing in a line across the street from the new girl. A tiny frown appeared across Laurel's forehead.

"My mother tied this bow," Laurel said. She turned around to show them a large, fat bow tied at her waist.

"I can tie my own bows," Gracie said.

"I can read," Laurel said.

"Everybody can read!" Adam said.

"I can write!"

"Stop it!" Bonita cried.

Instantly there was quiet. Uneasy, Bonita darted a glance over her shoulder to see where her sister was. Mary had slipped back to the side of the porch and was watching them intently with her fists clenched. What would their mother do in a situation like this? Bonita gave Adrienne a small shove. "Say something nice."

Adrienne, who had refrained from any shouting, stepped forward. "I like your braids," she said. "Did your mother do those for you, too?"

"No," Laurel said. "My daddy did."

"Your daddy knows how to make braids like that?"

Laurel nodded.

The idea that any of the fathers they knew might braid hair caused Bonita and Adrienne to look at each other and widen their eyes.

"My daddy can make pancakes," Laurel said. "He always cooks my breakfast. And he can cook dinner, too."

Contemplating their fathers going into the kitchen to do anything more than pour a cup of coffee or mix a martini, all of the children fell silent.

"My daddy made me memorize my new address and my new telephone number in case I ever got kidnapped," Laurel said. She looked up and down the street. "I don't think anyone ever gets kidnapped in this place." Her face had lost its open quality, and her eyes had narrowed.

"We might get kidnapped just as much as you," Frankie said.

Bonita looked around, trying to see the neighborhood through this stranger's eyes. Everything—houses, trees, shrubs, grass—seemed curiously pale and diminished.

"We had bigger houses where I lived before," Laurel said. "And our streets were this wide!" She threw out her arms. "Everybody there was rich, rich, rich. I might have been kidnapped every single day in New Orleans, Louisiana!"

"Is that why you moved here?" Bonita said.

They never found out why Laurel moved to Baton Rouge, for Mary dashed across the street, yanked hard at the sash in the back of Laurel's dress, threw a handful of sand from the sandbox on her, and then ran home.

"Who did that?" Laurel cried. She brushed the sand from her chest and shoulder.

Bonita looked up and down the quiet street for cars and then ran across. "Stay right there!" she called back to the children behind her. "And don't let Mary come over here!"

Bonita knelt in front of Laurel and brushed the sand from the bib of her pinafore. Up close, Bonita could see that tiny tendrils had escaped Laurel's braids and formed a damp crowd of curls about her ears and cheeks. Laurel's hair was the color of the toasted pecans Bonita's mother put on each bridge table when the Oleander Avenue Couples' Club met at the Gabriels' house. Across Laurel's nose were freckles as fine as the nut dust left in the crystal bowls when the party was over.

"My mother tied this bow," Laurel said.

Laurel said this over and over as Bonita struggled to form another bow. When Bonita turned Laurel around by the waist and, still kneeling, looked up into Laurel's face to say, "There, now. It's as good as new," tears ran down Laurel's cheeks, and the look they exchanged acknowledged that they both knew this was not so.

"Who was that?" Laurel said.

Bonita lowered her eyes. She picked a few grains of sand from Laurel's shoes and stood. "That was my sister, Mary," she said. She tried to take Laurel's hand. "Do you want me to walk you to your house?" she said.

Laurel did not permit Bonita to hold her hand. "No," Laurel said and walked home by herself.

Bonita went back across the street without looking both ways. She didn't wonder why Laurel was so distressed over her bow; sooner or later Mary made everybody cry.

"I see the Landrys got moved in," John Gabriel said.

"Did you know them from before?" Bonita said. She was setting the table for dinner in the dining room.

"We've known them for a long time. Your mother was at Sophie Newcomb with Dr. Landry's wife," her father said.

As a child Bonita had been nourished on romantic stories of her mother's girlhood. Born Lottie Dollier in Iberville Parish, Bonita's mother was the daughter of a wealthy sugar planter, and although Bonita's grandparents had died before she could remember them, the house on Oleander was full of their china, silver, and crystal. Lottie's vocal talents had been discovered early, and she had been sent while still in high school to board at a Catholic convent in New Orleans so that she could study privately with a world-renowned voice teacher.

Lottie came from the kitchen with a platter of fish and placed it on the table. "Ellen Allendorph was the most beautiful girl I ever saw," Lottie said.

"Did you like her? Was she nice?" Bonita said.

"Ellen Allendorph was always a little . . ."

Bonita waited as her mother sought the right word.

"A little detached," Lottie said. "But we all forgave her for it because she was so sweet."

"Was she shy?" Bonita said.

"Bonita, could you take time out from grilling your mother about our new neighbors and get us some napkins, please," Dr. Gabriel said.

Because Bonita was so curious, her father called her "the inveterate snoop." Once, a year earlier, Bonita had discovered a metal box in her parents' closet that contained their marriage license, both Gabriel children's vaccination records, and a birth certificate for a female child named Diana Dollier who was born in 1918, two years before Lottie's birth. When Bonita asked about this hitherto unknown aunt at supper one evening, her father told her that her mother's beloved older sister had died young. "How did she die?" Bonita had said, and her mother abruptly got up and left the table. "Your mother doesn't like to talk about it," her father said, and the question went unanswered.

Dr. Gabriel blessed the food and then took a white Haviland china plate from the plate warmer at his right hand and placed a serving of baked red snapper on it.

"Bonita, do you want sauce on your fish?"

"No, sir," Bonita said. "Is this fish going to have a lot of bones? I don't want any bones."

"Just be careful how you eat it, sweetheart," her mother said. "You must learn how to debone a piece of fish properly."

"You always help Mary with her fish. Why don't you help me with mine?" Bonita complained.

"I have to take the bones out of Mary's fish because she's still too young to do it properly," Lottie said. "You are old enough to do it yourself."

"No peas," Mary said when her plate came around. "No. No. No. No. No. No peas."

"Mary, Mary, quite contrary, how does your garden grow?" Lottie said. "With a little pea here and a little pea there," she went on, until she had ringed the fish on Mary's plate with peas. She passed the plate to Mary.

Mary lifted a spoonful of peas as if she were going to throw them on the floor.

Lottie took it from Mary. "I want to see you eat a pea," she said. "I want to see you busy as a bee." She made the spoon a circling insect that went to Mary's mouth.

"We probably ought to do something to introduce them to the rest of the folks in the neighborhood," John Gabriel said. "I feel responsible for them being here. When he called to talk about setting up a practice in Baton Rouge, I told him the Garner house was empty. I should have kept my big mouth shut."

It sounded to Bonita like her father was sorry that Laurel's daddy and mother had moved in across the street.

Lottie frowned at her husband and shook her head. "Why don't we have a little party here tomorrow afternoon? It would be a good way for them to meet everybody on the block," she said.

"What's a practice?" Bonita said.

"It's when you see patients. Like I do," her father said.

"I thought all doctors had patients," Bonita said.

"Larry's been doing research in a hospital in New Orleans," John said.

"What's research?" Bonita said.

"He's been studying an illness," John said.

"What illness?"

"It's too complicated to explain, Bonita."

"I want to know," Bonita said. "How does he do it?"

"Dr. Landry has been studying families," John said.

"You mean families like us?" Bonita said.

"Not exactly like us, Bonita. He traces a particular illness in certain families. He tries to see how this illness develops and why."

"Like measles?" Bonita said. "I've had the measles. He could study me."

"Not measles," John said. "Not that kind of illness. It's not something you would understand right now."

"What kind of a doctor is he?" Bonita said.

"Dr. Landry is a psychiatrist," her father said.

"Is that the same kind of doctor you are?" Bonita said.

"I'm just a plain old GP," John said.

"What's a psychiatrist?" Bonita said.

"He treats the mind," John said.

"How does he do that?" Bonita said.

"He talks to people," her father said.

"Maybe he could talk to Mary and ask her why she didn't want to talk like the rest of us," Bonita said.

"Certainly not!" John said, and the minute he said this, he shot a look at Lottie, who was still entreating Mary to eat her peas. If Bonita had not been in the habit of watching her parents' every gesture, she would have missed it.

"I'll give Larry a call after supper and see if tomorrow afternoon suits them," John said.

"They have a little girl," Bonita said.

"I know. I want you girls to be nice to her. She's the same age as Mary," her father said.

"She's older than Mary," Bonita said.

"Just a few months," Lottie said.

Bonita thought it might as well as have been a few years for all

Mary and Laurel had in common. Briefly, she considered telling her parents that Mary had already introduced herself to the new girl with a handful of sand, but decided against it.

"How come they left New Orleans?" Bonita said.

"We don't know why they left New Orleans, Bonita," Lottie said. "That is none of our concern."

"When Larry called me to ask about our schools, I gave him a big thumbs-up for the nuns, so she'll be in first grade at Holy Angels in September," John said. "Now Mary can have a friend of her very own in the neighborhood."

"She can read," Bonita said.

Her father laughed. "I'm not surprised. Larry Landry is a brilliant man. What's her name?"

Bonita was visited by the disloyal thought that Laurel Landry was the sister she would have wanted had she been given a choice. It would have been fun to have a sister who read books instead of marking them up with crayons. Bonita looked at Mary, who was engrossed in mashing her fish with her fork, her blond head bent over her plate. Her hair shining under the light, pale custard-colored strands over darker butterscotch tones, made her seem defenseless, and Bonita blinked to keep the tears from her eyes.

"What's her name, sweetheart?" her mother said.

Bonita swallowed. She put her hand to her brow and bent her head to conceal her eyes. "Laurel," she said. "Laurel Marie."

"What a pretty name," Lottie said. "Don't you think that's a pretty name, Mary?"

"Name name name name name name," Mary said.

Bonita glanced up in time to see her mother catch her father's eye and give him a small, sad smile.

John and Lottie cleaned up the kitchen. Together, they washed and dried and put away the china, crystal, and sterling. They once employed someone to do these chores, but after two goblets were broken and three silver knives were lost, the maid was fired and John and Lottie went back to doing it themselves. Bonita thought they probably liked that better, anyway, because as they worked, they talked. Sometimes Bonita hid behind the door and listened through the crack.

"I don't understand it," her mother said. "Why on earth do you suppose Larry Landry decided to pick up his family and move to Baton Rouge?"

"He said he wants to see patients. He said he's tired of research, but who knows what thoughts were in the great man's head," her father said. "Larry Landry always was an arrogant son of a bitch."

Bonita caught her breath. She had heard her father use that term only once: driving on the River Road to visit her paternal grandparents, he pulled out to pass a slow-moving car, and a pickup truck turned out of a side road and headed straight for them. "Son of a bitch," she heard her father mutter right before he drove them into the ditch that ran beside the road, avoiding a head-on collision.

"He is brilliant," her father continued. "I give him that. But the rules never applied to him. To you and me, yes. We are mere beaten-path followers in his eyes, and I'm a lowly GP to boot. But Larry belongs to that elect who choose to break the rules. He married a patient, for God's sake!"

"She wasn't his patient," Lottie said.

"But he was the one who admitted her," John said. "He was the first one to see her after her breakdown. Even if she did go on to work with someone else, that bond is never broken."

For a while there was only the silver sound of knives and forks touching one another and the deeper, ivory sound of plate against plate. "John," Lottie said. "We've got to do something about Mary."

"Mary is going to be fine. Look how far she's come since last summer. Don't worry so much about her, Lottie," John said.

"I went to the library at the hospital and read some of Larry's articles in the medical journals. He's saying the mother's to blame."

"Larry Landry's just jumping on the bandwagon with that bunch of doctors up East at Chestnut Lodge. He'll get over it," John said.

"But he says that the schizophrenic patients in the families he's been following all had early autism. And that it's because the mothers are distant."

"He's got a sick wife. He's looking for somebody to blame. I think that's probably why they left New Orleans. As long as Senator Allendorph was alive, he could keep a firm foot planted on Larry Landry. But after he died last summer, Ellen's mother probably got tired of hearing how her daughter's problems were all her fault. I think Larry realized that if he knew what was good for him, he'd better get out of Dodge."

"I don't want Bonita to go through what I did. We must never do to her what my parents did to me," Lottie said.

"Lottie, I promised you that if you would come back to Louisiana and marry me, you would never have to hear the words 'DePaul Hospital' again, and I meant it."

"But John, we can't just ignore it. Maybe we could find a good child psychiatrist in New Orleans. It doesn't have to be at DePaul. Maybe I should talk to someone myself. What if I'm causing it? What if I'm doing something to make Mary sick and I don't even know it?"

"No," John said. "It's not your fault. We don't know what causes mental illness. Schizophrenia is an act of God. Your mother didn't do anything to Diana. Your sister got sick! It could just as easily have been cancer. DePaul Hospital happened to be the best private hospital in the South. It was one of fate's cruel jokes that you happened to be in school six blocks away."

"It wasn't fate! You're being much too generous to my parents. Or else you've forgotten. They sent me to Dominican and then to Sophie Newcomb so I could be the one to keep an eye on Diana. My parents couldn't take it, so they sent me. Every afternoon when school was over, I rode my bicycle over to DePaul Hospital to see my sister on Rosary Three for four years. I was way too young to see and hear what I heard and saw on the third floor of that place!"

"They were ignorant, Lottie," John said. "And scared. That's what folks in the country expected of their children—to help out. That's why they had them. I'll never forget how proud your father was because he made enough money to hire help to work the land and he hadn't had to put you and Diana into the cane fields the way his father had him."

"I don't want Bonita to have to 'work the land.' "

"I know. I'll do my best to see that what happened to you doesn't happen to Bonita," John said. "But I have to tell you, I really think that's what families are for: to look after each other. I see it in my practice all the time. When somebody gets sick, if the family doesn't step up and take on the responsibility, it gets turned over to strangers."

"John, I don't want Bonita used," Lottie said.

Bonita heard the sound of silverware being flung down hard, and she winced and moved back a step.

"I wish I had never told Larry about the Garner house," her father said.

"Well, we have to be nice to them now that they're here," Lottie said.

Bonita slipped away to her room. Sometimes she heard more than she wanted. What was "schizophrenia"? It was an ugly word, and Bonita knew it would be stuck in her head for days. She shut her door and got into bed, but when she closed her eyes, she saw Laurel Landry looking at her sadly. And what, she wondered, had happened to her mother's sister, Diana?

At three o'clock the next afternoon, the neighbors began to arrive. Lottie assigned Bonita to welcome guests at the front door, in order to grow proficient in graciousness. All of the children were invited and came right on time.

Gracie had brought her second-grade reader and said, "I want to see her read." Then she turned to show Bonita that in her pocket was a tiny notebook and a stubby pencil. "And," Gracie added, "I want to see her write. In script."

"Me, too," Adam said.

By three-thirty all of the neighbors were there; the only ones missing were the honorees.

Bonita stood in the kitchen doorway, nervously watching her parents. She felt particularly anxious because of all that she had overheard the night before.

"Do you think they might have forgotten?" her mother whispered to her father.

Bonita's father closed his eyes and wrinkled his nose. Bonita recognized it as the face he made when he was thinking and didn't like what he thought.

At that moment Gracie ran in, hard heels clacking. "They're coming!"

Bonita raced, as fast as was possible on the waxed wood floors, to her post at the front door.

Laurel stood on the porch with her father, her hand resting lightly in his. That day she was dressed in blue. Dr. Landry wore a rumpled brown suit that nearly matched the color of his beard. His eyes were concealed by darkened glasses.

"Hello, Dr. Landry. My name is Bonita Jane Gabriel. Hi, Laurel. It's nice to see you again. We are so happy to welcome you to our home today. Isn't it a beautiful afternoon?" Bonita said, brightly miming a gracious smile. She resisted the wish to ask why Laurel's mother was not with them.

To Bonita's great surprise, Laurel walked right into the living room, took Bonita's hand, smiled up at her, and said, "I want to play with you. I like you."

Bonita's company smile turned into the real thing. "I like you, too. Do you want to come see my books?"

"Yes, please." Laurel's eyes shone.

Hand in hand, Bonita and Laurel led the other children away.

"Bonita," John said.

Bonita stopped but did not turn.

"Don't forget to include Mary."

"Yes, sir," Bonita said.

Laurel pulled on Bonita's hand to make her bend down. Laurel put both hands around Bonita's ear and whispered, "My daddy says I don't have to play with that baby who threw sand on me. I just want to play with you."

Bonita was flattered, but she knew that if she didn't include Mary, her father would be angry. Mary was nowhere to be seen.

"Adrienne, take Laurel back to my room and show her my books. I'll be there in just a minute," Bonita said.

Bonita pressed herself against the wall next to Mary's room. She leaned around the doorway to see what her sister was doing. Mary was seated on the floor in the corner of her room with her back to the door, constructing an elaborate tower of blocks. Bonita withdrew without speaking and went to her own room.

Gracie opened the second-grade reader to the last story in the book. "Read this," Gracie said to Laurel. "This story right here: 'Forest Friends.' "

"Not that," Bonita said. "That's too hard."

"I can do it," Laurel said.

Frankie, Gracie, Adam, and Adrienne crowded around to listen.

" 'Three gray squirrels . . .' " Laurel read.

Astonished, Gracie turned to Adam. "She knows 'squirrels.' " Gracie snatched the book from Laurel and turned several pages. "Here," she said, pointing with a finger. "What's this word?"

" 'Chipmunk.' " Laurel said.

All of the children looked at Laurel with respect.

Gracie took the book and closed it. "Now," she said. "About writing."

"Let's go out to the front steps where she'll have more room," Bonita said.

Outside, Gracie put the pad down on the second step and handed Laurel the stubby pencil.

"That pencil is too ugly," Laurel said.

Bonita went inside to ask her father if she could sharpen a new pencil in the sharpener on his desk. Her father said yes, they could have a new pencil, and were they playing nicely with Laurel, and Bonita told him yes they were.

Laurel was not as good with pencil and paper as she was with the three gray squirrels and the chipmunk. Laboriously, she produced a script that used the entire page of the pad for her first name.

Bonita said, "Maybe you could try to write a little smaller."

Laurel managed, on her next try, to get her full name on one page. Surprised and pleased that the girl had taken her suggestion, Bonita said, "You write pretty good."

Laurel smiled at her. "Thank you," she said.

"Who taught you to do that?" Bonita asked.

"My daddy," Laurel said.

"Did he teach you to read, too?"

"Yes," Laurel said. "I love to read."

"Me, too," Bonita said. "Sometimes I wake up before anybody else and read a whole book before breakfast."

"What grade are you in?" Laurel asked.

She sat on the step just above Bonita, and when she talked, her eyes were exactly level with Bonita's. Bonita, who had grown accustomed to Mary's sidelong glances—to her sister's swerving, hit-and-run gaze—found Laurel's direct regard pleasant. "I'm in fifth grade," she said. "Next year, in sixth grade, they elect hall monitors."

"I'll be in first grade in September," Laurel said. She frowned and looked past Bonita into the backyard. "I heard that first grade at Holy Angels is hard," she said.

"It won't be hard for you because you're so smart. My sister's going to be in first grade and she can't read or write," Bonita said and was immediately dismayed that she had told Laurel these things about Mary.

"Want to go over to my house to play?" Laurel said. "We can't go inside because my mother doesn't feel good, but I have some good games I can bring outside."

"Sure," Bonita said. "Is she sick? Is that why she didn't come to the party?"

"My daddy said I didn't have to talk about my mother," Laurel said.

The children trooped across the street and went to the back of the Landrys' house. Laurel permitted them to climb the steps with her to the back porch.

"Where's your mother?" Adrienne said, peering through the screen door into the kitchen.

"She's resting," Laurel said. "Wait here. My daddy told me to make sure nobody goes inside."

Laurel was gone a long time. The children amused themselves by opening the storage cabinets on the porch, but there were no surprises there, only dust mops and brooms. They were left alone so long that Bonita said, "Maybe I should just look in the kitchen."

"Yeah," Adam said.

Bonita eased the screen door open. When she saw there was no one in the kitchen, she tiptoed in and closed the door behind her. She found herself in a large room with many windows. White cabinets were stenciled with red hearts. Painted green ivy went all around the walls. She saw a maple table with four captain's chairs and a dainty desk. As Bonita walked carefully across the floor, the fact that she was in a house where she was not supposed to be both terrified and thrilled her.

Something was not right. Bonita saw everything in the kitchen with unusual clarity. As she tried to identify what was wrong, she became aware of a rhythmic thumping sound that she recognized but could not recall the activity that accompanied it. Drawn by an overwhelming impulse to penetrate farther into the house, Bonita entered the hall. On her right was a passage that went to the front of the house, and a flight of stairs. The rhythmic thumping was coming from a partially closed door to her left. Constantly casting glances at the staircase, Bonita tiptoed toward the sound. Adopting the same technique she had used for seeing into Mary's room, Bonita pressed herself to the outer wall and soundlessly eased her head around into the doorway. A dark-haired, naked woman with her back to Bonita sat on the floor playing jacks. Bonita could see the silver stars that had just been thrown spread out about the woman's right knee. The red rubber ball, the source of the sound, bounced, and the woman's right hand swept up four jacks. Laurel's mother—Bonita assumed it was Laurel's mother—had advanced to fivesies when Bonita heard Laurel's footsteps at the head of the stairs. Heart pounding as if the red ball had bounced into her chest, Bonita fled.

Outside on the back porch, as she leaned against the wall, panting, the children surrounded her, whispering, "What did you see?"

Bonita put her finger to her lips. "Sssshh. Laurel's coming. Pretend nothing happened." But an image of the kitchen came to Bonita, and she saw that the face of every clock—the small one in the stove panel, the large one on the wall, the crystal clock on the dainty desk—had been covered with black cloth.

Chapter Five

October 1995

We drove past the Stop-N-Go Mary had walked to last summer, thirsty for something red and sweet and without any money to pay for it. In the parking lot a gang of teenaged boys stood astride bicycles, laughing and smoking. Mary turned to look back at them as we went by.

I stole so many little looks at my sister that she put up her hand to shield her face and said, "Don't."

"I'm sorry," I said. "I'm trying to get used to seeing you again."

Mary said nothing, only cupped her hand closer to her cheek and hunched her shoulder to block my gaze.

"I've missed you," I said and was surprised to find that it was true.

At these words Mary straightened up, took her hand from her head, put it in her lap, and stared down the highway. She didn't say anything, but I told myself that she looked pleased, although it was hard to tell with only half her face to go on.

We passed a new subdivision in which all the freshly cut and paved streets were named after women whose names began with the letter

"M." Mary read them aloud: "Mildred, Martha, Marcia, Mary—look, they named a street after me!"

At the corner of Wilkerson Road and Highway 23, I had to slow down and stop for a red light.

"This is fun," Mary said. "I like riding in this car."

We looked at each other and grinned.

"That's Ortlieb's," Mary said, pointing to a brick building with white columns set way back from the road on her right. "That's where they'll take me when I die." She turned and showed me her whole face. "If I die," she said.

"Planning to live forever?" I said.

"I might," Mary said. "If I want to."

"Good luck," I said.

Carved into an unnaturally green lawn before the funeral home was a circular driveway in which a line of cars waited behind a gray limousine and a silver hearse. At the head of this procession, so close that Mary could have lowered her window, put out a hand, and touched him, was a Livingston Parish sheriff's deputy on an enormous black motorcycle. The man's eyes were concealed by black glasses, and his hands on the motorcycle grips wore black leather gloves.

"Ummm," Mary said. "He's nice-looking. Don't you think he's handsome, Mr. Sister?"

"He's sure got a big machine," I said.

Mary giggled. "Maybe he could be my new boyfriend. I need a new boyfriend. My other one died. They brought him to Ortlieb's. That's where they bring everybody who dies out there." She jerked her head in the direction we had come, then peered through the car window. "Maybe he's still there," she said. She looked at me again, but this time it was a strange, sliding kind of glance. "I know he's still there," she said. "Let's go look for him."

"When did he die?" I said.

"Last summer," Mary said. "July twenty-first at seven-thirty-six P.M."

"He's not still there," I said.

"He could be," Mary said. She continued to look hard at the funeral home.

"No, he couldn't," I said.

"He could," Mary said.

"He's not still there, Mary! If he died last summer, he's been dead and buried for months." The light changed to green, but the deputy rose up in the saddle of his big bike, stomped down on the starter with one big black boot, and gunned his motor into action. He signaled for me to move back and blocked my car with his bike, then the entire funeral procession pulled out in front of us. As the cars reached the street, each driver put his headlights on.

I slammed the steering wheel with the palm of my hand. "Damn!" I said. "We're going to be here all day."

"It was Adam Moak," Mary said.

"Who was Adam Moak?"

"My boyfriend," Mary said.

"It couldn't have been," I said.

"It was," Mary said.

"That's impossible," I said. "Adam Moak died years ago. He drowned in the Amite River. You remember that."

Mary looked stubborn, set her chin and mouth in a way I remembered well. "It was," she said, in the tone that brooked no interference; the tone that had led me into countless quarrels with her when we were children, to words I regretted to this very day.

"What are you doing with a boyfriend, anyway? I thought you were supposed to be married to Dan Rather."

Mary didn't answer, just looked straight ahead.

"Poor Dan," I said. I immediately regretted my words. What was wrong with me? Johnella told me that Mary longed to be in New

York, and the first thing out of my mouth was a joke about Mary and the fashion world of New York, a world she could never, ever hope to enter. And now I had made fun of her hopeless, painful passion. Why was I so mean? "I'm sorry," I said.

Mary stared straight ahead, ignored my apology.

The last car pulled out of the circular driveway, and the funeral procession began to move. The deputy turned his head toward us. I searched for his eyes behind the black glasses but could find no spark of human light, just the reflection of our car. He brought his arm down in an arc that told us we were now permitted to fall in behind the cortege. Then he wheeled about and sped away.

Mary pointed toward the mortuary and cried, "Look!"

I looked in the direction of Mary's pointing finger.

"Daddy!" Mary cried.

I searched the green lawn.

"There's Daddy!" Mary cried.

I looked and looked before I remembered it was impossible. "No way," I said.

"He's coming over here," Mary said.

I moved the car forward.

"Wait!" Mary cried. "Wait! He wants to get in!"

I wanted to drive away faster, but our path was blocked by the funeral procession. "No!" I knew better, knew there was no one there, but I was terrified and furious at Mary for scaring me.

Mary pulled my hands from the steering wheel. "Wait! Wait! Wait for Daddy!"

"It's not Daddy, and he's not getting in the car with us," I said. I flung her hands away from mine and drove faster. I shot a glance behind us, though I knew full well the lawn was empty. "Damn it, Mary."

"It was Daddy," Mary said. "You left him there. You went off and left him there."

"It was not Daddy," I said. "And I didn't go off and leave him there." I took hold of her arm. "Tell me you know it wasn't Daddy."

Mary pulled away.

"Tell me!" I said. "Say it!"

But Mary wouldn't answer. She looked into the backseat, inclined her head, and began to whisper to someone she had created out of wishes and imagination. Mary's lips continued to move, and I knew that she was talking to a person only she could see.

As we crept along behind the cars with their lights on in the middle of the sunny morning, I looked at Mary and said, "You know, don't you?"

An elderly black man in a dark suit, coming out onto his front step to find a funeral passing, stopped still, removed his hat, and placed it over his heart. When the funeral had gone by and it was just us, he replaced his hat, gave Mary and me a wave, and came down the steps of the old weatherworn frame house. A flowering red rose clung to the tattered screen of the side porch. Mary turned to watch him walk along the sidewalk. She waved back for a long time. "I know. You know. We know," she said.

"You heard Johnella talking about it to somebody, didn't you?" I said. "She said you didn't know, but you do, don't you?"

Mary said nothing.

"Don't you, Mary?"

But Mary maintained her silence.

The line of cars inched along the main street of the small town. Just when I felt I would scream if we didn't move faster, I heard Mary say in a perfectly normal tone, "Sometimes I like to go slow."

I willed myself to be calm. I reminded myself how confined Mary's life was and said, "I guess you do, don't you."

"When you're going slow, you get a chance to see everything— every little thing," Mary said.

"There's not much to see around here," I said. We went by a shuttered movie theater, an office-supply store with nothing left in its dusty window but a desk chair and a crumpled piece of paper.

"I liked looking at that security guard," Mary said.

"He was just a deputy," I said.

"I liked looking at him anyway," Mary said.

"Me, too," I said.

As we drove along I watched my sister take everything in.

"That's McArthur Drugs!" Mary cried, pointing to a newly re-modeled building bright with red and white paint. "That's where my medicine comes from." Mary went into my purse, removed the fluted medicine cup, lowered the car window, and held it up as we drove past. "I've got all my pills!" she cried, rattling them in their container. "Thank you very much!" An elderly white woman with tightly curled gray hair who was balancing herself with a cane as she struggled with the drugstore door looked after us, bewildered.

Mary pointed to a small frame house between an Exxon station and the Celestial Light Baptist church. "That's where Johnella gets my makeup." A sign, hand-lettered in red paint, was tacked to a black shutter: NEW WORLD BEAUTY SALON.

We crossed a railroad track, and Mary raised both feet from the floor of the car. "Put your feet up," she said. "Or you'll lose your boyfriend."

"Drivers don't have to put their feet up when they go over railroad tracks. They get a special dispensation from the pope."

"That's not true," Mary said. "Do you have a boyfriend?" she asked as we bumped across.

"Not right now," I said. I thought of all the men I had known, of all the men I had left behind.

I opened my purse and held out my hand. "Give me back that cup so we don't lose all the pills you're supposed to take at lunch."

Just past the railroad tracks, the funeral procession slowed to a stop. Waiting, I watched a woman with two little girls come out of a florist's shop. The woman was young and pretty. She wore black high heels, a black suit, and a white blouse. A red necklace hung around her neck. She reminded me of our mother when Mary and I were young. One child, maybe five years old, was small and yellow-haired. She carried a shiny red plastic purse and skipped along the sidewalk while holding tightly to her mother's hand. The older child was dark-haired, taller, walked alone and more carefully. "I wonder what that woman and those children were doing in the flower shop?" I said idly, more to myself than to Mary.

"They were buying flowers for a funeral," Mary said.

"I wonder where they're going now?" I said.

"They're going to Jumping Jack's to get some lunch," Mary said.

I looked at my sister. "They are?"

Mary nodded.

"Where are they going after they eat lunch?" I said.

"They're going to King Dollar," Mary said.

"What for?" I said.

"To get some clothes that fit right," Mary said.

"Then where are they going?" I said.

"Then they're going to go home with that man," Mary said.

"What man?" I said.

"That man on the motorcycle," Mary said.

I saw that the deputy, like a shepherd tending his sheep, had ridden to the rear of the column of cars to see that each had safely crossed the railroad tracks, that all remained with the flock, and then, in an exquisite figure eight, had turned and roared back to the head of the procession, ready to lead the hearse and its companions to the place of peace.

"Do you think he's their daddy?" I said.

"No," Mary said. "He just looks out for them. Their daddy's dead."

Chapter Six

Spring 1954

After the party to welcome the Landrys, Bonita's father came to her room near bedtime, closed her door, and sat in the rocker next to her bed. "I gave you specific instructions to include Mary in your games with the new neighbor. Do you want to tell me why you disobeyed me?"

"Yes, sir," Bonita said. She put the book she was reading facedown on the bed beside her. "Yesterday, right after Laurel and her mother and daddy got here with that big truck, some of us got to talking with Laurel across the street. Mary ran over—she didn't even look both ways—and untied the sash that Laurel said her mother had tied for her. Then Mary threw sand on her, too. Right on her new dress."

"What happened after that?" her father said.

"I tried to fix her sash as best I could, but I couldn't tie a bow as good as her mother's, and she started to cry and went home," Bonita said.

"That was very kind of you, Bonita," her father said. "I'm proud of you for trying to help Dr. Landry's daughter. But you still haven't told me why you disobeyed me."

"When Laurel got here this afternoon for the party, she said, 'My daddy says I don't have to play with that baby who threw sand on me.' I didn't know what to do," Bonita said.

Bonita's father sat down beside her and put his arm around her. "I understand that you were put on the spot, hon, but Mary needs to make some friends of her own. Laurel Landry would be a good place for her to begin. Would you help her?"

"But I don't know how to teach Mary to make friends."

"You'll figure it out," her father said. "It sure would mean a lot to your mother to see Mary have somebody to play with. You know how she worries about your sister."

"Yes, sir," Bonita said. "I'll try."

Her father hugged her and kissed the top of her head.

Bonita was grateful for her father's confidence and affection, but beneath her gratitude lay dismay: she didn't have the faintest idea how to accomplish what seemed to her an almost impossible task. But because Bonita would have done anything to make Lottie happy, she devised a plan. With cardboard from her father's clean shirts, a box of watercolors, a roll of Scotch tape, a dozen Popsicle sticks, and some green florist's clay, she invented a game for Mary and Laurel. She painted trees on the cardboard and oranges on tiny pieces of paper that were numbered and placed facedown in the foliage. To gain points, Mary and Laurel would use a Popsicle stick with a piece of clay stuck on the end to turn the oranges over; the player who accumulated the most points won. Bonita wrote the name of the game, Fruit in the Trees, across the top and, inspired by a missal in the chapel at school, illuminated the "F" and the "T" with fruit, birds, berries, and leaves.

When the game was ready, Bonita brought Mary into her room and closed the door. "Sit here in the window seat, Mary," Bonita said.

"Why?" Mary said.

"Because I want to talk to you," Bonita said. She put Mary on the seat next to her.

"Why?" Mary said.

"Because we are going to invite Laurel Landry over to play a game," Bonita said.

"Why?" Mary said, grinning now.

"Because Laurel is new here and we want to be friendly to her."

"Why?" Mary said, laughing out loud. "Why? Why? Why?" she said, and she ran all around the room until Bonita caught her up and put her in the window seat again.

Bonita leaned close to Mary's ear. "Tomorrow we're going to walk over to Laurel's house. I'm going to wait on the sidewalk, and you're going to walk up on Laurel's porch."

"Then what am I going to do?" Mary said.

"You're going to ring the doorbell," Bonita said.

"Then what am I going to do?" Mary said.

"You're going to ask Laurel if she wants to come over and play," Bonita said.

Although it required all of Bonita's patience and skill to get through to her sister, she knew that by drilling this into her, she could bring Mary around to whatever she wanted her to do. At the end of the day, Bonita slept fitfully and dreamed the same dreams over and over all night long.

The next day, Mary did just what Bonita had told her to do. Laurel consented to come over, and the three of them played Fruit in the Trees on the floor of Bonita's bedroom. Mary played so well that these games soon took place on a daily basis and the other children in the neighborhood were invited to join them.

Lottie would bring in tall glasses of cold milk on a silver tray and thick pieces of warm gingerbread on a cut-glass plate. She smiled as she passed the food around. For the first time in a long time, Lottie looked happy. Bonita even heard her mother singing in the kitchen, a snatch of Mimi's old familiar song from *La Bohême*.

Bonita stopped going home with her school friends in order to come straight home and play with Laurel and Mary and the rest of the neighborhood children. She found herself looking forward to seeing Laurel. When Bonita would get home from school in the afternoon, Laurel was always waiting for her at the bus stop. She would put her hand in Bonita's, walk by her side, look up at her with her extraordinary hazel eyes, and engage Bonita in intelligent conversation. Bonita loaned Laurel books she had loved when she was five going on six. Laurel read these books and returned them promptly without any crayon scribblings on their pages. If Bonita happened upon a mysterious word during the course of her school day, she and Laurel lifted the dictionary from its stand, climbed into Dr. Gabriel's wide wingbacked reading chair with the big book on their laps, and looked the word up. Mary often played happily beneath them on the living room rug. Bonita observed that Mary soaked up other people's feelings as if she were a sponge: if Bonita was happy, Mary was happy; when Lottie smiled, Mary smiled.

Bonita and Laurel grew so fond of each other that Bonita invented a life in which Laurel was her real sister. That entire spring Laurel got up early in the morning to walk with Bonita to the bus stop. When Bonita got on the bus, she sat where she could see Laurel standing alone on the sidewalk. As the bus bore Bonita away, they waved and waved until the turn at Lantana Street separated them.

On their walks to and from the bus stop, Bonita told Laurel a continuing story about their life together as sisters. They each took new names, new birthdays, and new birthplaces. In these made-up stories, Bonita and Laurel lived in another city without adult supervision and with no visible means of support. Laurel was always interested in what they would eat, so Bonita would cook a pretend breakfast. It was often something exotic: sunset-limited French toast or eggs Benedict (they studied the cookbooks in Lottie's kitchen and made out imaginary menus for the entire week.) Then, after consulting the *Encyclopaedia Britannica* in Dr. Gabriel's bookcase, they went on make-believe trips. They visited a different place each time, and they always traveled and provisioned themselves alphabetically. Often, on the weekends, Laurel and Bonita played together under the ligustrums on the side of the Gabriels' house, which, when they bloomed in April, gave Mary terrible hay fever, so they were left mercifully alone. They never, ever went anywhere near Laurel's house.

"Get on the magic carpet, Arabella," Bonita would say as she sat down in the scuffed dirt between two tall shrubs.

"Yes, my darling sister," Laurel would say and sit down cross-legged behind Bonita.

"Close your eyes and hold on tight," Bonita would say.

"Where are we flying today, Evangeline?" Laurel would say.

"Today we are going to live in Brazil and we're taking Boston baked beans. You name something."

"Bananas."

"Boiled beef."

"Brownies."

"Biscuits."

"Bread."

"Biscuits are bread. Pick something else—maybe blackberries."

"Blackberries. I can't think of any more B's. Let's go live somewhere else."

"Okay. We're flying to Chicago and we're taking candy. Chocolate candy."

"Corn."

"Crabmeat cocktails."

"Caramels."

In order for these soothing dramas to have any semblance of reality, it was necessary for Mary to disappear, so Bonita imagined on a regular basis that Mary had been kidnapped and they never saw her again.

During the hours that passed while they were playing, Bonita's thoughts turned often to Ellen Landry. She could not escape the memory of Laurel's mother sitting naked on the floor playing jacks. Bonita pondered the meaning of the clocks covered in black cloth.

Apart from Laurel, the other members of the Landry household remained a mystery. In spite of the fact that Lottie and Ellen Landry had been in college together, each time Lottie called to chat with her former schoolmate, she was told by the housekeeper that Mrs. Landry was resting. Laurel's mother remained a mysterious figure. Her nomination by Lottie for membership in the book club, Capitol City Classics, was graciously declined by mail. An invitation to join the Current Events Forum, a club whose membership was limited to the wives of physicians, was also turned down through the Landrys' housekeeper by telephone.

Once, though, Bonita came face-to-face with Laurel's mother. One Monday afternoon when Laurel wasn't at the bus stop waiting, Bonita went to look for her. The front of the Landrys' house was not friendly. After they moved in, the Landrys had not pruned the azaleas that grew along the front of the house or the boxwood hedge that lined the walk to the front door. All of the venetian blinds in the windows were closed with their slats pointing upward so no light leaked through them.

Bonita decided to go to the back. Slowly, she trudged up the driveway, which, like the Gabriels' driveway—two lines of concrete for the wheels of the car with grass growing between them—led to the garage at the back of the lot. Bonita glanced uneasily toward the blank blinds of the windows on the side of the house. "Laurel!" she called.

Bonita put her book sack down in the grassy backyard and went up the back steps. She saw the storage cabinets along the wall of the back porch and remembered vividly the day she and the other children had investigated their contents before she sneaked into Laurel's house.

Bonita opened the screen door and hollered, "Laurel!"

As Laurel appeared in the doorway to the kitchen, Bonita realized that someone was huddled in a corner of the porch, partially concealed by the storage cabinets.

Laurel motioned for Bonita to leave. Bonita saw Laurel's raised arm moving forward, pushing her away, and saw Laurel's mouth move, saying, "Go home!" just as the huddled figure in the corner raised her head.

Again the woman was nude, but this time her long dark hair hung over her face, and her knees were drawn up with her arms clasped around them.

Bonita heard a car pull up in the driveway and come quickly all the way back to the garage. Laurel came out onto the porch. She wore a long-sleeved sweater with a high collar that went up to her chin. Her face was tear-streaked.

"Go away," Laurel said, just as Bonita's shoulder was grasped by a strong hand from behind.

Bonita, torn between her wish to comfort Laurel and her desire to run, looked up into Dr. Landry's harried face.

"Run home," he said. "And don't come over here again."

Dr. Landry thrust Bonita aside so roughly that she almost fell from the steps. As he entered the porch, Dr. Landry slipped his suit coat from his shoulders. The last thing Bonita saw after one last look straight into Laurel's anguished face was Laurel's father covering his shivering wife with his own clothes.

Bonita picked up her book sack and ran home. She told no one what she had seen.

Laurel didn't come out to play for almost a week. When she did come out, late one warm Sunday evening, she still wore the high-necked, long-sleeved sweater. She didn't want to play with Bonita. She wanted only to play with Adam, Frankie, Gracie, and Adrienne.

During a game of hide-and-seek, Bonita followed Laurel to the ligustrums where they always hid together.

"You can hide here if you want to," Laurel said. "I don't care." She looked not at Bonita but through the leaves of the shrubbery at the sidewalk.

"Don't you want me to hide here with you?" Bonita said.

"I don't care," Laurel said.

Bonita was puzzled. Laurel seemed angry with her, and Bonita didn't know why. "It's almost your birthday," Bonita said. "Are you still going to have a western party with a real pony to ride on?" Bonita was saving her allowance in order to buy Laurel's present, a boxed collection called Games from A to Z that contained everything from Animal Rummy to Zoo Lotto.

Instead of answering her question, Laurel said, "What's wrong with your sister?"

"There's nothing wrong with my sister," Bonita said. She slid away from Laurel to the edge of the shrubbery.

"You said yourself that Mary can't even read yet," Laurel said.

"My daddy says Mary just needs a little extra time. Pretty soon she'll catch up, and then she'll be just like everybody else."

"That's not what my daddy said," Laurel said.

"I don't care what your daddy said," Bonita said, moving out from under the shelter of the hedge.

"I heard my daddy tell my mama there was something wrong with her. He said, 'John and Lottie are going to have a pot full of trouble with that littlest Gabriel girl if they don't do something soon,' " Laurel said. "He said your mama needs to go to the doctor, too. He said, 'Lottie Gabriel is a classic case. She fits those studies I've done to a T.' "

Bonita put her hands over her ears. "I don't want to hear what your daddy said!"

Laurel moved closer and spoke louder. "He told my mama that your daddy ought to call him up and get some help. But he says your mama and daddy never will because they don't want to see it. He says Mary's just going to get worse and worse."

"That's not true!" Bonita cried. She felt as if her lungs were being squeezed. "If something was wrong . . ." She panted as if she had just run all the way home from City Park. "If something was wrong with Mary, my daddy would fix it. If she was sick, he would make her well," she finally got out.

"My daddy says doctors are the worst ones," Laurel cried. "He said doctors never want to tell anybody they have a sick person in their own family!"

"Why are you doing this?" Bonita cried. "Is it because I saw your mama naked? I don't care if she wears clothes or not. It doesn't make one bit of difference to me if she wants to be naked all day long. We're supposed to be sisters, and sisters don't care about things like that!"

"We're not sisters!" Laurel cried. "Your sister's just a big old meanie!"

Bonita stood up, all thoughts of hide-and-seek abandoned. "Is that why you moved here?" she said. "Did you move here because your mama won't wear any clothes?"

"My mama wears clothes!" Laurel said.

"She never goes anywhere," Bonita said. "Why didn't she come to our party?"

"She was tired," Laurel said.

Bonita knew her fury was spiraling out of control, knew her mother would have said "Stop! You're the oldest; it's up to you to see that things don't get out of hand."

But, recklessly, Bonita let herself go. "She wasn't too tired to play jacks!" she shouted. "She wasn't too tired to sit on the floor without any clothes on and play jacks. I saw her do it!"

"I'm gonna tell my daddy you went in my house!" Laurel cried. "Nobody was supposed to go in my house!"

"We don't ever see your mama because there's something wrong with her," Bonita said. "Isn't there? There's something wrong with her!"

"Don't you say that about my mama!" Laurel shouted. "There's nothing wrong with my mama!"

"Then what did you leave New Orleans for?" She shoved Laurel. "Why?"

Laurel came right up next to Bonita's face. "Because we wanted to!" She spat it out. "And I'm sorry we did, because now I have to play with you and your no-good, dumb sister!"

"She is not no-good!" Bonita said. "And she's not dumb. You take that back!"

Adam came around the side of the house and tagged Bonita. "You're It! All in free, all in free, Bonita's It!" All of the other children ran in and touched base.

Just then Bonita saw the watchman's black car come around the corner. She seized Laurel by the arm.

"Ow!" Laurel said, pulling away. "You're hurting me!"

"Do you see that car? Do you see that man?" Bonita cried. She shook Laurel, so furious she trembled.

Laurel began to cry. "Yes," she said, snuffling and wiping tears away with her free hand. "I see him."

"That man looks out for us! We would never, never, ever be kidnapped because he watches us all the time! He doesn't know you! He doesn't care if you're kidnapped! He doesn't care what happens to you! He only cares about us!"

As the watchman's car drew closer, Bonita dropped Laurel's arm and waved to Orlando to show Laurel how familiar she was with this source of security and power.

In the fading light, the man slowed the car, raised his hand, and waved. To Bonita, whose sorrow over Laurel's words about Mary and

Lottie had invaded her entire spirit, the gesture came as balm; her trembling subsided.

Bonita stepped into the street, walked right up to the watchman's car as he stopped, and put her hand on the open window. She glanced back at Laurel to make sure she was watching.

"Hey there, Miss Bonita," the man said. "I still got that match you give me." He reached into his pocket and held it up to show her.

Bonita smiled at him.

"I keep it just in case I ever need to light up," Orlando said.

"I'll give you another one if you ever lose it," Bonita said.

The security guard put the match in his pocket and patted her hand. "That would be real nice," he said. "Now, jump back on the sidewalk, sweetheart. So you won't get hurt out here in the street."

Bonita stepped back and the car began to move.

"You be careful, now," Orlando called back. He again gave the little wave, picked up speed, and drove away.

With a secret, satisfied delight, Bonita turned and looked at Laurel. She smiled at her memory of the gun: how it lay in the watchman's car in the dark, radiating energy, a source of light known only to her.

Chapter Seven

October 1995

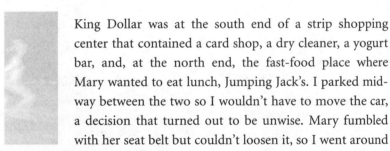

King Dollar was at the south end of a strip shopping center that contained a card shop, a dry cleaner, a yogurt bar, and, at the north end, the fast-food place where Mary wanted to eat lunch, Jumping Jack's. I parked midway between the two so I wouldn't have to move the car, a decision that turned out to be unwise. Mary fumbled with her seat belt but couldn't loosen it, so I went around the car to open her door and free her. On the sidewalk nearby, a slight, fair-haired security guard talked to a young woman who balanced a little girl on her hip. The guard wore a khaki uniform and carried a black revolver in a holster at his waist. One half of a pair of handcuffs hung out of his back pocket.

Mary paused with one foot on the curb, transfixed by the sight of the watchman in his uniform. She cast a glance back at me, a look of such authentic sadness and longing that, for an instant, I believed she was the Mary we had sought so long: the Mary who had been stolen away from us when only a child; the Mary who could read books without scribbling in them; the Mary who did not believe that she was married to a celebrity or that the dead walked and spoke; and who, when she got to a place, stayed put.

"Look," she said.

I closed my hand over her pointing finger. "He looks a lot like Mr. Orlando, doesn't he?" I said.

"It is Mr. Orlando," she said.

I shook my head. "No, you just want it to be."

"It might be," she said.

"It's not," I said.

"Dan told me Orlando would be here."

"I don't care what Dan Rather told you, it's not Orlando Duplantis."

"It is so," Mary said.

I touched her shoulder. "I know you want it to be, but it's not," I said.

She twisted away from my touch. "Want not. Not got. Got shot," she said, and the fully grown, perfectly normal Mary disappeared into the lost Mary.

The watchman reached into his left breast pocket, withdrew something, and handed it to the young woman with the child. At that gesture, I could bear no more. "Come on, Mary," I said. "Let's go."

"No, I want to go talk to him," she said.

"I promise you, it's not who you want it to be," I said. I chose a shopping cart, trying to get one whose wheels didn't wobble, took Mary's elbow, and urged her on. "Mary, you know it's impossible," I said.

Mary whipped her arm away from me and stalked into the store. "Dan told me it was. My husband knows."

We both fell silent inside. The collection of clothes and toys, shoes and cameras, Bibles and candy, hardware and housewares, the gathering of thousands of things under one roof, was almost more than we could take in.

Immediately before us were long tables piled high with maroon, cream, and baby-blue plastic coat hangers. There were hundreds and hundreds of them on rectangular tables that ran all the way to the back of the store. At regular intervals, someone with a quirky sense of humor had erected strange sculptures fashioned from twisted old-fashioned metal coat hangers that resembled fish and birds, and insects belonging to unusual orders. These twisted metal coat hangers rose up from the heap as if the outdated wire were being mocked by the more modern colored plastic. I took hold of Mary's arm for comfort.

Surprisingly, she didn't pull away. When I looked at her, her face was white. Too late I realized that the size of the store and the abundance of the merchandise might, after her long absence from the world, overwhelm her. We stood clutching each other. People flowed around us as if we were obstructions in a stream.

"Let's go," I said. "There's too much stuff in this store. I can exchange these clothes later."

"No," she said. "I want to stay and see what's here."

She still permitted me to cling to her, but the color was returning to her face, and I knew it wouldn't be long before she pulled away. She even began to look as though she might be enjoying seeing so many new things. I admired her courage; that morning, when I had come in to get her clothes, I was in and out of there in about two seconds flat. That's why everything had been too small. I had just picked out a bunch of dark-colored clothes and some underwear, paid for it, and bolted.

I looked about for someone to talk to about exchanging the clothes. I pushed Mary toward the customer-information booth at the back of the store. "This way," I said.

"No," Mary said. "I want to go over there." Pushing the shopping cart ahead of her, she set out for the dizzying array of games, puzzles, stuffed animals, and Tonka trucks in the toy aisle.

I caught up with her and said, "Okay, but wait right here for me. I'm going to exchange these clothes."

There was a line at customer service. When it was my turn to be served, I didn't have the receipt for the clothes I had bought earlier that morning. It must have fallen out when Johnella was getting Mary dressed, I thought. They said: no receipt, no exchange. I said: take these clothes and shove them where the sun never shines. I pushed the whole lot over the counter onto their precious paperwork and walked off.

When I got back to the toy department, Mary was gone.

I finally found her in the Halloween section. Into the basket Mary had piled costumes: a ghost, a black cat, and a witch. Now she was loading orange-and-black-decorated bags of M&M's, bubble gum, and Hershey bars; cartons of malted-milk balls, peppermint patties, and chocolate-covered raisins. On tiptoe to reach the top shelves, she plucked down wax teeth filled with orange sugar water, decorated Dracula suckers, and jack-o'-lanterns filled with candy corn. For good measure she threw in a witch's hat.

"Mary!" I stopped her, arrested her arm in midreach. The cart was almost three quarters full. "Whoa," I said. "What's up?"

"I want all this," Mary said. Beneath the candy I saw Monopoly, chess, checkers, a stuffed teddy bear, Tinkertoys, LEGOs, and Lincoln Logs.

"Well, you can't have all this," I said.

"But I want it," Mary said.

"You can choose two things, but all the rest of this stuff has to go back where it came from," I said. "I'm going to have to come back another time and get you a black dress."

The security guard we had seen outside came into the store, and I watched him as he walked toward us. Up close, he scarcely resembled Orlando Duplantis at all. His skin was pocked with old acne scars, and his eyes were not the clear blue Orlando's had been; his were dark and dead-looking. His mouth turned down at the corners. I never trust a person whose at-rest expression contains the ghost of a scowl. He walked up to us and stopped, hands on his hips, perpetual frown now in full bloom, mouth set to speak harsh security-guard words should the need for them arise.

"Hurry up," I said to Mary. "We need to get out of here so we can get some lunch." I pretended the man wasn't there.

Hastily, under the watchman's stern eye, we put everything back, and Mary trolled around the store looking for something to really want. Constantly at our backs was the watchdog.

Mary examined a Bible with an ornately carved wooden cover, a pound of malted-milk balls in a carton cleverly designed to look like a half-gallon of milk, and a T-shirt with a picture of a witch. She finally decided on a coloring book and a box of ninety-six Crayolas. I held on to Mary by her sleeve and forced her to wait with me while I paid.

Outside, on the sidewalk, the security guard stopped us. "I'm going to need to examine your packages," he said.

"Why? I just got through paying for these." I held the sack out for him to see as I withdrew the sales slip. He compared the two and then nodded.

"What's your name?" Mary said. "I think I know you. Do you have any brothers?" She moved her head so she could see his shirt. "You don't have your name over your pocket. We used to know somebody that looked just like you, and he had his name over his pocket. In red."

The man ignored Mary's questions. I knew they were inappropriate, but he didn't have to be so hard-nosed about it. I was disliking him more and more by the minute.

He held out his hand to Mary. "Let me see your purse."

Mary turned away from him, held her purse against her chest, and shook her head.

"Mary, give him the purse," I said.

She finally surrendered it, and the man opened it: Mary had a purse full of candy. "Oh, Mary," I said. "What have you done?"

"I wanted them," she said.

"You can't just take things because you want them, Mary," I said. My voice was starting to quiver. Oh Mother of the Word Incarnate, please don't let this terrible man see me cry, I prayed without thinking. I was horrified when I realized what I had done. I take it back, I thought. I don't need you. I can do this myself.

I drew the guard aside. "Look," I said. "This is my sister. Our father just died, and I came in here to try and get her a black dress to wear to the funeral. They wouldn't exchange what I had bought earlier, so we are going somewhere else. Can't we just take this stuff back inside? I'll pay for it and we can let that be the end of it?"

He pressed his lips together. "She's from that home for the ree-tards," he said.

"She's not retarded," I said. "But yes, that's where she lives. Please." I had to force the begging word around my teeth. It was hard to keep from letting him see how furious I was.

He finally agreed, and I took Mary back inside. The man stayed with us while we emptied the contents of Mary's purse onto the checkout counter so that the checker could see everything.

She was a sickly-looking white girl already wearing mules for bad feet. She stole looks at Mary from under lowered lids and then ex-changed a look with the guard. She took up a pencil and moved Mary's makeup and coupons—all of the contents of the drawer at the home that Mary had brought with her—around with it, as if she might catch whatever it was my sister had.

The guard escorted us to the door. "I already had one complaint about you from customer service," he said to me. "I don't want to see you in King Dollar again. Neither one of you."

My heart pounded as we walked away. I was so mad I felt as if the skin on my body was on fire.

Mary looked back and smiled at him—gave him a cheery wave.

How dare he talk to us like that? I thought of our mother, thought of how this would have humiliated her: her daughters taken to task by a nobody, lectured to by a common person who didn't even have the courtesy to tell us his name. I, too, turned to look back at him, but I didn't wave.

Chapter Eight

Spring 1954

When Bonita was in grammar school, confession at the Academy of the Holy Angels was heard by Father Michael, a retired priest who lived in a suite of rooms above the cafeteria. Once a month, a grade at a time, Bonita and her classmates filed into the chapel for confession. If Father Michael was pressed for time, he called in a younger priest to help him so two classes could receive the sacrament at once. Then, next to the altar, on the opposite side of the chapel confessional, Sister Veronica placed an ornately carved mahogany prie-dieu that had belonged to the order for over a hundred years. Behind it she put a wooden latticework screen with interstices so large that she always shook out a clean man's handkerchief and pinned it to the screen to protect the privacy of the penitent. If two grades were going to confession at once, Bonita would try to get a jump on the other group so she could lead her class to the old prie-dieu. The sides of the kneeler Bonita adored were ornamented with carved fruit and flowers. The mahogany shelf, worn smooth with use, held the arms of the petitioning student and formed the lid of a storage space.

Bonita loved confession more than any other sacrament the Catholic Church offered her. After confession, she always felt as if the world had achieved harmony. Outside in the sunshine, the sky seemed bluer, colors were brighter, and Bonita always had a brief but intense moment of well-being.

Once, in October of the third grade, Bonita had been the last one in her class to make confession. After receiving her penance, she genuflected, looked around quickly to make sure no nuns were watching, then lifted the mahogany lid to see what was hidden beneath. That was when she discovered where the supply of clean white handkerchiefs was kept. Casting furtive glances over her shoulder, Bonita lifted the handkerchiefs: a rosary of beautiful red crystal beads sparkled on the bottom of the box. Tenderly, Bonita touched the feet of the tiny silver Christ with the tip of one finger. Then, closing her eyes, she traced the shape of the red beads and committed them to memory.

At home, the memory of the vivid rosary made all of her own simple possessions seem pale. When the time for confession grew near again, Bonita decided to take something of her own and place it in the space with the handkerchiefs and the red rosary so that it could be infused with light from the glowing beads. Bonita examined all that she owned: her clothes, her shoes, a silver dresser set—comb, brush, mirror—her clock with the pink gingham face, the book she had gotten for her fifth birthday, *Picture Book of Exploration,* and a jump rope. She would have liked to take her book about the explorers to be blessed by the light, but it was too big. Finally she chose the plainest thing—the piece of rope. It was not a true jump rope, not one of the red-and-white braided ones with the red wooden handles she had seen in the dime store, but a plain, four-foot length of dirty, off-white hemp with a knot in each end to keep it from slipping through her fingers while she jumped.

In November, on the next occasion of confession, Bonita put the rope in her lunch box. Because third and fourth grades were the last to make their confession before lunch, students who had brought food from home were permitted to bring it with them to the chapel. Bonita contrived to be first so she could lead her class to her favorite kneeler, then slipped to the back of the line.

With her heart pounding, she waited to take her place at the prie-dieu. She made her confession: "I forgot to say my prayers Wednesday night; I talked back to my mother; when my father told me to stop reading and go to bed, I disobeyed him and finished my book with a flashlight; and I pushed Denise Matens so I could be first in line for the swing." She heard her penance, made an act of contrition, crossed herself, genuflected, and dropped to the floor. She opened the lunch box she had left next to the kneeler. Inside, with her lunch, was the coiled jump rope. Hurriedly, Bonita lifted the lid of the storage space in the prie-dieu. She inserted the rope and then, obeying an inner command she did not understand, she put in the orange from her lunch and closed the mahogany lid.

"My goodness, child!" Father Michael said as he came from behind the screen, his eyes cast down, folding his stole. "I almost stepped on you."

Bonita looked up at the priest. She put her hand on the prie-dieu that had belonged to the order for a hundred years. "I love to come here for confession because this kneeler's so beautiful. Isn't it beautiful, Father?"

"Yes, little one, it is beautiful. The sisters have cared for it well," Father Michael said.

Bonita ran her hand lovingly over the wood. "I love the way it feels, Father Michael," she said. "Feel how smooth it is."

"Yes, it is smooth, but I don't have time to feel it right now, my dear," Father Michael said, and he strode away.

Bonita got to her feet. She walked slowly to the door of the chapel. There, looking back at the prie-dieu, she raised her hand and waved. Then she ran outside to the cafeteria with her lunch box bouncing at her side.

It took several days for it to dawn on Bonita that when Sister Veronica opened the prie-dieu to get a fresh handkerchief for the next month's confession, she would discover the rope and the fruit. Then it occurred to her that someone had probably washed and replaced the handkerchief already.

Bonita didn't know what to do. She didn't know where the kneeler was kept, so she couldn't go look for it to remove the orange and the rope. She hung around Sister Veronica's office, hoping to hear the subject of confession come up in the conversation, but it never did, and she felt she was becoming conspicuous when Sister Veronica asked her twice, "Bonita, what can I do for you this fine day?" and smiled at her.

November passed. Bonita worried all through the month, but still no one said anything to her about the things she had left in the prie-dieu. When confession for December was over, Bonita lurked outside the chapel door until she saw Father Michael leave for the cafeteria. Walking rapidly on tiptoe, looking constantly behind her, Bonita approached the beautiful prie-dieu. She could hear the first-graders, already turned loose for lunch, shrieking and laughing and calling to one another outside.

Breathing hard, Bonita knelt and lifted the mahogany shelf. The rope, neatly coiled, lay on a bed of clean white handkerchiefs. The orange, neither withered nor decayed but studded with cloves, rested in a white tatted cradle atop the rope. Bonita lifted the orange by the Christmas-ornament hook attached to the top of the handwork. She rocked back on her heels and smiled, filled with delight at the sight of the transformed fruit. She brought it close to her face and inhaled its aroma. It smelled like the spiced tea her mother made during the holidays.

A holy card lay next to the red rosary. In the center of the picture, the Virgin Mary sat in a stable holding the baby Jesus on her lap. Behind her haloed head was a cobalt-blue sky filled with gold stars. On Mary's left was an ass, his head hanging over a stall; on her right a dark-haired child knelt in the folds of her white gown. Both the

Blessed Mother and the yielding girl were bathed in a beam of white light that fell upon them from the center of the indigo sky. The glowing face of the child so reflected what Bonita felt when she discovered the transfigured fruit that, for the whole arc of her life, when she imagined what she looked like, imagined what face the world saw, it was the face of this kneeling, joyful child.

Bonita turned the picture over. On the back was a handwritten message: "May you always be sheltered by our Blessed Mother's love. Holy Christmas, Bonita." Beneath this message was Sister Veronica's signature and the date, December 25, 1951. Bonita held the fragrant fruit to her lips and, with her other hand, pressed the holy card to her chest. It was the happiest moment of her life.

Three days after her quarrel with Laurel beneath the ligustrums, Bonita approached the confessional. She summoned the memory of that good child who knelt in the folds of Mary's gown, and of the fragrant orange, to sustain her.

Bonita knelt. Father Michael's duties had grown so few as he aged that the beautiful prie-dieu Bonita loved was never needed. Bonita remembered its beauty as she waited for Father Michael to open the window. She thought of her earlier confessions and longed for her simpler sins.

When she heard the priest open the sliding window, Bonita said, "Bless me, Father, for I have sinned. It's been a month since my last confession."

She hesitated. She was silent so long that Father Michael prompted her. "Yes, little one. You may begin."

"Father," Bonita said in a low, shaky voice. "I did something terrible."

"What have you done," Father Michael said.

"I had a fight with my best friend and I said some mean things," Bonita said. She did not know how to communicate to Father Michael the conflicting feelings of anger and guilt; nor did she know how to express her suspicion that Ellen Landry was hurting her daughter and that beneath Laurel's sweater were bruises. In spite of the fact that a housekeeper lived in the Landrys' home, Bonita felt that by withdrawing her friendship, she had deprived Laurel of the only person in the neighborhood she could count on while Dr. Landry was away at work.

"Go on," Father Michael said.

"I think I made her feel bad" was all that Bonita could find to say.

"Then you must go to her and beg her forgiveness," Father Michael said.

"Yes, Father," she said.

"And then try to get along better with your little friend," the priest said.

"Yes, Father."

"Now, for your sins, offer five Hail Marys and two Our Fathers and make a good act of contrition."

"Yes, Father. Thank you, Father Michael."

After Bonita offered up her prayers, she went outside. In the sunshine she saw first-graders swinging and waiting to go down the slide. She saw Sister Veronica go into the cafeteria. She heard third-graders chanting, "A my name is Alice, B my name is Barbara, C my name is Charlotte" as they jumped rope, and she thought how lonely she would feel if she never played Magic Flying Carpet with Laurel again. Bonita waited for the feeling of excitement at the beauty and variety of the world that had always followed the sacrament of confession in the past. But instead of the colors seeming brighter, sounds more bell-like, and smells more vivid, Bonita felt listless. The entire panorama of the schoolyard seemed dim to her, as if a fine gray dust had settled upon it.

That afternoon Bonita went to look for Laurel so she could do Father Michael's bidding. She found Laurel drawing hopscotch squares on the sidewalk in front of the Landrys' house.

Bonita knelt down in the grass and watched as Laurel drew the design for the game with a long piece of white chalk. Neither said anything. When Laurel's chalk snapped and a piece flew into the grass near Bonita's leg, Bonita retrieved it and came forward on her hands and knees to the sidewalk. "Is it okay if I help you do that?" she said.

"I guess so," Laurel said.

Laurel had begun with the heart of the game: the three horizontal boxes that contained the most important square of all—the middle one—in which the hopping child could finally come down on both feet and find rest. Bonita put the cap on the "T" as Laurel extended it downward.

Still on her knees, Bonita sat back on her heels and said, "That looks pretty good, Laurel. All of your lines are really straight," which was only partially true.

"This one's not so good," Laurel said and moved to correct the side of one square.

"I'm sorry for what I said about your mother. I take everything back," Bonita offered.

Laurel rubbed out the offending line and redrew it again and again. As Bonita waited for Laurel to decide if she would accept her apology, she saw wet spots appear on the concrete between Laurel's fingers, as if it were beginning to rain, and realized that they were Laurel's tears.

"I just can't get this one to be straight," Laurel said, wiping her eyes with the back of one chalky hand.

"It doesn't have to be perfect," Bonita said. "It's still good for jumping. Look how nice and big you made the squares. Do you want to play?" She crawled over to the edge of the street and looked for two flat pieces of gravel in the crumbling asphalt to use for tars. She turned back, one hand outstretched with the blue-gray gravel in it, and their friendship could have been restored, for Laurel, who had remained undecided, reached out and took one of the rocks from Bonita's palm. But Mary, who had been watching from the Gabriels' front yard, suddenly dashed across the street, ran between them, threw a handful of sand on Laurel's head, and tore off back across Oleander Avenue.

Laurel stood up, shook sand from her hair, threw the little rock at Mary's retreating back, and shouted, "I don't want to play with you or your dumb sister ever again," and ran away.

A week later, there was one last game of Fruit in the Trees on the floor of Bonita's bedroom, but Mary kicked over the board when she lost, and Laurel whispered something into the ear of every child but the Gabriels. When Lottie brought in refreshments—tall glasses of lemonade with a stemmed maraschino cherry floating in each tall tumbler and plump, puffy sugar cookies still warm from the oven— the other children snickered as she left the room.

When everyone had left but Adam, Bonita blocked his path. "What did Laurel whisper to you?" she said.

"She said not to tell you," Adam said.

"You know, Adam, whispering is very rude," Bonita said. "It is almost the rudest thing you can do. I don't think your mother would want to hear about this."

"I wasn't whispering!" Adam cried. "I was only listening."

"Tell me what Laurel said and I won't tell your mother that you listened," Bonita said.

"Laurel said your mama needs to go to the doctor. She said if your mama would go to the doctor, we wouldn't have to put up with Mary." Adam punched Bonita in the stomach. "We're sick of Mary. Now get out of the way and let me out of here!"

Bonita hit Adam in the ribs as he ran from the room. "Get out! And don't ever come back!" she hollered after him.

Bonita turned back to Mary, who sat on the floor tearing Fruit in the Trees into pieces. Bonita knelt and tried to put her arms around her sister to calm her, but Mary shoved her away.

Chapter Nine

October 1995

It was quiet inside Jumping Jack's, early yet for lunch. The only customers were three men in paint-splattered white overalls, waiting for their food. The two older men were joking with a girl behind the counter. They ragged her about her short hair, which must have been a new cut because each man made head-tossing motions and then pulled long imaginary hair back from his forehead and tucked it behind an ear. The girl giggled as she wrapped their food. The youngest man read a magazine. I peeked at the back cover: vintage cars.

Jumping Jack's specialty was frankfurters: plain dogs, corn dogs, chili dogs, and a dozen combinations of toppings to go on them. Each item on the menu appeared in simplified shapes and primary colors framed in red behind the counter. Mary studied the pictures. She made the peculiar motion with her fingers that I had observed before and now knew was a symptom of anxiety. I should have planned this entire excursion a little more carefully, I thought.

"What do you want to eat?" I said, hoping to distract her.

"I don't know," she said. "Aura Lee's brother always brings one of each. I want them all."

The painters laughed. "Go for it," the young man said. He closed the magazine and tucked it under his arm.

Startled, Mary looked at them and then laughed, too, as if she had just understood the punch line of a joke. Anxious to repeat her success, she repeated it. "I want them all," she said again. But their laughter had faded and she was unable to retrieve it.

Mary leaned over the counter and spoke to the young woman, who was sacking the painters' food. "I need to use the telephone," she said. "Can I come back there and use your telephone?"

The girl pointed to the rear of the restaurant. "The pay phone's back there by the bathrooms."

"Why do you need a telephone, Mary?" I said.

"I have to call Aura Lee," she said abruptly.

"Why?" I said.

"I need to tell her we're at Jumping Jack's. I need to know what I should eat," she said.

"You can't eat without Aura Lee telling you what to get?" I said.

Mary ignored me and turned to the young man who had spoken to her before and was just being given his change. "I need a quarter. Can I have a quarter?"

"Sure, hon," the young man said and held out a handful of money.

Mary plucked a quarter from his palm. She gave him a coy look. "Do you have a girlfriend?" she said.

The other two painters hooted with laughter. "Not if he pulls any more stunts like he pulled last night," one of the older men said. He banged the young man on the back.

I pulled her away. "Mary, you don't ask a perfect stranger for money," I said under my breath. "And you certainly don't ask him about his girlfriend."

"Why not?" she said. She looked back at the young man. "I need a new boyfriend. My other one died," she said and walked away with her odd, stomach-forward gait.

I opened my wallet and took out a quarter to repay the young man. He waved it away. "Don't worry about it," he said. "She's like my sister's girl. If they were out someplace getting some food, I'd want somebody to be nice to her." He gave me a wink and walked toward the door. The other two men smiled benignly as they passed. I resented the hell out of Mary making me into a person men in paint-splattered overalls could feel sorry for.

I found Mary in the space between the men's and women's restrooms. She held the receiver out to me. "Aura Lee wants to say hey."

"Hey, Aura Lee," I said, grateful that she couldn't get at me through the telephone; the memory of that wet kiss made me shiver. I promised myself that if she started in on my sins again, I was hanging up. "How are you doing?"

"Hey, Mary's sister! I'm doing A-OK. What are y'all up to?"

"Getting a hot dog at Jumping Jack's," I said.

"What kind?" she said.

"Well, that's why Mary called you, Aura Lee. She said you were the expert on the hot dogs here."

Aura Lee turned away from the telephone, and I heard her say in a loud voice, "Mary says I'm the expert on hot dogs." Then I heard her laugh and say it again.

I put my hand over the receiver and said to Mary, "Where is she? Did you call her at the nurses' station?"

"She's in the dining room," Mary said.

"Hadn't we better get off the telephone? I don't want to tie up an important line. What if they need to call an ambulance?"

"She's at the patients' phone," Mary said. "We can talk as long as we want."

There goes that excuse.

"Tell Mary to get a corn dog," Aura Lee said. "And a Coke to drink."

I put my hand over the receiver. "Aura Lee says to get a corn dog and a Coke," I said to Mary.

Mary nodded. "Okay," she said.

"Mary says she'll get a corn dog and a Coke, Aura Lee."

"Eat, this is my body," Aura Lee said.

I interrupted her. "Aura Lee," I said.

"Drink," she said. "This is my blood, shed for you."

Through the window I saw a Livingston High School bus pull into the parking lot and stop. It was that awkward orange-yellow color that always stayed sharp and pointy in the crayon box because it could be used only for cheddar cheese and public vehicles and was an ugly color to boot. The door of the bus opened and at least forty students poured out and every last one of them made for Jumping Jack's.

"Oh, shit," I said. "Sorry, Aura Lee. Gotta go. There's a whole mob of people heading this way."

I hurried back to place our order, but Aura Lee was not finished with me yet. "Sister! Sister! Sister!" Mary bellowed at the top of her voice. "Aura Lee wants to talk to you again."

I ignored her and stepped up to place our order. But then it came again, louder than before. "Sister! Sister! Sister! Aura Lee wants to say a prayer for you!" As the teenagers came inside, each looked in the direction of the shouting.

The students, both black and white, male and female, were of that buoyant clan who dress and decorate themselves to avoid pleasing as many adults as possible. Their jeans were carefully ragged at the knees and seats; one boy had artfully arranged for a red heart on his white underwear to peep out. Multiple golden rings and studs adorned ears and noses. I hotfooted it back to talk to Aura Lee, no matter what she had to say about my sins, just so I wouldn't have to be swept up into the life and excitement the students radiated.

"You should let her do it," Mary said. "You need it."

"I'll decide that for myself, thank you very much," I said and yanked the receiver away. "Aura Lee, I appreciate you wanting to look after my soul, but now is not a real good time for it. We're going to have to leave here and find somewhere else to eat because this place has filled up with people," I said. I saw Mary frown at that.

"Lord have mercy on us," Aura Lee said.

"Aura Lee, I'm hanging up now," I said.

"Say it," Aura Lee said. "Lord have mercy on us."

I turned my back to the students. "No," I said in a hissing whisper. "Aura Lee, I'm hanging up."

"Christ have mercy on us," she said.

"No, Aura Lee."

"Say it," she said. "Christ have mercy on us."

"Here's Mary," I said. "Talk to her." I held the phone out. Mary took it.

Mary listened a minute and then said, "She wants you to say 'Christ hear us.' "

"I know what she wants. Just hang up and let's get out of here."

"She wants you to say it," Mary said.

"I don't care if she wants me to say it or not, we're leaving. Tell her she can pray over me when we get to the house."

"We're going home?" Mary said.

"If we can ever get out of here," I said. I took the receiver. "Bye, Aura Lee. We'll call you later." I hung up.

Mary looked sulky.

I grabbed her by the hand. "Come on, let's get out of here and get some food somewhere else."

Mary's lips set in a stubborn line. She pulled her hand away. "No! No! No! No! No!" she shouted. "I want to eat here!"

The students fell silent and watched us. I was so furious with Mary I could have hit her. For thirty years I had successfully avoided this kind of spectacle, and now I was being forced back into it again. I longed to be back in the safety of my office, longed to be looking down on a world where everything was too tiny to wound you.

Mary opened the door to the ladies' room. "I have to go in here," she said. "I want two corn dogs and some fries." She disappeared for a minute and then stuck her head back out. "And a large Coke."

I got in line to order food. I'll bet those kids are getting a big kick out of this, I thought, furious with myself for caring. I looked down at the floor in order to avoid their eyes. One girl, whose hair was a beautiful, complicated masterpiece of braids and beads, said, "She be from that home, huh?"

"Yes," I said.

"She your kin?"

"Yes," I said. "She's my sister."

"My auntee work there. Johnella Johnson?"

"I know her," I said. "I met her this morning."

The girl smiled. "She love those people out there. She call them all her babies."

"I know. You can tell she does. She's real good to my sister. Even brings Mary some of her own clothes to wear. That dress my sister has on?" The girl nodded. "Johnella brought it from home this morning. Our daddy just died." Why had I said that? Tears filled my eyes. God damn it, I will not cry, I thought.

The girl hugged me. Then she escorted me to the line the students had formed to order food. She urged them to move aside. "This lady know Johnella. Let her go on ahead."

The students parted for me. "Let her go by," each one said. They passed the words from one to another gently, like a blessing. I had to work hard not to cry. I would have preferred rudeness. "Thank you," I said. I passed through the path they made for me. "Thank you."

I ordered four corn dogs, fries, and Cokes and paid for them. The students returned to being their noisy selves. While I waited for the food I saw Mary come out of the bathroom; she had repainted her eyebrows purple. When she joined me in the line, one of the students said, "Hey, girl, I like the way that stuff go over your eyes." The speaker plucked at a companion's sleeve. "Look here, how she got all that purple on her eyebrows."

Mary looked pleased. "I'm going outside," she said, and as I watched helplessly, glancing back and forth from Mary to the girl bagging our food, she walked out the door. So much for all of Mary's hollering about wanting to eat at Jumping Jack's, I thought. Christ, we were hardly started on this terrible day and Mary was yanking me around like a yo-yo. I didn't know whether to abandon our lunch and go after her or not. Finally, I decided I had worked too hard to get this food, so I waited. When everything was ready, I gathered it up and quickly went out to he car. I turned over both of the Cokes, cursed, righted them, and headed out to look for Mary again, muttering all the while that the next time I would park right at the door so I wouldn't get so far behind Mary. I looked in the window of the dry cleaner, the card shop, and the yogurt bar. There she was! With her face repainted into the terrible mask, Mary was inside holding a giant cone of soft strawberry yogurt, and it appeared that, just as at the Stop-N-Go last summer, she had been thirsty for something red and sweet and had no money to pay for it. I went inside and took care of it.

Just outside of the Baton Rouge city limits, we stopped at a small park. As we sat at a dirty picnic table eating our lunch and shooing flies away, I told Mary that Daddy was dead.

Chapter Ten

June 1954

After school was out for the summer, Bonita grew to dread the days when she saw Laurel with her arms covered, for it was then that Laurel led the other children in elaborate tricks on Mary. On one occasion Laurel told Mary that there were some brand-new little dogs on Poinciana Avenue, and when Mary went to see them, they turned out to be fictitious. The next day Gracie Davis rang her bicycle bell as she rode down the sidewalk, while Laurel ran in front of the Gabriels' house hollering, "Popsicle Man!" Mary took off running to catch an ice-cream truck that continually eluded her. Even so, Bonita missed Laurel so much that, in spite of all the pranks, she waited every day for an invitation to Laurel's birthday party. She even bought Laurel the box of games with her saved allowance. But no word came.

In mid-June the other children bragged of their invitations, came to the Gabriels' back door, called Bonita out, and sang, "We're going to the party at City Park. We're going to ride the pony on Friday. You're not invited."

Bonita did not tell her parents of their exclusion from the celebration, but when the day drew near, she told Mary that if she would zip her lips, she would ask Lottie if they could go to City Park to play that day and then ride there on their bicycles and take a look at the little horse. Bonita planned to take the present with her because, secretly, she believed that if Laurel was happy when she saw Bonita, their friendship could be mended.

"I'll be gone for lunch. I left sandwiches for you in the refrigerator." Lottie kissed first Bonita's cheek and then Mary's before she left. "Have a good time at the park. Be home by four o'clock."

"Yes, ma'am."

After lunch Bonita wrapped the box of games. She wore pink shorts, a white shirt, and white sandals. To mark the occasion, should they be invited to join the party, she put a pink grosgrain ribbon under her hair in the back, pulled it up, and tied it in a bow on top of her head. She pictured Laurel holding the reins of a Shetland pony, smiling at her, saying, "I want to play with you, Bonita." She imagined all the good times she and Laurel would have now that she was out of school. They could play Flying Carpet all day long.

At one-forty-five they set out on their bicycles for the park: Mary on the small bike that had only recently had its training wheels removed; Bonita with the present in her bicycle basket. As they came in sight of the park, its lawns already summer-thick and lush and lined with long rows of orange daylilies flowering up out of graceful, dark green fronds, Bonita's heart raced.

"Where's the little horse?" Mary said. "I want to see the little horse!"

Concentrating on the daylilies, counting their beauty as a manifestation of the Blessed Mother's love and protection, Bonita whispered under her breath, "Please, Mother of Jesus, let us see the little pony and make Laurel like me again."

The park was teeming with tennis players, golfers, roller skaters, swimmers, and picnickers, but there was no Shetland pony to be seen. Bonita and Mary rode from the roller-skating rink to the tennis courts, from the clubhouse to the picnic tables, and then they rode the same path all over again.

From time to time Bonita stopped to ask if anyone had seen a Shetland pony. "Nope," one man said. "Haven't seen hide nor hair of a horse around here."

It was almost two-thirty when they went to the bike rack in front of the clubhouse. Mary got down from her bike, kicked down the stand, and retrieved the box of games from Bonita's basket. Holding the wrapped present before her like an offering, Mary looked at Bonita with such anguish in her eyes that Bonita turned away. "Let's go inside and ask somebody," she said.

They found a woman typing in a small office. She was impatient at the interruption and brusquely said, "People don't have to sign up to give a birthday party in the park."

Bonita turned to her sister. "They're not here, Mary. Let's go home." The sight of Mary's pain-darkened eyes made Bonita's throat contract. "I have to go to the bathroom," Bonita said, turning away to hide her tears. "Come with me, Mary, and then let's go home."

Mary shook her head. "No! No! No!"

"I can't leave you here by yourself," Bonita said. She looked around for someone she could ask to look after Mary while she was gone. A trio of older girls in wet bathing suits with towels slung round their necks ate orange Popsicles while their wet hair and wet suits made puddles on the tile around their bare feet. Bonita went to the ticket booth, where one girl sold tickets to swimmers while the other girl looked into the mirror of her compact and applied her lipstick.

"Would you watch my little sister for a minute while I go to the restroom?" Bonita said.

The girl with the compact mashed her lips together to distribute the lipstick, then smoothed it out with the tip of her little finger. "Sure," she said, not taking her eyes from the mirror.

"Hold this present and wait here, Mary. I'll be right back."

But when she returned, Mary was gone.

"Where's my sister?" Bonita cried to the girl.

"She was right here. She started to cry while you were gone, and I told her, 'Your sister is coming right back.'" The girl leaned over the counter and looked around. "Where could she have gone? Boy, is she fast!" She turned to Bonita and shrugged. "I'm sorry."

Bonita ran to the door. Mary's bicycle was in the daylilies, but she was nowhere in sight. Bonita ran across the street to the skating rink, but Mary was neither outside nor inside. Panting and crying, Bonita ran from the roller rink to the tennis courts, from the tennis courts to the picnic tables, from the picnic tables to the swimming pool, and as she ran, she whispered frantically over and over: "Please, Blessed Mother, please help me find my sister."

Bonita ran until she could run no more. Finally, she went back to the clubhouse. Sweat trickled down her back and along her legs. She walked to the ticket booth. "Has my sister come back in here?" she said to the girl. The teenager shook her head.

"I'm going to have to call my daddy. Could I use your telephone?"

The girl pointed to a pay phone outside the golf shop.

"I don't have any money," Bonita said.

The girl pointed to the office. Bonita went to the door and interrupted the woman typing again. "May I use your telephone?" Bonita said.

Without taking her fingers from the keys, the woman jerked her head in the direction of the lobby. "There's a pay phone right outside the golf shop."

"I don't have any money," Bonita said. She was near tears again. "My sister is lost. Please?"

"Oh, all right," the woman said, and she moved the telephone on her desk so Bonita could reach the dial.

"Mrs. Pyburn, this is Bonita," she said when her father's receptionist answered the telephone. "May I speak to my daddy, please?"

"He's with a patient," Mrs. Pyburn said.

"It's an emergency," Bonita said.

"Just a minute," Mrs. Pyburn said.

When Bonita's father came on the line, he said, "What's wrong, Bonita?"

"Mary's lost. Mother said we could come to City Park and play while she went to her luncheon, and when I went to the bathroom, Mary ran away. I asked this girl to watch her, but when I got back, she was gone!"

"Where are you now?" her father asked.

"I'm at City Park by the swimming pool."

"Go wait outside, Bonita. I'll take care of it."

"Are you going to call the police?"

"I don't know what I'm going to do yet, Bonita. You just go out and wait in front of the building."

"Yes, sir." Bonita hung up and turned the telephone back toward the woman. "Thank you," she said.

The woman said, "Uh-huh," without looking at her.

Bonita pulled Mary's bicycle from the orange daylilies and set it upright next to hers in the bike rack. Sweat soaked her shirt and the waistband of her shorts. She sat down on the clubhouse steps where she could watch the street and wiped her upper lip and her forehead with her sleeve. She thought of the orange Popsicles with longing. She wished she had taken a drink from the fountain inside. Now she was afraid to leave her post for fear Mary would come back while she was gone. Bonita waited on the steps, watching, for what seemed forever. She was so tired she finally put her head down on her knees and closed her eyes. When someone touched her hair, Bonita looked up.

"Your daddy said that little sister of yours has escaped again," Orlando Duplantis said.

Bonita jumped up. "Do you think she's been kidnapped?"

"I don't see any cause to think that yet. Most likely she's running down the sidewalk somewhere, having herself a good time looking over her shoulder and waiting for us to catch up to her," he said. "How long has she been gone?"

"A long time. What time is it?"

"It's three-thirty," he said.

"It's been almost an hour. That's her bicycle over there." She was too embarrassed to tell him that Mary had run off while she was in the bathroom. Swallowing hard and blinking tears from her eyes, Bonita turned away.

"We'll get it in a minute." Orlando went to his car, reached through the open window, and took a small notebook from above the visor. "What's she wearing?"

Bonita told him, and he wrote it down.

"How old is she?" he said. "Four?"

Bonita shook her head. "Five. She'll be six in August."

"And you think it was two-thirty or thereabouts when you saw her last?"

"Yes, sir. I looked at the clock on the wall in there," Bonita said, pointing back to the clubhouse.

"Anything else?"

"She's probably carrying a birthday present, because I gave it to her to hold and it wasn't in my bike basket."

Orlando closed the pad and stuck it in his shirt pocket. "Okay," he said. He put his hand on her back. "Come on. Let's go inside."

Bonita could feel the pressure of his hand through her sweat-soaked shirt. "Aren't we going to start looking for Mary?"

"We'll get to huntin' her as soon as I get you something cool to drink and talk to whoever's in charge around here. You look bushed," he said.

"I don't have any money."

Orlando took some coins from his pocket and handed them to her. "Run get yourself something. I'll be over there." He pointed to the park office.

The orange Popsicle—it was what Bonita wanted most. The paper pulled away easily, and as she brought it to her mouth, Bonita had the sensation that the orange ice glowed.

"I left the secretary some numbers to call in case little Miss Houdini shows up around here," Orlando said when he came back.

Bonita gave him back his change. "Thank you very much for the Popsicle, Mr. Orlando."

"You're very welcome, Miss Bonita. I told the secretary in there to hang onto her if she comes back here."

"I don't like that lady." Now that she had someone to help her, Bonita dared to feel cross.

"How come?" he said.

"She didn't want me to use her telephone. She made me beg." Bonita sucked on the Popsicle as they walked back outside, remembering how she had run frantically from place to place, begging the Virgin Mary to help her find Mary, and felt cross with the Blessed Mother, too. She was glad to have a real person on her side. If they found Mary with a kidnapper, she knew the watchman would take his gleaming gun from the dark glove box and get Mary back.

Bonita sucked thirstily on the Popsicle as the watchman opened the trunk of his car and first put Mary's little bicycle inside first, then Bonita's bigger one. The trunk lid wouldn't close completely over the two bicycles, so Orlando pulled a piece of rope from inside and tied the lid down.

"Let's get cracking," he said.

Bonita finished the Popsicle in one big bite, threw the stick into a trash can, and quickly got in the car.

"Cheer up," Orlando said. "We'll find her."

At this, Bonita sat back in the seat and began to relax.

Orlando retraced their ride from home.

"What were y'all doing in the park?" he said.

Bonita looked down at her hands. "Somebody told us that Laurel Landry was having a birthday party at City Park with a Shetland pony. Mary and I weren't invited, but I told Mary we would come and see if we could find the little horse. I guess Gracie and Adam were teasing me when they said the party would be here, because we never even saw a pony. That birthday party's probably going on someplace else right now. They're all riding a pony and having fun while Mary's lost. I even had a present just in case we got invited when we got there." Bonita blinked hard to keep from crying.

"You were planning on going to a party you weren't invited to?" the man said.

Bonita shrugged. "I guess I was." A few tears slipped out onto her folded hands.

Orlando Duplantis looked over at her. "After we track that little sister of yours down and get her home, maybe it would be best if we didn't mention that fact to your mama and daddy."

Bonita wiped her eyes with the back of her hand. "You're probably right." She tried to smile at him, but tears filled her eyes again.

Orlando tapped the bow she had tied on top of her head and said, "I like your pretty hair ribbon."

At the corner of St. Rose and Broussard, Bonita was wiping her nose on her sleeve when she suddenly cried, "Wait! There's the wrapping paper from my present!"

Bonita jumped from the car and ran over to look at it. The paper, wadded into a ball, had blown up against the azaleas in front of the screened porch of a house. Bonita picked it up and, with her eyes on the ground, searched the yard for some other sign that Mary had come that way. Near the sidewalk she found a pile of red checkers. She picked them up and held out her hand for the security guard to see.

Orlando got out of the car, walked up to the front door of the house, and rang the bell. Bonita ran up the steps with the paper in her hands. A woman with curlers in her hair answered the bell but talked to them through the screen door.

"Have you seen a little girl, about five years old, in a yellow play-suit?" Orlando said.

"She's my sister," Bonita said, crowding in close to the screen door, so close she could see each tiny mesh square. "And she's lost."

"I did see a little girl out there. She was sitting down playing over there on the grass."

"Did you see where she went?" Bonita said.

"No, I sure didn't. I went to the kitchen to get a cup of coffee, and when I came back, she was gone."

"Thank you," Orlando said.

"Thank you very much," Bonita remembered to say, flinging the words back over her shoulder as she ran down the steps behind the security guard.

"You walk along the grass here and look for more clues while I drive slow behind you," Orlando said.

They followed a trail of animal-rummy cards and red and black checkers to the Academy of the Holy Angels. "She's playing at my school!" Bonita cried when she saw the lid to Games from A to Z on the front lawn.

Orlando stopped the car and they both got out. Bonita ran to the playground behind the school. Orlando followed her.

"There she is!" Bonita cried.

Mary stood on the top rung of the slide, gripping the metal bars on either side. When she saw Orlando and Bonita coming toward her, she quickly clambered up the steps.

Bonita started to run, but Orlando put out a hand to slow her. "Whoa. Don't spook her."

Mary laughed out loud as she climbed. But near the top of the slide, Mary's sandal slipped from the rung, and she fell to the ground.

"Mary!" Bonita screamed. When they got to her, Mary's cheek was bleeding and her left forearm was strangely bent. Bonita knelt to try and lift her.

Orlando held her back. "No!" he said. "Don't pick her up. That arm's broken. Stay here while I go get help."

He soon returned with a nun walking rapidly beside him. Bonita jumped up. Even in her distress, she remembered to put the toe of her right sandal behind her and bend her left knee. "Sister Veronica! Mary fell off the slide."

Sister Veronica looked down, smoothed Bonita's damp hair back from her forehead, and said, "Mr. Duplantis called your father. He's sending an ambulance. It should be here any minute. In the meantime, we're going to have to keep Mary still."

Mary moved and opened her eyes. Sister Veronica knelt down in the dirt next to the steps of the slide and put her hand gently on Mary's waist. "Don't try to move, Mary."

"I want my mother!" Mary began to cry and tried to rise.

Orlando knelt down. "Don't get up, little Miss Houdini." He put his hand on Mary's head. "Just be quiet as a mouse. That's my good girl," he crooned.

Mary smiled up at the watchman and, to Bonita's amazement, never even stirred.

When the ambulance arrived, the men immobilized Mary's arm, lifted her onto a stretcher, and slid her into the back of the vehicle.

"You ride with your sister, Miss Bonita," Orlando said. "I'll follow you in the car." He extended his hand to the nun. "Thank you, Sister."

Sister Veronica waved to Bonita as the ambulance pulled away.

Dr. Gabriel was waiting for them at the emergency room. He looked at Bonita. "Are you hurt, Bonita?" he said as nurses rolled Mary away on a gurney.

"No, sir. Just Mary. She fell off the slide."

"Duplantis told me," he said. "I'm going to stay with Dr. Johnson while he sets Mary's arm. Your mother should be along soon, Bonita.

Sit down right over there in the waiting room so she can see you when she gets here."

At that moment Orlando Duplantis came into the emergency room. Bonita watched as her father went to meet him and extended his hand. "I appreciate you looking out for my girls," she heard her father say.

"Glad to be able to help, sir," Orlando said. "If you'll give me your keys I'll put the girls' bicycles in the trunk of your car."

When Orlando returned, Bonita saw her father take his wallet from his pocket. He took out five bills and handed them to the watchman. Bonita watched as Orlando removed his own wallet from his back pocket and put the bills inside. Bonita looked away when Orlando looked up and saw her looking at him.

Dr. Gabriel walked through the swinging doors and left them alone.

"They got your sister in okay?" Orlando said, tucking his wallet back into his pocket.

"Yes, sir. They took her off somewhere."

When Orlando sat down beside her, Bonita said, "Daddy told me to stay here while he and another doctor fix her."

"Then I'll just wait here with you for a minute until we find out everything's going to be okay," Orlando said. He took a cigarette from his pocket, put it in his mouth, and leaned back in the chair.

Bonita grew drowsy. Her eyelids closed, opened, and closed again. Finally, she leaned against Orlando's arm and slept.

Exhausted, Bonita went to bed without even eating supper. Near midnight, when she got up to go to the bathroom, she heard her parents talking in their bedroom.

Bonita didn't want to overhear her parents ever again. She put her hands over her ears and crept away to her room.

Chapter Eleven

October 1995

We parked behind Singleton and Son's funeral home and went in the back door. The air in the corridor, laced with carnations and disinfectant, pricked my eyes and throat. In the ladies' lounge, a tiny lamp with a Tiffany-like shade of crimson glass and a bulb no bigger than a nightlight cast a red glow on the burgundy carpet. When we stood in front of the mirror in that ruby light, Mary's purple eyebrows and red cheeks looked just right, pleased the eye, like a ballerina's face when viewed from the audience. But, just as the dancer's black-rimmed eyes, pale, powdered brow, and fervid cheeks would startle backstage, so would Mary's face in ordinary light.

I sat Mary down before the mirror on a stool covered in red velvet. I took a comb from my purse, subdued my own hair, and then turned to taming Mary's. I wiped her face with a wad of wet toilet paper. When Mary's hair was calm and her face was clean, I leaned down, and briefly, we regarded our reflection in the glass. An image, one of Mary and Mother and me looking at ourselves in another mirror, broke memory's black pool. I fancied for a moment that we were normal, ordinary people: our dear father had just died and we, his loving, grieving daughters, had come to arrange his funeral. Mr. Singleton awaited us in his office and would sympathize with us on our loss. We would cast our eyes down and, from time to time, wipe tears away with white linen handkerchiefs embroidered with dainty sprays of lilies of the valley. When we were gone, he would say of our father to his assistant, "Did you know that Dr. Gabriel was an expert on the poetry of Longfellow? The older daughter told me that he could recite *Evangeline* by heart."

But the truth was that the Barely Beige face powder and the Call It Red lipstick that I had applied earlier that morning had flown away, fleck by fleck. It didn't seem fair to wipe Mary's face clean of makeup and then reapply my own. Consequently, I looked not only old but exposed, every line, pore, and blemish unconcealed.

Feeling suddenly on the brink of tears, I plucked a handful of pink tissues from one of the boxes placed in every conceivable corner a mourner might weep, and we went back out into the corridor.

Mr. Singleton was waiting for us. I guessed that he was in his early fifties; my age, give or take a few years. His suit and tie were of subdued tones, his demeanor solemn. "Mrs. Mitchell?" he said. He extended his hand. "Jim Singleton."

"Hello, Mr. Singleton." He shook my hand and then took Mary's hand as I attempted to introduce her, but she interrupted me.

"Mary Rather," she said. "My name is Mary Rather. Mrs. Mary Rather."

"Mrs. Mitchell. Mrs. Rather. Let's go in here."

I had to decide quickly whether to expose Mary's appropriation of Dan Rather's name or let it pass. I chose to let it go by and hope that Mr. Singleton didn't have the opportunity to find out he had been duped. As far as I was concerned, we were going to have a short, private service at the graveside and get this ordeal over with as little commotion as possible.

He led us into a room with a long wooden table. We sat down, Mary and me on one side and Mr. Singleton on the other, as if we were going to eat a meal. Overhead, fluorescent lights buzzed. One of the long bulbs struggled to come on and occasionally cast a sudden brilliance upon us, as of a heavenly light, but then took it back. Mr. Singleton placed a gold-rimmed leather-bound book on the table. It was the size of the three-ring binders we used to have in school. He did not open it, just placed his hand flat on the cover. His spread fingers fit perfectly into the center leather square; one finger a little to the right or a thumb moved a fraction to the left and he would have touched gold.

"You sent me no information for the notice in the paper," Mr. Singleton said.

"We are just going to have a small private service," I said, still fascinated by the way his hand fit so well into the leather square. I tilted my head a little to read the gold writing on the spine. I couldn't make it out.

Next to me, Mary was shaking her head violently.

"Where do you plan to lay your father to rest?" he asked.

"Roselawn Cemetery. That's where our mother is."

"Put it in the paper," Mary announced. "It has to go in the paper. There are people who want to come. There are people who want to see me."

That's exactly what I was afraid of: the prospect of standing next to our father's casket while people from all over Baton Rouge— Daddy's patients, our neighbors from Oleander Avenue, old friends from Holy Angels—came to offer their condolences and Mary intro- duced herself as Dan Rather's wife. No way, I thought. Not if I can help it.

And what about the people from work? No one at the state capitol knew I had grown up in Baton Rouge, or my real name. Nor did they know I had a sister, much less one like Mary.

"You look familiar," Mr. Singleton said to me abruptly. "I know you from somewhere. Ever since you sat down, I've been trying to remember where it was."

I looked at him again. Like the light overhead, the face of the boy flickered into the face of the man; exchange that suit for a pair of khaki pants, a white shirt, and a black tie, widen that grin, muss that smooth hair until the cowlick in the back stood straight up, and I was standing in the hall at the door of the Academy of the Holy Angels, and Sandra Bonifanti and I were giggling and jumping up and down with excitement because the eighth-grade boys from Catholic High had come over with Father Michael to help put up the chairs for the annual back-to-school assembly: PeeWee Singleton.

"It'll come to me," he said. He turned the leather-bound book to us and opened it.

"This will be yours to keep," he said. The first page was a color reproduction of *The Last Supper*. It was not the one by da Vinci that we were accustomed to seeing, the one with the commanding Christ and the perfect proportions. This *Last Supper* was by some lesser artist who had placed Judas in the extreme right foreground, looking furtive and clutching his cloak to his side, so close it seemed possible that his betrayal could contaminate the viewer. The artist had so weighted the picture toward faithlessness that it had taken three standing apostles on the left side, representing fidelity, to restore the balance. Even then, the picture conveyed a feeling of deception. In the center, at a much shorter table than the one we were used to, was the figure of Jesus. In spite of his halo and golden chalice, he was a decidedly puny figure.

Mary stood. "This is not the right picture!" she said. She placed a finger on the page, squarely on Christ's chest. "Who painted this picture? This is not the right Jesus! We don't want this one!"

"Mary. Mary," I said. I pulled at her sleeve. "Sit down."

Reluctantly, Mary sat. I kept my hand on her arm; I could feel the tenseness and impatience rippling through her muscles.

Jim Singleton seemed uncomfortable when I looked back at him.

He had already turned the offending page. I wondered how long it was going to take for him to realize who we were. If things had been different, not just Mary but all of the circumstances of our life, it would have been comforting to plan Daddy's funeral with a childhood friend. The community could have gathered so that the rites of passage were eased, the rituals summoned to console, but now I saw nothing on the way but embarrassment and humiliation.

The page before us bore the name of the funeral home in elaborate script. Below it were lines for the name of the deceased and the date and time of the service. Moving right along (we were receiving a much hastier explanation than was usual, I suspected), we saw pages titled In Memoriam, Bearers, Mass of Resurrection, Final Resting Place, Floral Tributes, Music.

"Stop!" Mary cried. "What kind of music?"

"You may choose from several different tapes," Jim Singleton said. "We have organ music–that's very calming. It's classical music: Bach, Beethoven, and Henry Mancini."

"What else?" Mary said.

"We have a tape of a tenor singing the good old hymns, accompanied by the organ. We also have one of old hymns just on the organ itself." He paused, thinking, I suspected, that he had provided us with a generous array of choices. But he didn't know Mary. I suspected she probably knew a lot more about music then Mr. Singleton did. I knew she never forgot anything she heard. She could probably still identify every note of the music our father had forced upon us. I, on the other hand, had refused to listen to music for almost thirty years, and I had no intention of letting music into my life now.

"We'll worry about that later," I said, turning to the next page. This one was titled "Friends and Family" and was the first of a daunting number of blank, lined pages. I hated to disappoint old PeeWee, but all of those pages were destined to remain empty.

"Yes," I said. "This is all very nice. But what we really want is just a basic funeral. No music. No visitors."

"Not me," said Mary. "I want music, music, music. I want friends, friends, friends. I want everybody to come and meet my husband, Dan." Mary leaned forward and spoke confidentially to Jim Singleton. "He's coming all the way from New York," she said.

Jim Singleton looked as if he longed to be elsewhere. I was acquainted with that feeling but not lucky enough to indulge it. I desperately wished that I could stem the flow of words from Mary's mouth. Each time she spoke, the clanking machinery of her thought processes became visible, as associations passed directly from her brain to her mouth.

Jim Singleton looked from Mary to me. I looked away. He said quickly, "I will contact the people at the cemetery for you. There are a couple of things there that need to be taken care of: a little paperwork to make sure you have clear title to the plot, an okay to hire the grave diggers, and I'll need you to bring me some of your father's clothes: a suit, white shirt, tie, underwear, socks, and shoes. But now let's go down the hall and you can choose a casket." Jim stood before all of these words were even out of his mouth, so anxious was he to get away.

The long room was filled with caskets in muted colors. Each rested on a silver bier, blues, grays, greens and golds all softened with a pearly glaze—what I would call frosted in a lipstick. They were beautiful. The velvet linings echoed not only the color of the casket but the hue. The gray carpet, cushiony beneath our feet, and the light thrown upward by shell-shaped sconces softened the lines and angles of the coffins.

Mary turned to me. Her eyes reflected the light; her face was softened by it. Here was one beautiful thing I could not deny Daddy.

"You choose," I said.

Mary went directly to a pale blue one. She ran her hand along the blue velvet lining, then along the side; a pattern of maple leaves running all the way around adorned it. The casket was so beautiful, so inviting, that I envied my father.

Mary and I then proceeded straight through the center of the room, and Mary touched every casket: lavender, gray, gold, bronze. Then she looked at those against the right wall. The first one was a warm, rosy color. It resembled pale raspberry sherbet. Along each side a raised frieze of leaves and fruit glowed with a kind of brushed radiance. Mary smiled and turned to look at me, her hand flat on the lining. We nodded to each other but moved on.

We stayed in there longer than we should have. After surveying every casket, after laying her hand on every single one in the room, Mary returned to the rose-colored coffin. She was extremely agitated. She put her hand on the lining and inclined her head. Her lips moved. Either she was praying or she was talking to Daddy. I suspected it was the latter.

"Daddy says he wants this one," she said. She caressed the pink velvet, a rose color so warm it actually seemed to soothe her and even calmed me.

I turned to look at Jim Singleton, who waited in the doorway. "We'll take this one," I said.

Mary nodded. For the first time she seemed pleased.

We went back to the room that contained the long table and sat down. Again, the overhead light flickered and flickered. We all looked up as if it signaled some coming revelation, but none was vouchsafed to us.

At Mary's request, Jim handed her the leather-bound book with the inadequate Christ and the cowering Judas. I wouldn't look at it. I never wanted to see it again. Mary studied it while Jim and I attended to a few more details and then I wrote him a check. Twice Mary interrupted us to insist that we let Jim Singleton send an obituary to the paper with the place and the time of the service. Twice I refused.

Finally, I stood up. "No!" I said. "I don't want to talk about it anymore."

Jim Singleton saw us to the door. As he pulled it open, he snapped his fingers. "Gerry Winborn," he said. "You and Sandra Bonifanti used to meet Gerry and me on Saturday mornings at the picture show . . . at the Louisiana Theatre."

I watched him remember what it was he knew about me. He looked away quickly and then looked back as if to assure me that his memory contained nothing that would cause me pain.

"That was a long time ago," Jim said quickly. "Been a lot of water under the bridge."

But it was too late. Now that he knew who we were, there was no getting away from the terrible sadness of it. "Yes," I said. "A lot of water under that bridge." And I hustled Mary out to the car without looking back.

Chapter Twelve

July 1954

In late July, when it was time to celebrate her birthday, Bonita refused her mother's offer of a party. All she wanted, she said, was to go with Mary to Third Street, pick out some paper dolls at Kress's, go to a movie and then to eat a grilled-cheese sandwich at Walgreen's.

So, on the Saturday of Bonita's birthday, John Gabriel passed eleven one-dollar bills over the backseat and said, "Here you go, sweetheart. Here's a dollar for every year you've been on this earth. Your mother and I will be either at home or at the tennis court at City Park. Call my service if you need us. We'll pick you and Mary up in three hours. Let's coordinate our timepieces."

Bonita looked at the face of the gold watch that her mother had wrapped and slipped under her pillow that morning. "I have ten o'clock sharp, Daddy."

Bonita's father pretended to adjust the hands of his watch. "Ten o'clock . . . sharp," he said. "We'll pick you up right here at one P.M."

"John, are you sure this is a good idea?" Lottie said.

"Lottie, an eleven-year-old girl needs to learn how to get about on her own in the world. Just leave a message with my answering service if you need us." John put his hand on Lottie's knee. "Would you care to join me in a game of tennis, my precious?"

Bonita could see her mother looking back anxiously as they drove away. She blew her mother a kiss, pulled Mary onto the sidewalk, and then held out her hand. "Want to carry some of the money?" she said. "Take four of them."

Mary's eyes gleamed as she carefully lifted four bills from her sister's hand. "Money," she said. The cast had recently been removed from Mary's arm, leaving the skin beneath wrinkled and white.

"And we can do anything we want!" Bonita cried.

Third Street was bustling. People walking fast veered around them. Heat shimmered in the exhaust of the constant cars. At the traffic light, when Bonita and Mary crossed, they could look down the long street all the way to the state capitol building.

Bonita took Mary's hand, and together they entered the five-and-ten-cent store. For a moment they paused, still with wonder. On the left was a popcorn machine. They could hear the corn popping and smell the warm scent of the cooking oil. Next to the popcorn was the candy counter: panel after panel of clear glass against which were pressed peppermint patties, licorice whips, stars of chocolate, and chocolate-covered raisins. On the right was an entire wall of cosmetics and hair-care products.

"Hold me up. I want to see," Mary said.

Bonita put her arms about Mary's waist and, bracing her knee against the brown wood of the counter, lifted her sister so she could see the rows of ribbons, combs, and lipsticks.

A man and a woman came in the door.

"I need some nail polish," a female voice said. "Help me pick out a new color, Orlando?"

"Florette, what I know about polish would fit on the end of my little finger," a familiar voice said.

Mary wiggled down from Bonita's grasp. She ran over and threw her arms about the man's left knee.

"Would you look at this, Florette?" Orlando said, gazing down at Mary. "This here's the kid from my route. Where's your sister? You haven't run off again, have you?" Mary raised her arms to be picked up, and Orlando swung her onto his shoulders.

Bonita shyly joined them.

Florette held a card of nail-polish samples. "Are these colors true?" she said to the saleslady.

After Orlando told Florette who Bonita was, Florette glanced at her and said, "Good. I need another woman's opinion." She tapped one of the colors on the card with a perfectly shaped pale pink fingernail. "I've got to get rid of this pink. What do you think of Red as Sin with this dress, darlin'?" Florette held the card close to her clothes and studied it. The dress Florette wore was a narrow, sleeveless sheath covered with flowers. The red poppies on Florette's dress looked gigantic to Bonita. Their yellow stamens were long and full and curved and had five little black dots at the end representing pollen.

"It looks nice," Bonita said.

Florette handed Bonita the samples and, putting a hand on Bonita's shoulder for balance, took off one of her red shoes and held it close to the card.

Bonita looked down at Florette's bare foot; the toenails were painted the same fragile pink as her fingernails. It made Bonita worry that Florette's toes, so exposed in the bright red shoes, might get hurt.

"You don't think it might need a little more orange in it, do you?" Florette said.

"Maybe," Bonita said.

Bonita was so close to Florette that she could smell her dusting powder. Bonita scented cigarette smoke, too, but it was faint, and she thought that beneath it the woman smelled sweet and clean.

Florette moved the shoe along the card. "How about Coral Madness? Don't you love these names, darlin'? I could look at this stuff all day long. Or this one: Pretty as a Poppy?"

"That's it!" Bonita cried. "It's perfect!"

Florette pointed her shoe at Orlando. "See, I told you I needed another opinion. Find me that color, darlin', and let's look at the real thing."

Bonita searched the rows of bottles topped with their brushes, tiny as little pots of paint, until she found Pretty as a Poppy. She held it up for Florette to match to her shoe.

"You're right. This is the one," Florette said. Holding onto Bonita's shoulder again, Florette put her shoe back on, wiggling her toes until it fit exactly as she wanted it. Bonita watched with fascination as Florette made the final adjustment to the thin red straps that fit over her toes and ran behind her ankle.

"Thanks, darlin'," Florette said. When her balance was restored, she gave Bonita's shoulder three little taps and let go.

Bonita shot a look up at the woman's face. Florette had on bright red lipstick and vivid aqua eye shadow. Her dark curly hair was pulled back on the right side and secured behind her ear with a red comb. Bonita looked at Florette's hand. That this absolute stranger had touched her and called her "darling" made the woman's hand look soft and warm. She wished Florette would touch her again. Under the pretense of examining the new nail polish, Bonita edged a step or two closer to Florette.

Florette looked down at Bonita and, as if she had felt her yearning, took Bonita's chin in her hand. "You got good bones," she said. "You wearing makeup yet?"

Bonita shook her head. "No, ma'am," she said.

"Don't start out too heavy or you'll end up with no place to go," Florette said. She reached over the rows of lipstick and plucked up a tube of Petal Pink. "You should start with this on your mouth. I wouldn't put anything on your cheeks yet. But when you do, put a little dot of rouge right here." Florette touched the top of Bonita's cheek under the outside corner of her left eye. "Then you want to spread it lightly, lightly," Florette said, and she ran her finger like a feather up to Bonita's hairline. "You never want it to look made up when you're young. You just want people to think God gave you a great face." She laughed and patted Bonita's cheek.

Bonita stood still but the moment was over. Florette turned away as if she had lost interest in children. "I'll take this one," she said to the saleslady. She looked over her shoulder at Orlando, who put Mary down and reached into his back pocket for his wallet.

When the transaction was accomplished, Bonita said, "I want this one," and she pulled a dollar bill from the pocket of her pinafore and paid for Petal Pink.

"A little bird just told me it was your birthday, Miss Bonita," Orlando said. "Me and Florette made some sandwiches for a picnic. You all want to come along?"

"Orlando," Florette said. "I thought we were going to spend the day at False River."

"We don't have to go that far, Florette. We can go out to the Amite," Orlando said.

"We've got to go by the house and pick up the food," Florette said. "We don't have enough sandwiches."

"We can make more. How did you kids get here?"

"Mother and Daddy dropped us off," Bonita said.

"What time are they picking you up?"

"One o'clock. But you and Miss Florette go on to False River. Mary and I were going to Walgreen's anyway."

But Mary wanted to go on the picnic and wouldn't take no for an answer.

"See, they want to go," Orlando said.

"I don't know why I have to spend my day off looking after somebody else's kids," Bonita heard Florette mutter as they left the store. "These people can plenty well afford baby-sitters."

"We're just pretending we're a family, Florette."

As they passed the Brunswick, Florette said, "Orlando, when you get done baby-sitting, come get me. I'm gonna have a beer." She paused in the doorway of the bar, gave Bonita a little smile, and went inside.

"Okeydokey," the watchman said.

Watching Florette walk off in her high heels and tight flowered dress made Bonita feel sad. "I'm sorry we ruined her day off," she said.

"Don't worry about it. Florette's perfectly capable of entertaining herself. She wasn't real big on this picnic idea, anyway. Southern Bell might strike. If they do, she'll have to go round up a bunch of operators so they can get a picket line together."

"How will they know where to find her?" Bonita said.

"Everybody knows Florette hangs out at the Brunswick."

"Where do you live?" Bonita said when they were in the watchman's car.

"I live on Bungalow Lane. Down by the river. Right in the shade of the capitol building," he said.

When they got to Orlando's house, Bonita rolled down the window and looked up at the white building that rose high into the sky.

"Just think, you could go see the capitol every day if you wanted to," Bonita said.

"Sure could, if I wanted to. Happens as I don't want to," he said.

The state capitol dominated the landscape in Baton Rouge. The land was so flat that whenever Bonita was out riding in a car, her eyes went looking for the top of the building whether she wanted them to or not. At Christmas, the windows of the offices on the top floors were lit in the shape of a huge cross, and people from all over the city drove to the river to see it, then said, "Now the Christmas season is really here."

Orlando Duplantis lived in the small side of a white frame duplex. A concrete birdbath with a sea horse in the center stood in a bed of bushy chrysanthemums. In order to get to Orlando's front door, they had to go through a screened porch with a broken tile floor. A sagging red-and-yellow-striped canvas lawn chair stood next to a small black iron table on which rested a metal ashtray overflowing with cigarette stubs. "Some of Florette's mess," Orlando said.

Bonita felt uneasy. She knew her mother wouldn't approve of them going into this man's house. She thought about backing out of the picnic altogether, but she knew Mary would pitch a fit, and they had already made Florette mad. "We'll just wait out here on the porch," Bonita said.

The shock of seeing the watchman had made everything about him seem more intense to Bonita: his eyes were so pale, his hair cut so short, his language so startling. She could hardly bear to think what her mother would make of him; her mother, who guarded their grammar with the sharp blade of her tongue, ready, at their every word, to slice out each impurity. She wondered what this man's mother must have been like. She imagined him in a house in the woods; a house with no plumbing; a house with no books. Quick images—wood walls like Lincoln Logs, a fireplace, an outhouse— made her feel melancholy.

After they picked up ice cream and cake and put them in a cooler with the sandwiches, they drove all the way out Florida Boulevard to the traffic circle. Bonita liked the sensation of moving away in the car. Even though she was right next to Mary, it seemed to her that she was leaving behind the terrible fear that she was trapped by her sister forever. Soon they were in the country. Bonita began to wonder where they were going.

There was not much traffic on the highway. Two cars came toward them and swished past. Then the highway ahead was empty as far as Bonita could see. Immediately after they crossed the bridge over the Amite River, Orlando took them off the road onto a rutted path full of weeds that brushed the underside of the car. They bumped along for a hundred yards until they came to a clearing near the river. He stopped, got out, and came around to open their door. Mary clambered out over Bonita, who followed close behind.

Insects, disturbed by their passage, flew up, buzzing and whirring. Birds called warnings to one another. A bluejay swooped past. A squirrel fled up a tree and, from a branch above their heads, complained. Over all Bonita saw—weeds, trees, grass, water—heat made the air shimmer.

Orlando took an old quilt from the trunk of the car.

"Did your mama made that quilt?" she said.

Orlando looked down at it. "Somebody must have made it. We sure never bought nothing. Maybe some old cousin. I never knew my mama. You carry the quilt. I'll bring the food. Don't run off, Houdini," he said.

"Were you an orphan?" Bonita said, running along beside him on the narrow path. "Where were you born?"

"I was born in Slaughter, Louisiana," Orlando said. "Know where that is?"

Bonita shook her head.

"That's in East Feliciana Parish, and no, I wasn't no orphan. I had a daddy and a mother, but my mother got TB when I was a baby, and they packed her off to Greenwell Springs Sanitarium."

"What happened to her?'

"She died," Orlando said.

"How old were you?"

"They told me I was about three."

"Did that make you feel sad?"

"Don't remember," he said.

"I would be sad if my mama died," Bonita said.

"You're a regular curiosity box, aren't you?" Orlando said. "I suppose you want to know how old I am, too?"

"Not if you don't want to tell me," Bonita said.

"I don't mind telling you," Orlando said. "I was born in 1910. I'm forty-four years old."

"Are you married?" Bonita asked.

"Nope, me and marriage don't get along too good."

"You're not married to Miss Florette?" Bonita said.

"Nah," he said. "Florette's just a good-time girl."

Bonita turned the phrase over in her mind as the three of them stood on the riverbank looking down at the dark, swiftly flowing water.

"This is one mean little river," Orlando said. "I don't want neither one of you to ever go swimming here by yourself." He tapped Mary on the head. She took his hand and looked up at him. "You hear that?" Mary nodded.

He looked at Bonita. "You hear that?"

"Yes, sir," Bonita said.

"And when both of you get older and some boy wants to bring you here for a swimming party, you say, 'There'll have to be at least six people at this party,' because you'll need every last one of them to pull people out of the whirlpools," Orlando said and pointed. "Like that one."

Before their eyes, the water began to swirl as it approached a sandbar, carrying bits of branches and twigs into a vortex that darkened as it went down. To Bonita, it looked like dirty dishwater being sucked down the drain after she had removed the plug.

"And don't think just because you're standing in water up to your ankles on a sandbar that you're safe, because right next to you can be a hole six feet over your head." Orlando pointed to a quiet section of the river. "See them ripples on the water, out in the middle where it looks so ladylike and innocent?"

"Yes, sir," Bonita said.

"That's what you got to watch out for. Them ripples means there's a strong current way down under the water where you can't see it,"

Orlando said. "So when you come out here to drink beer and have a good time, keep your eyes peeled for them little lines moving on the water."

"Did you come here a lot?" Bonita said.

"I came a fair number of times. Right after I took that job with the state troopers, I moved to Baton Rouge, and I used to run with a crowd that liked to come out here."

Maybe a "good-time girl" was someone who liked to drink beer and go swimming, Bonita thought. "Did Miss Florette come with you?" she said.

"Didn't know Florette then," he said. "You remember all these things I'm telling you, Miss Bonita." Orlando shook out the quilt.

"Yes, sir, I will," Bonita said as she took one side of the quilt and they spread the pallet out on the patchy grass above the bank. She took off her sandals and sat down. Carefully, she crossed her legs in front of her and pulled her dress down over her knees. Even with the puffy cotton under her, she was poked by twigs and burrs.

Mary, ignoring all of Orlando's warnings, was climbing down the bank with a handful of small rocks and stones to throw into the water. Orlando leaned over, scooped her up, and took her by herself to the edge of the woods. Bonita could hear the hum of his voice, but she couldn't make out what he said. Mary stood quietly, concentrating on his words. As she watched, Mary ran her forefinger along her mouth, put her thumb and finger together, twisted them over her lips, and pretended to throw something away. Then Orlando swung her up onto his shoulders and came back to the picnic. "Miss Houdini has zipped her lips, locked 'em up, and thrown away the key."

"I know what we could do," Bonita said. "To keep Mary from running away."

"What's that?" Orlando said as he put Mary down in the middle of the quilt. He opened the cooler, took out a sandwich, and put it in front of her. "Eat this and then we'll have some ice cream," he said.

"Handcuff us together," Bonita said. "That would keep her still."

"Or keep you running," Orlando said. "Here." He handed Bonita a sandwich.

When they had finished their sandwiches, Orlando said, "You really want to see them cuffs?"

Bonita nodded. "I never saw any handcuffs up close," she said.

Orlando took out the ice cream and cake. He put a cup in front of each person. "Mary, here's your spoon."

Bonita looked at Orlando. "What will we do if she gets dirty?"

"She's not going to get dirty. She's already promised. But wait," he said. "We forgot to sing. And I didn't get any candles."

"That's okay," Bonita said.

Orlando began to sing in a low, toneless voice, "Happy birthday to you." He tapped Mary on the top of the head with a forefinger. "Sing," he said.

"Happy birthday to you," Mary said. She ran all the words together. "Happybirthdaytoyou."

From his back pocket Orlando took the handcuffs and handed them to Bonita. "Take a look up close so you can say you've seen the real thing."

They were heavier than Bonita expected. The watchman handled them so effortlessly that she was prepared for something with no more substance than a plaything. When her hand wobbled under their weight, she realized that her idea of handcuffs had the same relationship to the reality as a toy stove with painted burners had to a real stove with gas jets.

Suddenly, Bonita was frightened. What were she and Mary doing with this strange man out in the middle of nowhere? She felt lightheaded and thought she knew now what a grown women meant when she said she might faint.

"Want to put them on?" Orlando took a key ring from his pocket. "I've got the key right here."

Dizzy and terrified, Bonita gave the handcuffs back to him. She held out her hands with her closed fists together as if she concealed a bean in one of them and it was up to Orlando to guess which one. When Orlando saw that her fists shook, he drew back. "Are you scared of me?" he said.

Bonita bit her lip, but her fists remained outstretched. "A little," she said.

"What do you think I might do to you?" he said.

"Kidnap us," Bonita said.

"And then what? Ask your daddy for a million dollars?"

Bonita nodded, her eyes cast down.

"Hon, you're describing the exact thing I was hired to prevent. Don't you know your folks checked me out with my old boss in the state police? Your very own daddy was the one called me in the first place. It was him that got your neighborhood all together to do it."

"Why did he do it?" Bonita said.

"Your daddy didn't say so when he hired me, but I think now he was worried about her," Orlando said softly, nodding toward Mary. "I wouldn't hurt you for nothing." He put his hand on Mary's head. At his touch, Mary looked up and smiled at him. "And her. You know I would never hurt her." He studied Bonita's face.

Bonita's heart was pounding.

"Want to go?" Orlando said. "We'll throw this ice cream and cake in the river and I'll take you both back right this minute."

"I want to stay," Bonita said. "Put the handcuffs on me. I want to see what they feel like."

Orlando looked worried. "If you're sure," he said.

"I'm sure," Bonita said. She was having trouble getting her breath. The blood in her body was rushing everywhere. One of the heels of her crossed feet was pressed between her legs beneath her skirt. She pushed it in closer to still the pounding there.

Orlando put the handcuffs on her wrists. He held them so that they encircled her lightly, watched her face to see if she wanted to continue. Bonita nodded. When she heard them snap and felt their coolness and their weight, the pulsing sensation between her legs reached a crescendo and she pressed harder. All about her, trees and water dissolved and ran and became fused with the pulsing spot between her legs. She eased her foot away. A bead of sweat trickled slowly down her forehead.

"Want 'em off?" Orlando said.

"No," Bonita said.

"You like having them on, don't you," he said. "I know what else you would like."

"What's that?" Bonita said.

"You'd like to take a look at my gun, wouldn't you. You been wanting to see that gun since that very first night you got in my car and we followed your sister down that dark alley, haven't you?"

"I would like to see it," Bonita said.

"I'll let you take a look at it," he said. "That'll be your birthday present. I might even let you hold it."

When he returned, Orlando said, "A gun is a different breed of cat entirely from a pair of handcuffs. A gun can do you some real harm." He lifted the gun so that it pointed upward and was level with his shoulder. "Always hold a gun pointing straight up. You don't want to carry it here"—Orlando patted Bonita at her waist—"because you might swing it around until it's pointing at somebody. And you don't want to carry it pointing at the ground because you might shoot yourself in the foot. Most lawmen carry only five bullets in the cylinder. If they don't expect any trouble—and as long as I've been patrolling your neighborhood, I've never had one speck of trouble—they keep the sixth cylinder, the one under the hammer, they keep that one empty. So the gun you're looking at in that glove box is safe as long as you don't pull the hammer back. If you cock it, the bullet in the next cylinder is going to fall into place under the hammer, and even if you ease it back as carefully as you can, you're loaded for trouble at that point."

During Orlando's lecture, Bonita had been watching the barrel of the gun with a fascinated horror. She found the shadowed blue-black color sinister—it conjured up memories of both the dense black shadows beneath her house, from the night she had gone under it to get Mary, and the starry shiny indigo sky that had promised precious freedom when she burst out from under the house.

"Why is it that funny color?" she said.

"It's blued. That's just the way this kind of gun is." Orlando leaned down and lifted Bonita's handcuffed hands so that she could touch the barrel.

Bonita snatched her hand away. "Ugh! It feels awful." She made a face and shook her head.

"You don't have to touch it if you don't want to," Orlando said.

Bonita watched the muzzle of the gun. She looked up at Orlando. His pale eyes were fixed on hers. Bonita lifted her cuffed hands. "Take these off," she said. "So I can get a good feel of it."

Orlando unlocked the handcuffs.

"I want to hold it, too," Mary said.

"You'll get a turn, Houdini," Orlando said.

Bonita put her hand on the revolver. It was the coldest thing she had ever felt in her life. Again she was so repulsed that she pulled her hand away.

"You don't have to hold it," Orlando said. He turned toward the car as if to take the gun back.

"No, wait," Bonita said. "I can do it. I want to hold it."

Orlando put the gun in her hand. Like the handcuffs, it was heavier than Bonita had expected, and she had to put both hands on it to hold it up.

Orlando removed one of her hands from the butt and took her other hand into his and raised it. "Remember, always pointed up at shoulder level. That way, if you've screwed up and the thing is loaded after all, you won't be as likely to hurt anybody."

Bonita closed her eyes. As long as his hand supported hers, she was not afraid of the gun; she even liked it. "What kind of gun is this?" she said dreamily.

"It's a .38 Smith and Wesson service revolver."

"Where did you get it?" Bonita asked, her eyes still closed.

"I bought it in a pawn shop in 1929, when I was nineteen."

Orlando let go of her hand and she was holding the gun by herself. Bonita shivered. The gun shuddered also, turned sideways, pointed at her head. Quickly, Orlando straightened it. "Too heavy for you?" he said. "Want me to take it?"

"I guess so," Bonita said, reluctant to give it up, although fear of the gun's unholy darkness was making it hard for her to get a deep breath.

"Here, Miss Mary, you can hold it for a minute. Put your hands together."

He put Mary's small hands between his own and let her pretend to hold the gun.

What am I going to say if Mary tells that she got to hold a gun? Bonita thought.

"Come on," Orlando said. He led them to the bank of the river. "Hold on to your sister, Miss Bonita."

Orlando went down on one knee. He held the gun with both hands and brought it up until it was level with his right eye. "See those roots under that biggest willow tree, the ones that make a circle?" he said.

"I see it," Bonita said.

"Watch," Orlando said. "I'm going right for the center of it." He fired the gun, and a halo of dirt flew up around his target. Mary shrieked and clapped her hands over her ears.

"That was loud. Doesn't that hurt your ears?" Bonita said.

"If I was to be doing this very long, I would put some stoppers in my ears. Once or twice isn't going to hurt you." He shook out the cylinder and turned it until there was no bullet in the chamber beneath the hammer. Carefully, he put the gun into Bonita's hand. "What you're going to have is a controlled explosion in your hand," he said. "This gun's going to smack you pretty good when it goes off, so you need to get ready for it. You sure you want to do this?"

"Is it going to hurt?" Bonita said.

"Might. You don't have to do it. You can watch me shoot it again if you want."

"I want to do it," Bonita said. "I can do it."

Orlando knelt on one knee beside Bonita. With his right hand, he steadied the gun in Bonita's hands. With his left, he pulled Mary to him and said, "Get over here behind me, Houdini." Then he whispered, "And stand still as a mouse."

"Still as a mouse," Mary whispered back. "Is it going to be loud again?"

"Yes," Orlando said.

Mary put her hands over her ears and peered around Orlando's shoulder to watch.

"What do you see over there on that bank that you want to shoot at?" Orlando said.

"I'm going to shoot at the same place you did," Bonita said. "Right in the middle of those tree roots, right there where it makes that circle."

"Okay," Orlando said. "What you need to do is this: keep hold of the gun with both hands and bring it up to where you can close one eye and sight down that barrel. I'm going to keep hold of your hands, but loose, so when you pull the trigger, you are going to be in full charge. Got that?"

"Yes," Bonita whispered. She was so scared that the roots she had chosen for her target seemed to be jumping all over the riverbank.

"Take a deep breath," Orlando said.

Bonita did as he told her.

"Bring it up now and take your sight down the barrel."

Again Bonita did as he told her. The gun shook as she raised it, but Orlando steadied it with his hand.

"Got your target in sight?"

"Yes, I've got it."

"Now pull the hammer back with your thumb."

Bonita felt a clunk as the cylinder turned, and she knew she had a bullet under the hammer. The world went dark, contracted to a tiny point of light at the end of the gun barrel. Saliva poured into her mouth; she swallowed twice, but it filled again and again.

"Ready?" Orlando said.

Bonita couldn't speak. A groan rose up out of her chest.

"Now!" Orlando said.

Bonita pulled the trigger, and the dark world exploded into a million pieces of light. She gasped in pain and surprise at the recoil but stood her ground. "Did I hit it?"

"You got close," Orlando said. "You hit the trunk. I think you might be pretty good with a gun if you decided to take it up."

Bonita smiled at him, proud of herself.

"We'd better get going," he said. He returned the gun to the car.

"What if Mary tells somebody that I shot your gun?" Bonita said when he came back.

"She won't," Orlando said. "We already talked about that." He sat down on the quilt and took Mary onto his lap. "Remember what I told you when we got here?"

Mary nodded.

Bonita was uneasy now that they had to leave. As long as she had been absorbed in what they were doing, excitement had overridden her anxiety, but now she was afraid. And her hand hurt. She rubbed it.

"Sore?" Orlando said.

"A little," she said.

"It'll be gone soon," Orlando said. He stood up and put Mary on her feet. "We got to get this stuff cleaned up so we can get back to the picture show. Here, Houdini, carry this bag of trash to the car."

As Bonita and Orlando walked along behind Mary, who was racing for the car, Bonita said, "Mr. Orlando, can I ask you something?"

"Sure can," Orlando said.

"Is there something wrong with Mary?" Bonita whispered.

Orlando looked down at her. "I wouldn't go so far as to say there's something wrong, but I do think she is going to be different from most everybody else," he said finally.

"Different bad or different good?" Bonita said.

"Probably some of both," Orlando said.

When they got back to town, he pulled the car over to the curb two blocks away from the theater. "You better get out here," he said. He looked at his watch. "You got ten minutes before the movie gets out. You can walk from here in plenty of time."

From the backseat, Mary put her arms around Orlando and squeezed him hard. He pretended to be choking, and then she released him and climbed out onto the sidewalk.

"Thank you very much for the birthday party, Mr. Orlando," Bonita said. "I had a nice time."

"Did you have a nice time out there in the big wide world?" her father said when he and Lottie picked them up in front of Walgreen's.

Bonita and Mary looked at each other. Mary ran her finger along her lips, pretended to lock them, and threw away the key.

"Yes, sir," Bonita said.

Chapter Thirteen

October 1995

In the alley behind the house on Oleander Avenue, all of the garbage cans lay scattered on their sides. Somebody, probably Mrs. Moak, had put out Daddy's trash.

"We'll have to go in the back, Mary," I said. "That's the only key I still have. I hope Daddy hasn't gotten new doors and locks."

I got out, leaving Mary in the car, and went to bring in the trash cans. As I got close to the house with them, I saw that time and neglect had brought the house to the edge of ruin. No need to worry about new doors and locks; no need to worry about new anything. I carried the cans to the back steps and put them where we had always kept them, in the nook between the stoop and the west corner of the house. The paint was peeling from the back boards. Some, under the windows, were stained a greenish black with mildew.

I looked in the car window to see how Mary was taking this return home. She stared straight ahead. Her hands rested in her lap. She was hammering out a rhythm with the fingers of her right hand onto the back of her left hand. I watched the ritual tapping until I grew detached from the painful tasks that lay ahead. I blinked and opened the car door.

"Come on, Mary, we have to go in. We have to pick out a suit for Daddy to be buried in."

"You do it."

"I need you to help me."

When Mary made no effort to get out of the car, I rested my forehead against the door. "Mary, please."

Mary did not interrupt the pattern of her tapping.

Forgetting how my sister hated to be touched, I put a hand on her hands to still whatever ceremony she was conducting.

Mary jerked her hands away. "No! No! No!"

I looked around to see if any of the neighbors were watching. No one could see us. What had been, in our childhood, one long green backyard running the entire length of the block was now interrupted by fences.

Averting my eyes from the driveway, I left Mary for a moment and walked to the front sidewalk. Most of the other houses on the block had been repainted in muted vegetable shades: the St. Germains' old redbrick house was now mushroom gray, the Fish house a pale green the color of lettuce. Laurel Landry's former white frame house was now eggplant, with a large glassed-in addition on the south side. From a corner of the new porch flew a silk flag bearing an orange jack-o'-lantern. The Davis house was gone completely. In its place was a huge beige brick house that took up the entire lot. Only the Moak house and Daddy's were not up to date. Only our two old houses seemed caught in the past.

I went back to the car. Mary was still unresponsive. I couldn't bring myself to go in and leave her alone outside. Or maybe it was just that I couldn't bring myself to go in the house at all. I went to sit on the bottom back step. In the grass against the lattice that now covered the large crawl space beneath the house lay an assortment of broken flowerpots, dead plants, and rusty garden tools. One weathered garden glove indicated that sometime in the years I had been gone my father had taken up gardening and then abandoned it. In the backyard were fruit trees and berry bushes I did not remember. But I did remember the last time I came down these steps, and that memory brought me to my feet.

I fled back to the car with my heart pounding. "This is a terrible idea! Let's get out of here!" I cried.

In a flash Mary was out of the car and up the steps. I got out quickly and followed her. "These steps are treacherous," I said. "Be careful."

Mary continued up the steps, and I went up right behind her, ready to grab for her if she lost her balance. The screen door squeaked when she pulled it open. When we were both safely on the back porch, I looked back through the screen at the backyard.

The fruit trees were lit by a hard bright light that was not the light of ordinary day but the distorted light of memory. The fig tree at the end of the yard against the fence was older than I was. Its leaves were too big. Blowsy and unkempt, they looked like the leaves of trees in nightmares. Worse was the overgrown persimmon tree outside the window of my old room. Its overred fruit looked obscene. I put my hands over my face and turned away. I leaned against the back wall of the screened porch and gasped for breath.

Mary, too, was having trouble. She stood frozen in the middle of the porch. I pulled myself together and, careful not to touch her, eased around her to the back door.

"It's okay, Mary. Everything's going to be okay," I said in the singsong voice one would use to quiet a baby.

I shook the keys that unlocked the doors of my present life from around the big dull gold key that unlocked the back door of Daddy's house. It was a key I had carried since I had left home, unable to use it and unable to throw it away.

The jingling sound startled Mary, and she stomped heavily across the boards of the back porch. I handed her the key. "Here, you want to do it?"

Mary tried to insert the key in the lock three times, but her ability to direct the fine motions of her fingers had been destroyed by years of medication. Finally she slammed the keys to the floor. "You do it!" she shouted. "You could always do everything!"

I bent down, retrieved the ring, put the key in the lock in one smooth motion, and opened the door. We both gasped at the familiar smell of the house. With the twist of a key, thirty years were wiped away and we were back where we had begun.

I reached for Mary's hand. In the brief moment that she permitted her hand to be held, I took comfort from the warmth of my sister's flesh. I took heart from the fact that Mary had been able to sustain the momentary contact. I hoped that she had been not only comforted by the touch, as I had, but fortified by it.

Mary plunged through the kitchen into the dining room. But I stood just inside the kitchen, caught up in the familiar smell of the house. What was it, I wondered, that gave every house its own particular odor. To me the house smelled of cypress planks, dust, mildew, a sweet moth crystal our mother had favored, and even, many years after her death, her perfume, a scent I had dearly loved for its flowery smell.

The kitchen was clean and neat. I saw that my father's coffee, normally brewed in a small French-drip pot and kept warm all day on the stove in a saucepan of barely simmering water, had been moved to the deep old-fashioned sink. I opened the cabinet that had held our juice and water glasses—still there; the cabinet that contained the yellow plates with the bluebirds and orange flowers we had used for breakfast—still there. I stood on tiptoe and opened the cabinet over the stove; the platinum-ringed jigger full of kitchen matches was still there. Nothing appeared to have been changed in the years I had been gone: the sterling silver was still in a tarnish-proof box on the counter; blue-and-white-striped kitchen towels were carefully folded and hanging on the rack next to the sink; a set of graduated knives with worn wooden handles still hung on the wall under the window.

I turned to look out across the back steps. I wondered what my father had thought as he fell. Did he have time to think of Mary? To think of me?

I followed Mary into the dining room. My sister's clumsy steps on the uneven wood floor, and then the clanging of her heels on the metal floor furnace in the center of the house, together with the sight of the white china on the mahogany sideboard and the sun glinting on the crystal in the glass-fronted cabinet, brought back a day in 1965, the day of Mary's high school graduation luncheon. Brought that day back with such force that I took a few faltering steps into the dining room and grasped the carved back of one of the mahogany dining chairs for support, fighting the sensation that those thirty years had fallen into a deep hole and that I, the person I had so painfully created, was poised to step directly into darkness. I took deep breaths until my heart had slowed and the proper progression of years had been restored.

On the way to our father's room, I saw Mary taking stuffed animals from her closet and dumping them on her bed. She had emptied the contents of her purse onto her dressing table, skirted with gathered, lace-trimmed cotton that had once been white but was now cream-colored with age and stained by some unseen source of dampness.

"Mary, don't take all of that stuff out of the closet. We won't be here long enough for you to put it all back," I said, knowing even as I spoke that my words were useless, that Mary would do exactly as she pleased, and indeed she ignored me and continued her trips to and from her closet to her bed.

My father's room was dark, the venetian blinds drawn and locked into their cradles on the sill, the paint on the old-fashioned wooden slats faded into off-white and water-stained. I loosened each blind and then drew them straight up to the top of the window, hard. Light poured into the room, which was neat. It was exactly as it had been when he shared it with my mother. On his desk was a picture of my grandparents on the back steps of the farmhouse on the River Road, in an oval silver frame that had been there as long as I could remember. Next to it was an old gray egg basket filled with marbles that had belonged to my father when he was a boy, and a wooden elephant with movable metal legs that leaned forward on his knees, as if performing a trick for a circus audience. It was a Christmas present, my father had told us, from his own grandparents when he was six years old.

I opened the door of his closet, pulled the string that turned on the light, and moved his suits on the bar until I came to a dark blue one with a gray stripe. I fingered the material of the jacket, touched the tiny round Kiwanis pin in the lapel.

I tried to summon the memory of my love for my father. It had the quality of something ancient, of something fixed and frozen so far back in time that it made my thoughts hurt in the same way that it strained my mind when I attempted to imagine the historical past, tried to picture Hernando de Soto wandering all over Florida and Alabama and Louisiana and then dying of fever. I had done these things easily as a child. Once I had loved my father effortlessly. Once, before Mary was born, I had opened my picture book about the explorers of the New World and listened to my father tell their stories. It had been real to me when he told how de Soto got so worn out from looking for gold that all he wanted to do was just get home without everybody dying. And how de Soto got sick himself, trying to follow the Mississippi River to the Gulf, and how he died, leaving what remained of his men out there in the middle of nowhere. And de Soto's men were so scared that they buried him in the Mississippi River in the middle of the dark night so the Indians wouldn't know their leader was dead and that now they were vulnerable. That story had always frightened me because I could imagine how his men would feel, abandoned like that. But now the effort to remember that I had once loved my father and that de Soto had really existed and been buried in the river that ran right past my office, and that all of the land under the houses in which people lived so easily had once been wild territory, all of it exhausted me.

I took the dark blue suit from the closet and put it on the bed. I ran my fingers through the silky ties that hung on the inside of the closet door, and their cool smoothness felt so good that I prolonged the search just to touch them. Finally, I chose a narrow silk tie with a design of blue and gray diamonds. Memory made me so sad that I left the room and went to look in on Mary.

She had pulled back the covers of her bed and gotten into it. She was surrounded by dolls and animals. "I'm going to live here now," she said. "With you. We can live here together."

"Don't get your hopes up," I said. "I don't think it would work out. Come help me find a pair of Daddy's shoes to take to the funeral home."

"You do it."

But then we heard someone at the back door.

"Yoo-hoo, Bonita." Adam Moak's mother stood on the back porch gripping a Pyrex casserole with two mitted hands. "I thought you might get here this afternoon. I brought you something for supper."

Alma Moak had become a handsome woman. When I was a child and knew her, she had short, wavy, no-color hair and a good, useful face—kind but plain, not nearly as beautiful as my mother; no one in the neighborhood had Lottie Gabriel's charm and carriage. But Alma Moak, unlike my mother, had survived the tragedies of her life and now looked upright and strong. We went into the kitchen.

"Thank you very much, Mrs. Moak," I said.

Mrs. Moak put the casserole on the counter and removed her oven mitts. Her unmemorable hair had turned a beautiful slate color, and her nondescript features displayed what must have been there all

along: wisdom and compassion. As we spoke of the past, I was over-
come with grief that Adam was lost to us, and I could not control
my tears.

Mrs. Moak embraced me as I cried without restraint over her dead
son. She patted my back and, seeming to think that I was grieving
for my father, said over and over, "I'm so sorry, my dear."

If she thought it odd that I had been gone so long and was only
now reappearing, she did not show it.

I wiped my wet face with my hands and then with the blue dish
towel Mrs. Moak plucked from the rack over the sink.

"I was the one who found him," Mrs. Moak said. "I saw him at
the bottom of the back steps. I ran inside and called 911. I'm so sorry,
dear," she said again.

"Thank you, Mrs. Moak. And thank you for the food."

"I'll bring you some hot bread and a salad when it's time for
dinner. I just wanted to make sure you knew you didn't have to worry
about food. When is the funeral? Mr. Moak and I will surely want to
be there."

"It will be a private service at the graveside," I said. "Just my sister
and me."

"Whatever you think best, my dear. How is your sister?"

"Mary's a little upset. I wanted her to go with me to choose the
casket, and we decided to come by the house, so she's here. Would
you like to see her?"

"Oh, I don't think so, my dear. I'll just run on along now. Will
she be here for dinner, too?"

"No," I said. "I'm getting ready to take her back to the nursing
home in just a minute. As soon as I pick out a pair of shoes, we're
going to take Daddy's clothes by the funeral home, and then I'll run
her back out there."

"Is it a nice place?" Mrs. Moak said.

I thought of the patients I had seen. I thought of Aura Lee and
Johnella. "It's okay. There's a nice black girl who seems to like Mary.

She looks after her pretty well, I think. And Mary has a roommate."

I heard Mary's steps in the dining room. I had turned around to see where she was when the telephone rang.

"I'll just run along now," Mrs. Moak said. She went down the back steps hastily while I went to the telephone table.

"Is this the residence of John Gabriel?"

It was a female voice I did not recognize.

"Yes, it is," I said.

"My name is Libby Marshall. I'm a real estate agent. I have a client who is interested in your wonderful old house. She would like to see it if possible," the woman said.

I heard Mary walking in the dining room, crossing and recrossing the floor. Then I heard the screen door to the back porch open.

"Excuse me," I said. "How did you find out that this house might be available?"

"Word of mouth," she said. "I know this is a difficult time for you, and I would like to offer my condolences. But my client and I have been looking for a house like yours for some time." I pictured the two women driving up and down the street waiting for my father to die.

I held the receiver away from my ear and tried to see around the door. I was pretty sure that Mary had overheard me tell Mrs. Moak that I was going to take her back soon.

"Could we make an appointment to see the house? Perhaps run by for just a minute this afternoon," Libby Marshall said.

"It would be more convenient if you called me later," I said. "This is not a really good time for me to talk."

"Could we just set up an appointment, and then I'll let you go," the realtor insisted.

I heard glass breaking. I hung up on Libby Marshall and went out to the kitchen. I could see the back of my sister's head at the foot of the steps. When I went outside, I saw that she stood with a stack of white china over the garbage pail.

"Mary!" I cried. As I went down the steps, I saw that the garbage pail was filled with Waterford crystal. "Mary, what are you doing?"

Mary turned. She had repainted her face. It had never occurred to me to be afraid of my sister, but now, when Mary turned to me, the baleful eyes that glared at me from under the purple eyebrows made me think of blows and cries and then of pain and blood. I felt violence in the air like a cloud.

I ran down the steep steps and grabbed Mary's arm just as she dumped the plates into the garbage can. "Mary, why on earth are you doing this?"

"Daddy told me to do it. He got in the car with us at Ortlieb's. He told me to do it. He wants a real funeral. When I told him you wouldn't have one, he said, 'When you get home, throw out all of the crystal and china. That'll make your sister sorry for not having a real funeral.' "

"You've broken everything!" I cried.

"He wants it in the paper!" Mary shouted. "Daddy wants people to come to see me."

"You've broken everything we had to remember them by, Mary." I sank down on the bottom step. "You've broken it all," I said, and I put my head on my knees, and once again, I wept. In all of the years since I had left that house on Mary's graduation day in 1965, I had not cried once, and now I could not stop.

"Not everything," Mary said as she stepped over me. I heard her mount the steps and go back onto the porch. "I left you a few. Daddy told me to save you a few plates."

Chapter Fourteen

September 1954

 Early in the morning on the first day of sixth grade, Bonita was awakened by sunlight filtering through the leaves of the persimmon tree outside her window. The shadows moving on the floor reminded her of other Septembers when exciting school events lay ahead, but Bonita didn't bound from her bed. The night before, Dr. Landry had called to ask if Laurel could ride with Mary and Bonita to school.

After Dr. Landry's call, Bonita asked her father if she could talk to him privately. They went out to the front porch and pulled two white rockers together, and he had listened while Bonita, speaking softly, told him of her quarrel with Laurel beneath the ligustrums the previous spring. Bonita repeated, word for word, everything Laurel had heard her father say about Mary and Lottie and her father. When she got to the part where Laurel had quoted, "Lottie Gabriel is a classic case. She fits those studies I've done to a T," her father slapped the flat arm of his rocker and said, "For God's sake, Bonita, why didn't you tell me this sooner?"

"I was afraid you'd be mad," Bonita said.

"I am mad."

In the fading light, Bonita could see her father thinking. "Okay," he said. "Look after your sister at school for the next few days, Bonita. And try to keep a lid on that little Landry girl. I don't want your mother hearing anything that might hurt her feelings."

"Yes, sir," Bonita said.

"Maybe you could eat lunch with your sister and play with her at recess until she gets used to being in school."

Bonita thought of the conversation she had overheard between her parents, of everything she had looked forward to in sixth grade. "Daddy," she said, "what made Aunt Diana get sick?"

In the deep dusk Bonita could feel her father's displeasure.

"Little pitchers with big ears," he said. "The next time your mother and I have a private conversation, I'll look behind the door to see if anyone is listening. Diana is a person from the past, Bonita. I'd appreciate it if you would keep your mind on the people in the present."

"Yes, Daddy," Bonita said.

"Sisters have to look out for each other," her father said. "Family is the glue that holds the world together, Bonita."

"Hello, Laurel," Lottie said when they arrived with Adrienne to pick up Dr. Landry's daughter. "Don't you look nice in your uniform. Did you tie that bow yourself?"

When Lottie turned to smile at Laurel, Bonita saw that her mother looked particularly beautiful. Lottie wore a red linen dress piped in black. Her dark hair was tied at the base of her neck with a red-and-black-checked silk scarf. She wore silver bracelets and silver earrings in the shape of coins. Her cologne scented the entire car.

"Yes, ma'am," Laurel said when she had settled back in the seat.

She stuck her feet straight out. "And I tied my own shoelaces."

"Aren't you a smart girl," Lottie said. "Are you excited about first grade?"

"Yes, ma'am," Laurel said.

As they rode, Laurel and Adrienne began to whisper and giggle. Bonita, concerned there was a conspiracy brewing against Lottie, leaned over and whispered in Laurel's ear, "If you say anything about my mother going to the doctor, I will take a gun and shoot you dead."

"I didn't say a word about your mother," Laurel whispered.

"Well, if you do, I will kill you," Bonita whispered.

"You don't know how to shoot a gun," Laurel whispered.

"Sure I do," Bonita said. "I shoot guns all the time."

"No whispering," Lottie said from the front seat.

Sister Genevieve took the roll and passed out textbooks. She set a date for the first meeting of Saint Teresa's Little Flowers, a club that encouraged imitation of the saint through good works and fellowship. When the bell rang at ten o'clock for little recess, Bonita was writing her full name and "1954–55" in a textbook on Louisiana geography. The book had been used before; another name was above hers: Diane Hudgins, 1953–54, a good omen, for Diane glittered in the seventh-grade firmament. But the workbook that went with the text was new.

This paperback pamphlet was dark green and bore on its cover a frieze of Louisiana fruit in the center of which was a large red strawberry. Even after the bell rang, Bonita could not resist leafing through. There were chapters on cotton, rice, fruit, sugarcane, fish, and furs. There was a foldout map to be traced and transferred to cardboard, each parish to be colored and then cut into a puzzle. It was the most beautiful schoolbook Bonita had ever seen, and it had been written by a nun named Sister Dorothy Acosta who taught in New Orleans. Carefully, Bonita placed it on top of her desk and then ran outside to the playground with a light heart.

Denise and Darlene Martens, twins who lived across the street from the school, ran up to Bonita. Darlene said, "Mother's bridge club is tomorrow, and she's fixing shrimp salad, tomato aspic, and cheese straws. It's going to be on the screened porch, and everything will be blue and white. She's practicing today, and you're invited!"

"I can't come," Bonita said. "I have to eat lunch with my sister."

"You have to come," Darlene said. "There'll be blue tablecloths and Grandmother's Blue Willow china. She's even going to have blue goblets."

A shriek from Mary, near the swings, fighting to get the ribbon that went beneath her collar from Laurel while Gracie Davis waved her hands before Mary's face to distract her, only served to reinforce their father's instructions.

"My daddy would be mad if he found out," Bonita said. "I have to go get Mary's ribbon back."

After recess, Sister Genevieve held the election for hall monitors. When Bonita was nominated, she raised her hand. After Sister Genevieve called on her to speak, Bonita asked permission to come to the desk.

"Sister, I can't be a hall monitor because today is my sister's first day of school and my father wants me to make sure that she has someone to eat lunch with," Bonita whispered.

"I understand," Sister Genevieve said. "All children are nervous on the first day of school, but there are plenty of students her own age to keep her company."

Bonita was ashamed to tell Sister Genevieve that no one from their neighborhood wanted to play with Mary, so she said, "It's also to see that Mary eats all of her lunch."

"Sister Alice will make sure that Mary eats a good lunch with all the other first-graders, Bonita. That's what teachers are here for. Your sister is not your responsibility while you're at school. You have your own friends and your own work to do. There's plenty of time for you to be with your sister when you're at home," Sister Genevieve said.

"Now, run along and sit down and let's get the hall monitors elected before noon."

Just before eleven-thirty, Bonita and a girl named Sandra Bonifanti were elected and sent to the cafeteria to eat an early lunch.

"Some eighth-grade boys are coming over from Catholic High during lunch hour to set up the chairs for assembly," Sandra said.

"How did you find that out?" Bonita said. She found Sandra's short, stocky, developing body, her too curly black hair and pimpled cheeks intriguing. Bonita had heard that Sandra Bonifanti already wore stockings and a garter belt and went out on dates.

"I heard Sister Veronica tell Father Michael that she needed three eighth-graders." Sandra drained her milk until the straw slurped. "Hurry, I need some time to fix my face before they get here."

"You're going to put on makeup?" Bonita said.

"Sure. Come on," Sandra said, and she left the cafeteria with Bonita close behind.

In the hall, Sandra gave a little hop from a black tile to a white one. "Three boys!" she said in a thick whisper. "Thirteen-year-olds." She twirled so that the pleats of her uniform whipped up about her sturdy hips. "I'll be twelve next month, you know."

"No, I didn't know," Bonita said.

"I'm really supposed to be in seventh grade," Sandra confided in the same hoarse whisper. She pulled the girls'-bathroom door open and said over her shoulder, "My parents held me back in first grade. I couldn't read. We lived in New Orleans then. Nobody else in class knows."

"I won't tell," Bonita said.

Sandra reached into her right blue and white saddle oxford and held up her lipstick. "I carry it in my shoe," she said.

"What shade is it?" Bonita said.

"Call It Red. You can wear some, too, if you want."

"I guess I'd better not," Bonita said. "I don't want to get in any trouble."

"Sister Veronica will send you home if she catches you with lipstick on," Sandra said with great satisfaction, as if the only reason for putting it on was to upset the principal. She leaned forward and outlined her lips with the lipstick, mashed them together, and then redistributed the color with her little finger.

It reminded Bonita of the teenager she had asked to watch Mary while she went to the bathroom on the day of Laurel's birthday party. She put out her hand. "Let me have some," she said.

"We'll wash it off before we go back to class," Sandra said. "I like to put a little on my cheeks, but that's probably why I'm getting these goddamned pimples."

Bonita blinked at the profanity. "What will we do if Sister Veronica sees us?" she said. She leaned toward the mirror and traced the outline of her lips. Then she filled it in, dabbed a dot on each cheek, rubbed that all around, wound the lipstick down, capped it with a click, and handed it back to Sandra.

"It'll be so dark in the hall that when the nuns pass us, they won't notice. Just turn your head," Sandra said, opening the bathroom door and waiting for Bonita to come, too.

Bonita couldn't help stealing looks at herself in the mirror. She seemed to be someone else, someone like Florette.

"You keep a lookout at this end of the hall," Sandra said. "I'm going down to the other end to watch out for Father Michael's car."

During the first fifteen minutes of the lunch hour, Bonita was busy. She took a second-grader who had fallen on the playground into the bathroom and washed the little girl's scraped knee, then sent her to Sister Veronica's office to get some antiseptic and a Band-Aid. Shadowing her face with her hand, she took a note given to her by Sister Thecla to Sister Gertrude in the safely dark chapel. Bonita spent so much time trying to hide her made-up face that she wished she had never tried out Sandra's lipstick. She was on the point of going into the bathroom to wash it off when Sandra shouted, "They're here!"

Bonita ran down the hall to look out the window with her. Father

Michael's old green Plymouth was just pulling into the circular drive.

"Oh my God, it's Gerry Winborn," Sandra said. "That tall blond boy getting out of the backseat. Isn't he adorable?"

Behind him came two more boys.

"The dark-haired guy," Sandra said. "That's Roland Brown. And the short one getting stuff out of the trunk, that's PeeWee Singleton. Dibs on Gerry. You can have the other two. They're going in the cafeteria. Watch my end of the hall while I run over there and take a peek."

Sandra returned with the news that the boys were busy putting up the chairs. She had watched through the window until Sister Genevieve waved her away. "And there's some ruckus going on in the cafeteria. Sister Alice came out with a kid who was squalling to beat all get out."

"Did she have blond hair?" Bonita said.

"Yeah, and a big mouth," Sandra said. "She was screaming her lungs out." She looked down the hall. "I'm going to see if I can sneak in and talk to Gerry. I know him from swimming lessons last summer at City Park. He taught me how to do the dead man's float." She ran back down the hall.

Again Bonita remembered her frantic day at City Park. Sandra was probably having a good time in the swimming pool with Gerry Winborn while I was racing all around looking for Mary, she thought. Let someone else worry about Mary for a while. She decided to stay right where she was.

"Are you Bonita?"

Bonita turned. "Yes," she said. "I'm Bonita."

It was the tall blond boy Sandra had called Gerry. Up close she could see that his blond hair was very straight and fell over his forehead into his eyes. A bead of sweat rolled down the side of his face. He brushed it away and pushed his hair back with one motion of his forearm.

"Sister Veronica said you could show me where Father Michael's chair is," Gerry said.

"It's in her office," Bonita said. She led the boy to the principal's office and pointed to the overstuffed chair that sat in one corner. "She keeps it here just for Father Michael, so he'll have a comfortable place to sit when he has to come to assembly."

"What do the sisters sit in?" Gerry said.

"They all sit in folding chairs like the ones we sit in. Father Michael is the only one to get a good chair."

Father Michael's chair had been in the corner of Sister Veronica's office for as long as Bonita could remember. It was an easy chair upholstered in gold brocade.

Gerry tried to pick the chair up. It was so heavy he put it down again. He looked at it with his head cocked to one side. "I think I'm going to have to go get PeeWee to help me," he said.

"I'll help you," Bonita said.

She took hold of one chair arm, and Gerry took the other. Together, with it barely an inch from the floor, they wrestled it out of Sister Veronica's office, out the back door, and staggered with it across the grass.

"I think I'll become a priest," Gerry said. "If they get the good chairs."

"Me, too," Bonita said.

"I'll tell Sister Veronica you're going to become a priest," Gerry said.

Bonita giggled. Her giggles made the chair wobble, so she had to lower her side to the ground. Gerry started to speak. Bonita held up her hand. "Don't say anything funny. If you make me laugh, I'm gonna get the hiccups." But it was too late, the hiccups were upon her.

The first two were so painful Bonita had to lean over the fat arm of the chair to suffer through them. Concerned, Gerry put down his side of the chair and walked around to her.

The pain lessened, and Bonita tried to speak. "I swallowed a giggle," she said between hiccups. "My mother says you'll get the hiccups if you swallow a giggle."

Gerry bent over to look in her face. "Are you okay?" he said.

Bonita straightened up. She took a shallow, experimental breath. "I think they might be gone," she said. But they weren't. She hiccuped again, hard.

Gerry turned away to conceal his laughter. Bonita banged him on one shaking shoulder. "I told you, don't make me laugh." But she was laughing, too. And hiccuping at the same time. They took up the chair again and stumbled across the grass with it, laughing all the way to the gym.

The other two boys were waiting outside the door. Just as they got there, Sandra pushed the door open. "Hide your face! Sister Veronica's coming," she said and she ran away.

"What's wrong?" Gerry said.

"I've got on lipstick. If Sister Veronica sees me, she'll call my mother and send me home."

"PeeWee," Gerry said. "Take Bonita's side. Quick!"

PeeWee shouldered Bonita away as Sister Veronica came outside. Bonita whirled, wiped her mouth with her hand, and started to walk across the grass. The boys headed into the gym with Father Michael's chair. Sister Veronica's voice brought them all up short. "Bonita, Sister Alice is looking for you. Your sister needs you."

Reluctantly, Bonita turned. "Yes, Sister," she said.

"One of the other first-graders untied her ribbon and she became very upset," Sister Veronica said.

"Mary has a hard time making a bow," Bonita said.

"All first-graders have trouble tying bows, Bonita. But they don't usually have hysterics. I had to call your mother. She's on her way."

"Where is Mary now?" Bonita said.

"Sister Alice took her back to the room. She thought she might be able to calm Mary if she were separated from the other students."

"May I be excused to go see about Mary, Sister Veronica?" Bonita said.

"In just a moment, Bonita. Come here to me."

Bonita walked slowly toward the nun.

"Did you have on lip rouge?" Sister Veronica said.

"Yes, Sister Veronica."

"Of all my students, Bonita, you are the last one I would have expected to disobey the rules."

"I'm sorry, Sister Veronica," Bonita said.

"Where did you get it?"

"I brought it from home in my shoe," Bonita said.

Sister Veronica looked at Bonita sadly. "Let's go inside. After you wash your face, I want you to come to my office. I'll have to talk with your mother about this when she gets here."

Bonita accompanied Sister Veronica to her office, where her mother was waiting with Mary.

Mary's face was tear-streaked. Bonita knew her sister was upset because she had permitted Lottie to hold her.

"I'm going to take your sister home," Lottie said. "Sister Alice suggested we let her take a good nap this afternoon and try again tomorrow."

Bonita watched Sister Veronica, waiting for the principal to tell her mother about the lipstick, but all Sister Veronica said was, "You may be excused, Bonita. Join your classmates in the gym for assembly."

Father Michael was in his car with the engine running when Bonita went outside to go to the gym. He tooted the horn and beckoned her over. "Tell those young men that we have to leave this very minute," he said. "They are going to be late for class if we don't, and I've got to get back to give the opening prayer for assembly."

"Yes, Father Michael," Bonita said.

The boys came out of the door as Bonita reached it. "Father Michael says you have to leave this minute," she said. "Or you'll be late for class."

Roland Brown and PeeWee Singleton took off running for the priest's car. Gerry Winborn handed her a note. "Read it right now," he said. And he, too, ran off toward Father Michael's car.

It was a folded piece of lined paper torn from an assignment book. Bonita opened it. Scrawled sideways across the page was the message "Meet me at the Louisiana Sat. morning. Ten o'clock." Bonita read it and looked up. Gerry was waiting behind the open car door. She nodded and then went inside to assembly.

Lottie didn't want Bonita to look after Mary at school. Her father disagreed, but Lottie prevailed. Bonita was permitted to remain a hall monitor, Mary allowed to take her chances with the other children. When Bonita asked for permission to go to the movies on Saturday morning, her father said that she could go, but that Mary would have to go with her because he and Lottie were playing tennis.

At school Friday morning Sandra said, "PeeWee Singleton called me and said you and Gerry were going to meet at the movie Saturday morning, and he wanted me to come, too, and sit with him. I told you I had dibs on Gerry."

"He came inside to get Father Michael's chair. I didn't do any-thing," Bonita said. She knew that wasn't strictly true. She didn't tell Sandra how quickly she had volunteered to help Gerry carry the chair. Nor did she tell Sandra they had laughed and she got the hiccups. Or that he had touched her shoulder. "That's the only time I talked to him. Cross my heart and hope to die."

"Well," Sandra said, "I'll forgive you this time because you didn't tattle on me about the lipstick."

Sandra was waiting in front of the Louisiana Theatre. She wore a short, flowered skirt, a white blouse, and red shoes with a little stacked heel. A red purse hung by a strap from her shoulder. To Bonita, the short, stocky Sandra Bonifanti in her red-flowered skirt looked exactly like a miniature Florette.

When Bonita and Mary got out of the car, Sandra whispered, "That's the kid who was screaming in the cafeteria. Is that your sister?"

"Yes. Mary, this is Sandra. She's in my class."

"Why did you bring her?" Sandra said.

"I had to," Bonita said.

"She'll tell," Sandra said.

"She won't tell," Bonita said. "She never tells."

"Does she know B-O-Y-S are coming?" Sandra let each letter leave her mouth silently like a smoke ring.

Mary watched both girls with bright eyes. Something in their manner alerted her to their excitement; it was as contagious as measles. Mary imitated Sandra: "B-O-Y-S."

Bonita shook her head. "Not yet."

"When are you gonna tell her?" Sandra said.

"Not until they get here," Bonita said. "They might not even show up."

"They'll show up," Sandra said.

"They? They who?" Mary said, twisting away from under Bonita's hand. "Tell me who."

Bonita knelt down, puffed her sister's sleeves, straightened her sash, and said, "Somebody's going to sit with us during the movie."

"Who?" Mary said. "Mr. Orlando?"

"No, not Mr. Orlando."

"Who's Mr. Orlando?" Sandra said.

"Somebody who looks out for us," Bonita said. "So we won't get kidnapped."

"You might get kidnapped?" Sandra said.

Bonita wanted to take the words back. The thrill of saying them had flared and flown like a struck match.

"Are you rich?" Sandra said.

"No, we're not rich," Bonita said.

"Rich," Mary said.

"Anybody could get kidnapped," Bonita said. "You could get kidnapped."

"Not me," Sandra said. "I'm not rich."

"Rich, rich," Mary said.

"Well, we're not rich, either," Bonita said.

"Rich, rich, rich," Mary said.

"Stop it, Mary," Bonita said.

Mary shook her head violently. "Rich! Rich! Rich!" she shouted. The other children going to the movie turned to look at her.

Sandra leaned close. "What's wrong with your sister?" she whispered in Bonita's ear.

"Nothing," Bonita said. "There's nothing's wrong with her. Just don't say the word 'rich' again."

Fortunately, Gerry and PeeWee appeared at that moment on their bicycles. Mary stopped shouting to take in this new development.

"We're late," Gerry said, dismounting. He was frowning. "We're way late. I'm sorry you had to wait out here on the street for us." He lifted his bicycle onto the bike rack at the side of the building. "Has the movie started yet?"

"I don't think so," Bonita said, looking around at the doors. "Everybody's still going in."

"We've got to get some tickets," Gerry said, locking his bicycle. He reached into the pocket of his blue jeans, approaching the ticket booth.

Bonita had been so preoccupied with Mary that she had forgotten completely about tickets. Horrified, she looked at Sandra. "We didn't get any tickets," she whispered.

Sandra whispered back, "They get the tickets. They asked us."

"But not Mary. Gerry didn't ask Mary." Bonita had noticed that, out of his khaki school uniform, Gerry looked much taller. As she walked toward the ticket booth, she realized that he looked taller because his pants were too short and his cotton shirt, worn from washing, was too small. His shoes were neatly polished, but they were worn, and his bicycle was decidedly not new. Bonita took the movie money from the pocket of her dress.

"I'm sorry you had to stand out here on the street waiting for us," Gerry said. He looked stern. He had not once smiled at her.

"That's okay," Bonita said. "We didn't mind." She put a quarter on the counter. "I had to bring my sister with me," she said. "I couldn't come if she didn't come, so here's some money for our tickets."

Gerry moved the quarter away. Bonita slid the quarter over to his hand; Gerry moved it away. Neither said a word, just engaged in a silent, awkward battle. Gerry won. Bonita ran back, took her sister's hand, and dragged her along so they could go in the door with Gerry.

At the candy counter, Bonita said she didn't want any popcorn, but Mary said, "I want popcorn!"

Gerry pushed Bonita's money away and paid for three boxes himself.

"This is for my sister," Bonita said to him. "I don't want you to pay for hers, and I don't want any popcorn."

Gerry handed her one of the boxes anyway and turned to go inside the theater. He looked so forbidding, Bonita wanted to run away. The ease and humor of their initial encounter were nowhere in sight. If she hadn't had Mary with her, none of these problems would have arisen. If she had been unencumbered by Mary, she thought, she could have found a way to talk to Gerry—after all, until the past spring, Adam Moak had been her best friend. She thought she could learn how to talk to a boy, but Mary was a rock tied to her tongue.

PeeWee and Sandra went in first, followed by Mary, Bonita, and Gerry. The lights went down and the children stopped screaming. Everyone had settled back to see the cartoon when Mary's voice sang out through the whole theater—"My popcorn's all spilled"—and she began to cry.

Bonita sank into her seat, slid down until her head was below the level of the seat's back. She pulled Mary down. "Sit down and be quiet," she said. "People can hear you."

Bonita was mortified when she saw that Sandra and PeeWee were giggling. Between the tickets, the popcorn, and Mary making a spectacle of herself, she was convinced Gerry was going to refuse to speak to her. Just let me get out of here and I'll never do this again, she vowed.

But Gerry, who had been a stiff presence beside her ever since they sat down, bent toward her instead of turning away. "What's your sister's name?" he said.

"Mary," Bonita said.

"Let Mary sit next to me. Change seats with her."

"Change seats with me," Bonita said to Mary.

The sisters exchanged places. Gerry leaned down and said something to Mary that Bonita could not hear. Mary giggled, sat back in the seat, and held out her empty popcorn box. Gerry shook popcorn from his box into Mary's. He spoke to her again. Mary laughed again and then was silent.

Outside, after the movie, the boys hung around.

"How are you all going to get home?" Gerry said.

"I'm riding the bus," Sandra said.

"We can give you a ride home, Sandra. My parents are picking us up," Bonita said. Bonita looked down Third Street for her father's gray Buick, which she recognized not by its color and shape but by its toothy grille.

Sandra opened her red purse, withdrew a small silver compact with sculpted roses on the lid, plucked up a powder puff, and said to PeeWee, "They might get kidnapped," as she powdered her nose.

"Who?" PeeWee said. "Them?" He jerked his head in the direction of Bonita and Mary, who stood together near the curb.

"Not really kidnapped," Bonita said.

Sandra took out her lipstick, traced the outline of her lips with it, mashed her lips together to spread the red around, and said, "They even have a bodyguard."

"It's not a real bodyguard," Bonita said, rigid with embarrassment, but secretly suspecting that this shame was the penalty for her boast. "It's just a man who drives around our streets at night. He helped me look for Mary a couple of times when she was lost. He's never seen a robber in our neighborhood, though. Or a kidnapper. And don't even bring up murder, because he's never seen that, either."

"Never ever?" Sandra said.

Mary looked up at Sandra with the smile and the gleaming eyes that forecasted her theft of words that rhymed.

"I don't know if it was 'ever,' " Bonita said. "He might have seen one sometime that I don't know about."

"That's why I didn't want you and Sandra left out here waiting by yourself," Gerry said. "My mother told me once, 'Never, ever leave a girl waiting alone on a street.' That's probably why she said that. Because you might get kidnapped."

"Never ever!" Mary said. "Never ever! Never ever!"

Bonita put her hand on Mary's hair. "Don't." She turned Mary's head so that she faced the street. "Watch for Mother and Daddy," she said.

Bonita was relieved to realize that Gerry's silence had less to do with Mary than his discomfort when he was unable to do what his mother had told him to do.

"Yeah," PeeWee said. "And then they would send your parents one of those letters asking for a million dollars to get you back. I don't know how much they would want if it was two of you—maybe a trillion dollars."

Bonita gave a small, disclaiming laugh. "My daddy sure doesn't have a trillion dollars," she said.

"And then, even if your parents paid them all that money, you might get murdered anyway," Sandra added.

"Stop," Bonita said.

"Yeah. And then they would stuff you and your sister in the trunk of their car," PeeWee said.

"Stop it!" Bonita said.

"And then they would ride across the Mississippi River on the ferry and throw your dead bodies in a sugarcane field, wouldn't they, PeeWee?" Sandra said.

"Yeah," PeeWee said. "And then . . ."

Gerry put his hand on PeeWee's shoulder. "She said stop it!" he said.

"You're making my sister cry," Bonita said.

Mary watched them, tears rolling down her cheeks.

"Now see what you've done," Bonita said.

"I don't want to get put in the trunk," Mary cried.

Gerry patted Mary's head. "Nobody's gonna put you in the trunk. My daddy's a policeman, and he would never let anybody hurt you."

When John and Lottie arrived, Bonita said, "Can we give Sandra a ride home?"

"Of course," Lottie said. "How about you boys? Do you need a ride home?"

"No, ma'am. But thank you very much," Gerry said. "We have our bikes."

While Sandra and Mary were climbing into the backseat, Bonita said, "Thank you very much, Gerry, for taking Mary and me to the movie. And thanks for the popcorn. We had a nice time."

"Meet me here next Saturday?" Gerry said.

"Even if I have to bring Mary?" Bonita whispered.

"Sure," Gerry said.

Bonita let out the breath she had been holding and said, "Yes. Yes, I will."

"Come on, Bonita," Lottie said. "We're waiting on you." And, when Bonita was in the car, "Introduce us to your friend, Bonita."

"Mother and Daddy, this is Sandra Bonifanti. Sandra, this is my mother, Mrs. Gabriel, and my daddy, Dr. Gabriel."

Lottie turned around, gave Sandra a smile, and said, "I'm so glad to meet you, Sandra. It's so lovely to see my girls with their friends. Who were those boys, Bonita?"

"Someone we met at school when they came to put up the chairs for assembly," Bonita said.

"They looked a little old for you," Lottie said. "How old are they?"

"Twelve," Sandra said before Bonita could answer. "They're big for their age."

Mary giggled. Bonita and Sandra looked at her. Mary zipped her lips, locked them, and threw away the key.

Chapter Fifteen

October 1995

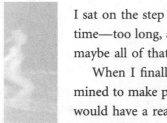 I sat on the step staring out into the backyard for a long time—too long, as it turned out. As I sat there, I thought maybe all of that china and crystal deserved to die.

When I finally got up and went in the house, determined to make peace with Mary—to tell her that yes, we would have a real funeral for Daddy, that I would put it in the paper so that she could see the people she had cared for in the past—I couldn't find her.

I looked in every room, in every closet, under every bed, under the back steps, under the front stoop, up and down the sidewalk; I looked everywhere, but it was all for nothing, Mary had taken off.

I took up one of the white Haviland plates Mary had spared and sat down at the dining room table. Holding the plate so that the light from the windows fell on it, I put my hand behind it. When I was a child and my grandmother Gabriel called these plates bone china, I thought it was because you could see the bones of your hand through them, as if the plate were an X ray. I saw the outline of my hand, but not one sign of a bone. I placed the plate on the table and put my head in my hands. I was out of the habit of looking for Mary as if every frantic minute that I couldn't find her was a debit entered in some terrible ledger kept by the gods of pain and terror. I stood up. I didn't want to do it by myself anymore.

"State Home."

"This is Mary Gabriel's sister. May I speak to Johnella Johnson?"

"Hold on."

Johnella came on the line. "Hey," I said. "This is Mary's sister. I've got a problem here."

"She got away from you, didn't she?" Johnella said.

"Yes," I said. "She got away from me."

"How long she gone?" Johnella said.

"Not long. Maybe fifteen minutes. I looked all around the house and all around the neighborhood, but I can't find her."

"You give her any money?" Johnella said.

"No," I said. "I didn't give her any . . . hang on a minute." I put the receiver down, went into the dining room, and looked in my purse. Damn! I returned to the telephone. "Johnella, she's got my wallet," I said.

"What she got? How much cash?" Johnella sounded calm.

"Almost four hundred dollars," I said.

"You keep credit cards?"

"No. All she's got is cash."

"I'll have to call the Baton Rouge police. And I'd better call the Livingston parish sheriff's department and the state troopers. And I better warn the local TV station."

"She's not going to hurt anybody," I said. But even as I said it, I remembered the baleful look in Mary's eyes, and I wondered if it was true.

"They don't know that," Johnella said.

She leaned away from the telephone to speak to someone. I heard her say, "I'll be there in a minute. Mary's sister done lost her." She came back to me. "I gotta go. We changing shift here. I'm gone be outta here before too long, so I'm gone give you my number at home. You call me if anything happen. Where you are?"

"I'm at Daddy's house in Baton Rouge."

"Give me that number. You don't have no telephone where you be living, do you? That man at the coroner's office said he looked for one everywhere."

"No, I don't have a telephone at home," I said.

"Where you going to be?" she said.

"I don't know. I'll probably start driving around looking for her."

"You let me know if you find her," Johnella said.

"I will," I said.

I was standing there considering what to do next when the telephone rang. I thought it might be that real estate person again, so I jerked up the receiver and said, "Yes? What is it?"

"Hey, Mary's sister. This is Aura Lee Lewis, Mary's best friend in the whole world."

"Hey, Aura Lee," I said. Oddly, I found the sound of her voice comforting.

"How you doing, Mary's sister?"

"Not so good, Aura Lee. Mary's run away."

"I know," Aura Lee said.

"You know? How do you know that, Aura Lee?" I said.

"She told me she was going," Aura Lee said.

"When did Mary tell you?" I said.

"Just awhile ago. Mary gave me this number and said to call you in ten minutes and say that she's not coming back until you put it in the paper about your daddy," Aura Lee said. "And that you say you'll have a real funeral."

"She called you before she left?" I said.

"Yes-siree bobtail, she did." Aura Lee was exhilarated. Outside of protecting her box, Mary's escape was probably the most exciting thing Aura Lee had been in on in a long time. I was glad she felt like she was slap-dab in the middle of life again after all that time isolated out there in that sad place, but I was sorry I had to be in on it with her.

"Did she say where she was going?" I said.

"She said she had some things to do," Aura Lee said.

"She's not heading for New York, is she?"

"Not yet," Aura Lee said.

"Because there's no point in having a funeral if she's not going to be here for it."

"She'll be there," Aura Lee said.

"Okay, Aura Lee, I'll do it," I said. "It will take me a little while, but I'll do everything Mary wants." I looked at my watch. "It's almost three o'clock. Tell Mary when she calls that I expect her to be back here at the house by five o'clock. Tell her we'll go someplace nice for dinner and I'll see if I can get permission for her to spend the night here at home. Have you got all of that?"

"I got it," Aura Lee said.

"When is Mary going to call you back?" I said.

"She didn't say exactly when," Aura Lee said. "Mary is slippery."

"That's the God's truth," I said.

Aura Lee yelped with laughter. "That's the God's truth!" she cried. "Mary is slippery! That's the God's truth!"

"Aura Lee!" I said. "Aura Lee, I've got to go. I've got to call the funeral home. Don't forget what I've told you. Five o'clock. I want Mary back here at five o'clock. And would you go tell Johnella that Mary called you, please, before the shift changes. I told her I'd let her know if I heard from Mary."

"Okay, Mary's sister. I'll tell Mary five P.M. when she calls. Five P.M." Aura Lee said the time again and again, emphasizing the initials as if she liked the rich sound of them, as if they amounted to something of substance.

I sat down at my father's desk and opened the bottom drawer, the deepest one. It was filled with manila folders, each neatly labeled: Gulf

States Utilities, Exxon, Shell, Anderson Drugs, Medical-Lottie Gabriel Medical—John Gabriel, Medical—Mary Gabriel (that one leaked letters out of every side), and a folder for me: Bonita Jane Gabriel.

Although I knew Dr. Scott had had no choice because I couldn't be located, it troubled me to think of him examining the contents of my folder. In it, indeed, were the four booklets I had written on Louisiana fruit, but also in that folder were other papers, legal papers and a sheaf of bills and insurance forms for the long hospitalization at DePaul Hospital in New Orleans during my teenage years.

I replaced my folder and closed the drawer. I turned sideways to the other side of the desk and pulled up the old typewriter. Carefully, I inserted a pair of canary-yellow sheets into the manual typewriter; long, long ago, when I had wanted to play at his desk, my father taught me that a sheet alone would be pierced by the typewriter keys and damage the rubber roller. I typed my father's full name onto the page. Embarking on this task brought my father back to me vividly in just the way that I had dreaded. I looked away through the window at a tall crepe myrtle whose boughs, heavily hung with round seedpods, arced downward as gracefully as water from a fountain.

Distracted almost before beginning, I got up and went to my mother's dresser. As it was with my room and Mary's, everything my mother had touched, worn, or lived with was completely intact. I opened a box of her face powder, lifted the fluffy puff, and loosed a cloud of dusty motes into the air. I pulled out one of her dresser drawers. Even her lipsticks were still there. I took one and turned it upside down to see the shade—Really Red. I opened it. It was dry. I replaced the top and opened a jar of Pond's cold cream. It was empty. I lifted the lid of a gold compact engraved with the initial "G," flanked by an "L" and a "D," and brought the mirror close to my face. The curtains behind me were reflected, and I remembered the party my parents had for the Landrys when they moved into the neighborhood.

I wondered where Laurel Landry was now. I conjured up an adult face for her, composed of her remembered childish features—the freckles, the ginger hair, and the eyes that always seemed to know more about sadness than any five-year-old should. I put the thought of Laurel Landry aside and got back to writing my father's obituary.

"I'm sorry I didn't recognize you right away," Jim Singleton said when I handed him Daddy's clothes and the typewritten pages. "The name 'Jane' threw me off. Mitchell is your married name?"

"Yes. It didn't last, but I use it for my work. I've gotten so used to it, sometimes I forget I ever had another name."

"I've read that column in the paper on native fruits for quite some time. I didn't realize it was you. My wife likes it, too. She was really happy to get that recipe you got from Rapides Parish for mayhaw jelly," Jim said.

"I'm glad somebody got some good out of that. I'm so isolated up there I never know if anybody's reading what I'm writing or not," I said.

All of the things I was saying were lies: I never, ever forgot that I had another name, and I didn't really care if anyone was reading what I wrote or not, but, unlike Mary, I could still make conventional conversation.

"Have a seat," he said. "I'll have my secretary fax this over to the paper."

It felt good to sit down and rest for a while. I leaned back and rested my head on the back of the chair.

"I think about those days at Catholic High," Jim said when he returned. "More and more as I grow older. I used to want to put the past behind me as fast as I could. Now I just want to get it back. You ever see anybody from back then?"

"No," I said with my head still against the back of the chair and my eyes shut. "Never."

"Sandra Bonifanti made it big in New York, you know," Jim said. I opened my eyes. "No, I didn't know. Doing what?"

"Painting. She's a big deal up there. They had a bunch of her pictures out at LSU, and my wife and I were invited to go see them. I liked them. At least I could tell what everything was supposed to be. Not like some artists, where you can't make out what you're looking at."

"That's good. I'm glad for her," I said. "Does she still live in New York?"

"No. She moved back to Baton Rouge a couple of years ago. Said she was ready to come home. Just like the rest of us, I guess. Now that the hardest part is behind us, we're ready to relax and enjoy the past a little."

Enjoy the past, I thought. You must be crazy. Aloud, I said, "Does she have a family?"

"No. She never did have children, although I think she was married two or three times. She was always a lot of fun. We saw Gerry Winborn when we went to see Sandra's paintings. He was with his wife. She's sick. She's been sick for a long time."

"I'm sorry. What is it?"

"Multiple sclerosis."

"Who did he marry?" I said. Just thinking about Gerry being married to someone else gave me a pang.

"Her name is Christine. I don't know what her maiden name was. She was from North Louisiana. Monroe, I think. Or maybe it was Shreveport."

I wondered where Gerry had met her, how he had met her. I remembered how nice he had been. He was sweet to me no matter what happened.

"Did they have children?" I said. Gerry had always said he wanted lots of children.

"No children. They haven't been married all that long. I heard she was sick when he married her."

Yes, Gerry would have done that. If I could have stayed married to anyone, it would have been Gerry. I thought of the life Gerry and

I could have had: a small house, probably, maybe one of those pleasant houses near Holy Angels like the one the Matens twins had lived
in. Then children. Lots of children, and they would have all gone to
the same schools we had, been taught by the same nuns and priests
Gerry and I had known. I would have hosted meetings of the Little
Flowers, baked cookies for the Christmas party, gone into the kitchen
of the cafeteria and cooked spaghetti to raise money for the new gym.
The world would have been full of bright colors.

"Where are you living these days?" Jim said.

I wanted to lie, but for reasons I could not understand, since
Daddy had died it seemed harder to lie than to tell the truth. "I live
here in Baton Rouge. On Bungalow Lane. Up by the capitol," I said.

"You live in Baton Rouge?" Jim said, astonished. "All this time.
You've been in Baton Rouge all this time?" Then he looked embarrassed. "Sorry," he said.

I shrugged.

Jim nodded and let it go.

I tried to think of something else to say. I remembered the day I
answered the door at the party for the Landrys, remembered saying
the stilted phrases my mother had written out for me to memorize.
"And how is your family?" I said. "Your folks doing okay?"

"My dad died last year," Jim said.

"I'm sorry to hear that."

"My mom's doing real well. She still lives on Hundred Oaks in
the house I grew up in," Jim said. "She's still able to live alone. I look
in on her every day on my way home. If I can't get there, my wife
goes by. I don't know how much longer we'll be able to keep it that
way, but she's fine for the time being."

I was overwhelmed with envy of Jim Singleton's life. I wanted
someone else's life. Any life but my own. These were the feelings I
had been dreading. This was why I hadn't wanted a funeral. Seeing
people from the past was going to be unbearable.

"Gerry liked you a lot. After you . . ."

I waited to see what he would say and how he would say it.

Jim finally settled on "weren't there anymore," then continued, "Gerry talked about you all the time. What happened to you really tore him up. He kept saying, 'If only we hadn't left that party. If only I had been there, maybe it wouldn't have happened.' Of course, Gerry and I haven't discussed it recently. That was all a long time ago."

I leaned back. Closed my eyes again. "I can't stay," I said without moving. "I have to get back to the house and wait for Mary to come back. She took off and sent word that she would only come home if I brought you this death notice for the paper and agreed to everything she wanted." I opened my eyes and looked at Jim. "Her name's not really Mary Rather," I said. "My sister has this delusion that she's married to Dan Rather. She thinks he wants her to come live with him in New York. She also thinks Daddy got in the car with us when we stopped for a red light on our way to Baton Rouge. She's been talking to him ever since. When we got back to the house on Oleander, she threw out all of our mother's crystal and china because she said Daddy told her to do it. She said he told her to do it because he wanted a real funeral. Then she lit out."

"I'm sorry," Jim said.

"She's supposed to come back this afternoon. She sent word that she would come back if I brought you that information for the newspaper and agreed to a proper funeral." I stood up. "Is there anything else I need to do?"

Jim stood also. "You'll need some pallbearers. Most people have about half a dozen."

"I'll see what I can do," I said.

Jim walked with me to the back door. "You don't try to keep her with you, do you? I would think that would be real hard."

"No," I said. "She lives in a place out in Livingston Parish. They seem to like her and take good care of her."

"Well, that's good," he said.

"That's why I wanted a private service. I don't want Mary to be put in a position where people will laugh at her," I said. In spite of my feeling that I'd already said too much, I couldn't seem to stop talking.

"I don't think anyone would do that," Jim said.

"They used to laugh at her. All the time," I said.

"People understand a lot more about these kinds of illnesses than they used to," Jim said. "They don't react the same way they did when you and I were growing up. I know this is none of my business, but I think you've made the right decision. You and your sister should look at this funeral as a time for both of you to feel better about your dad's going. It seems to cheer people up to see their friends at a time like this. I guess that's one of the benefits of living in one place all your life. Kind of outweighs all the bad things."

"Bad things?" I said. What bad things could this man possibly have in his life? From my angle, his life looked just about perfect.

"You think my life is great, don't you?" he said. "I can see it in your eyes. You think you missed out on a lot. Believe me, it's not so easy to live in a place where everybody still calls you PeeWee. I have buried the parents of a lot of my friends, and maybe when that generation is completely gone, I'll be treated as an adult. I'm fifty-four years old. That's way too old to be called PeeWee. In Baton Rouge, if you eat at the Picadilly without your wife, people want to know if your marriage is in trouble. If you don't make it to mass one Sunday, people call up to see if you're sick. Sometimes I wish I lived somewhere else. But you don't seem to have that problem."

I went to the door. "That's because I have no friends," I said. "And no life."

I was furious with myself. Furious for telling Jim Singleton I'd been living in Baton Rouge down a rat hole by myself for thirty years and furious for telling him just how crazy Mary was; furious that now he knew things about us. But I smiled to cover my fury. "Thanks again for your help," I said and got out of there.

Outside in the parking lot, the late-afternoon sun was pouring through the trees with that long look light gets in October. In that pale orange, all of the dying leaves glowed as if they were about to burst into flame. My heart beat hard for a minute because foliage was fading everywhere and my father would never see leaves green again.

Chapter Sixteen

Fall 1954

Bonita and Mary had been in school less than a month when the first meeting of the Little Flowers was held after school on the playground at the Academy of the Holy Angels.

"Morning Glories are over here!" Darlene Matens shouted.

All of the students had worn their dress uniforms. Little girls in white blouses that buttoned to pleated white skirts, with red bow ties under their collars and white beanies, ran all about the playground.

"Daisies come over by the swings!" Darlene's twin, Denise, cried.

Each student had put her hand into a goldfish bowl and withdrawn a slip of paper on which was either a Rose, an Iris, a Daisy, a Marigold, or a Morning Glory. Poster-sized illustrations of matching flowers painted by sixth-graders were scattered on the grass. In the coming months the Little Flowers would tour the Louisiana State Capitol Building, prepare Thanksgiving baskets for the needy, and, at

Christmas, have a party in a student's home and exchange gifts.

"Roses are here at the slide!" Sandra Bonifanti cried. Using only poster paints in primary colors, Sandra had created a rose so richly colored and striking in design that Sister Genevieve, in spite of her rule against singling a student out for praise, pinned it to the bulletin board.

Folding tables had been set up outside the cafeteria. As soon as the last bell rang, room mothers from all six grades arrived bearing thermos jugs of pink lemonade. Mrs. Matens brought over an enormous white frosted sheet cake.

Bonita, a Morning Glory, watched anxiously as Mary, a Rose, stood alone at the slide. She knew that Mary was growing sad and frightened; Mary never laughed anymore and spent every recess alone. The other Roses, led by Laurel Landry, ran all around Mary as she clutched the railing of the slide. Occasionally, a little Rose darted in to untie Mary's red bow tie or to snatch her beanie.

As each day passed, Bonita grew more frantic at her inability to protect Mary. She saw threats everywhere.

Bonita looked around for help. Sister Gertrude, the Rose sponsor, had gone to pour lemonade into paper cups. Bonita walked over to her. "Sister Gertrude," she said.

"Bonita, it's not time for cake and lemonade yet. Run on back and stay with your group, dear."

"It's not that, Sister Gertrude," Bonita said. "Would you make Laurel Landry stop teasing my sister?"

Sister Gertrude looked at the Roses encircling Mary, frowned, strode over to them, and said something that made Laurel shrug and the other children look down at the ground. Laurel handed back the beanie she had been waving just out of Mary's reach. Sister Gertrude retied the red bow under Mary's Peter Pan collar, replaced and adjusted her beanie, and then walked away, but it wasn't long before the children found ways to slyly tease Mary again.

Bonita walked over to join them. "Stop it, Laurel." All of her tender feelings for the girl had vanished.

"We're just playing."

"Leave Mary alone."

Laurel put her hands on her hips. "Make me."

"Okay," Bonita said. "I will." Bonita put her hands on either side of Laurel's collar, with its faultlessly tied red grosgrain bow, and shoved her to the ground. It felt good. It felt wonderful.

Laurel sat down hard in the loose dirt at the foot of the slide. Her mouth formed an "O" of pain and surprise.

With the exception of getting to shoot Orlando's gun, pushing Laurel Landry down into the dirt was the most satisfying thing Bonita had done since she and Mary had searched City Park for the Shetland pony. It felt so good that when Laurel got up, brushing the dust from her hands and looking behind her at the smudges on her white pleated skirt, Bonita shoved her down again. Then she leaned down and untied Laurel's perfect bow. "How does that feel?" She snatched Laurel's white beanie from her head and threw it as far as she could into the wide playground behind them. "Now, how do you like that?"

Laurel opened her mouth and howled.

"What's wrong? Who is that crying?" Sister Thecla said.

"She pushed me!" It was a long wail. "She pushed me down in the dirt! She made me get all dirty!"

"Who pushed you? Who pushed you down in the dirt?"

"Bonita did."

"Bonita, what's gotten into you, child?" Sister Thecla said. "Darlene, run get Sister Veronica."

Sister Veronica led Bonita into the chapel. Dark, diamond-paned ruby and sapphire stained glass transformed the sun's rays into muted patterns on the marble floor. The stifled light made Bonita want to run back outside into the bright sunshine.

Several upperclassmen—Bonita recognized Diane Hudgins—were waxing and polishing the order's carved prie-dieu that had once been the object of Bonita's adoration. Now she hardly noticed it.

"Would you girls excuse us for a moment?"

"Yes, Sister Veronica." The girls put down their rags and, after a curious look at Bonita, left.

Midway up the aisle, Sister Veronica stopped and motioned for Bonita to take a seat. Sister Veronica sat down beside her.

"You'll have to stay after school tomorrow and write 'I will not use physical force to settle disputes' one hundred times. That is to remind you of the truth of that statement," Sister Veronica said.

"Yes, Sister Veronica."

"You're very protective of Mary, aren't you?" Sister Veronica said.

"Yes, Sister Veronica," Bonita said. She looked at her hands. A tear trickled down each cheek. Bonita mashed her fingers together. "My daddy says sisters have to look after each other. My daddy says family is the glue that holds us together."

Sister Veronica stood, patted Bonita's shoulder, and said, "Don't try to take on all of your sister's problems. You'll have enough of your own to worry about. Save some of your tears for yourself. Now, you don't want to miss the cake and punch, so run on back outside to your group—what are you?"

"I'm a Morning Glory, Sister," Bonita said.

Gravely, Sister Veronica took Bonita's chin in her hand and looked down at her. "A morning glory is a beautiful creation, Bonita. Always remember that your soul is a beautiful, delicate plant that will prosper best in the shelter of Our Blessed Mother's love."

"Yes, Sister," Bonita said.

Bonita stood and watched Sister Veronica walk away. When the principal had almost reached the chapel door, Bonita said, "Sister Veronica?"

The nun turned back to look at Bonita.

"Is there something wrong with Mary?" Bonita said.

Sister Veronica paused at the door for a few moments. "Try not to worry about that right now, Bonita. Let the adults take care of it."

"Yes, Sister. Thank you, Sister Veronica."

But after several weeks, when nothing had changed, when Mary still cried before she went to school and after she came home in the afternoon, when Bonita could see no evidence that the adults had done anything at all, she who had once contrived to be first in line for confession now devised ways to avoid it, slipping in and out of the sixth-grade line as it snaked its way to the chapel until it appeared that she had made her confession when in fact she had not. With a series of feigned headaches and fictional upset stomachs, she also managed to evade the sacrament of communion when she attended mass on Sunday with her family. Bonita no longer cared whether her soul withered or not.

The only pleasure that remained was meeting Gerry, Sandra, and PeeWee at the Louisiana Theatre on Saturday mornings. Even though she had to take Mary with her, the atmosphere was lighthearted. Gerry accepted Mary's strangeness, and nothing Mary did bothered Sandra and PeeWee, who had exchanged I.D. bracelets and were in love.

During the week, Bonita and Gerry talked on the telephone every night. Gerry told her how he wanted to grow up and become a policeman like his father; Bonita told him that she wanted to grow peaches and oranges and strawberries after she finished college. Then they met on Saturdays to finish the conversations they had begun during the week. Once, during the most exciting part of *Guns of the Pecos*, Gerry picked up Bonita's left hand, placed an orange LifeSaver in her palm, and, after she placed the candy in her mouth, kept her hand cradled in his. The only flaw was that Mary was watching and nudged Gerry with her hand outstretched. He put a cherry LifeSaver in her palm, but when the candy was in her mouth, Mary put her hand out again. Gerry took her hand, too.

*　*　*

Early in December a rumor went around the neighborhood that Ellen Landry had seen a prowler in her backyard at dusk one Sunday. Five days later she reported that, shortly before dinner, a man had looked in her bedroom window. Both times the police were called, but no one was apprehended. The heads of the households on Oleander Avenue decided to extend the hours of the security guard from just before dark—between four-thirty and five in the afternoon—until two in the morning. It meant that instead of only one break at eleven o'clock, midway through his shift, now Orlando took two breaks— one for supper, sometime after eight o'clock, and another for coffee at midnight.

On the first night of Orlando's new schedule, Bonita slipped out after she was supposed to be in bed and waited in the shadows of the shrubs beneath the dining room windows until she saw Orlando's car come around the corner. She crossed the sidewalk and stood waiting for him on the grass in the same spot she had seen him for the first time.

Orlando stopped when he saw her. He lowered his window. It was cold, and Bonita had come out without a coat.

"Where's your sweater?" Orlando said.

"I forgot it," she said. "I want to ride with you."

Orlando looked up and down the street. "Run around and hop in."

He turned on the heater and left the motor running so she would be warm while he went in the Windmill Grill on Government Street to get a sandwich.

"Bring me something," Bonita called. She tried to sound cheerful and carefree, but as soon as Orlando left the car, she opened the glove compartment and stared at the gun in its pool of light. She glanced from time to time at the door of the diner, and when she saw him come out, she pushed the lid quietly closed.

"What is it? What did you bring me?" she said when he got in.

"A chocolate shake," he said. "Here." He handed her a milk shake and a long plastic spoon.

"Thanks," Bonita said. In the past she would have been embarrassed for him to buy her something and not pay him back. But now all she cared about was fooling him into thinking that she was just a greedy child and not a dangerous person who wanted his gun.

She tasted the milk shake and then held a spoonful out to him. "Want some?" she said, all the while keeping the gun glowing in a darkened compartment of her mind.

"No thanks," he said. "I got me a Coke." He put it on the dashboard while he unwrapped the waxed paper from around his food. When he was settled with his sandwich, he said, "So, what's new at school?"

"Not much," Bonita said. She closed the door on the image of the gun and let the school day flit across her memory. "Yesterday at lunch I went home with Denise and Darlene so their mother could practice on us for her bridge luncheon. We had chicken salad in a tomato cup. And Sandra got sent to the principal's office for wearing makeup again."

"That Sandra's just like Florette," Orlando said.

"How is Miss Florette?"

"Don't know. Florette took off," Orlando said.

"Miss Florette's gone?" Bonita cried.

"Gone but not forgotten," Orlando said.

"Where did she go?" Bonita said.

"Don't know that, either," Orlando said. "She took off for parts unknown about a month ago."

Bonita wondered where she would go if she decided to leave Baton Rouge. She thought that if she could visualize Florette in some congenial landscape, preferably one with flowers and fruit, perhaps she wouldn't feel so trapped. She placed Florette near a pond filled with water lilies, eating a peach. Maybe Florette had gone to Ruston. One of the chapters in their new workbook said that Lincoln Parish was home to many peach orchards, and every summer her father always said, "I'll be glad when the Ruston peaches come in."

"But you could find her if you wanted to," she said. "Because you could track a person down, couldn't you?"

"I'm kind of out of the habit of that," he said. "Most all I'm good for now is driving around watching out for robbers and kidnappers."

"And murderers," Bonita reminded him.

"That, too," he said.

"I would like to see Miss Florette again," Bonita said. "There was something I wanted to tell her."

"What's that?" Orlando said.

"I wanted to tell her I was sorry about that time we ruined her day off. Remember when Miss Florette didn't get to go to False River? She stayed at the Brunswick to drink a beer while you and Mary and I went on the birthday picnic."

"Want me to find her for you just so you can tell her you're sorry she didn't get to go to False River?" he said.

"Not only for that. I would just kind of like to see her again," Bonita said.

Bonita was a little disappointed that it was Sandra and not she who called to mind the vanished Florette, but she supposed that, with her low spirits, she would never be associated with a woman strong enough to organize telephone operators to strike against Southern Bell.

"Me, too," Orlando said. "Although I wouldn't tell it to anybody but you." He crumpled up the wrapping from his sandwich and stuffed it in the paper bag. "That Florette. She was sure somebody who went for men," he went on. "And she knew every last thing in the world there was to know about makeup. I'll promise you that." Then he got out of the car and put the bag in a trash container at the side of the store. When he returned, he came around to her window, took a cellophane-covered mint from his shirt pocket, handed it to her, and said, "Give this to your sister. It's too bad she can't come out with you."

Bonita took the candy and put it in her pocket. "I'm not sorry," she said. "This is about the only time in the whole world that I don't have to worry about her."

"You worry too much about her," Orlando said.

Bonita recalled the image on the gun, fortified herself with its strength. "How can I worry too much about her? Laurel Landry has turned everybody in the whole school against her."

"You don't know that for sure. You got to be careful you don't start imagining things," Orlando said.

The Friday night before Bonita and Mary were scheduled to go Christmas shopping the next morning, Gerry Winborn called Bonita.

"I haven't seen you in a long time. You never come to the movies anymore," Gerry said.

"I've been sick," Bonita said.

It was true that Bonita and Mary had missed the November meeting of the Little Flowers because they were both sick. But Bonita was convinced that the only way she could protect Mary was to isolate her, so she and Mary spent most of their time indoors.

"I'm sorry. I hope you're feeling better," he said. "Can you come to the movie tomorrow?"

"I can't. I have to take my sister Christmas shopping."

He was silent.

"We have to pick out presents for the Christmas party," Bonita said. "For the names we drew for Little Flowers. We'll be downtown. Right across from the movie, probably. Mary likes to go to Kress's. Why don't you come over to the toys? You can help us shop."

"What time will you be there?" he said.

"My mother and daddy have a tennis game at ten o'clock, so they'll drop us off right before then, I guess. We should be there by ten-thirty."

"Okay," he said.

Saturday was cold and clear. The sun shone down strong through the sharp air, and when the sisters got out of the car, Bonita, accustomed to the many months of warm air that seemed to her to fray the bounds of things, thought for the first time all winter that the cold defined the sidewalks and stores with a hard edge, as if there were a black outline about them, just as things were outlined in coloring books.

Bonita wanted to get the presents for their parents before the crowds got too heavy in the department store—it was hard for her to wait in line and keep her eye on Mary at the same time—so they went first to the men's section. There they bought a tie clasp, some handkerchiefs monogrammed with the letter "G," and a pair of slippers for their father. For their mother, they bought a bottle of cologne and a red silk scarf.

They went across the street to the five-and-ten-cent store shortly after ten-thirty. The store was filled with children. Mary struggled to get close to the counter that held the dolls. Bonita remained outside the fray and thought about a present for Orlando. It had to be something small. Something he could carry with him all the time. Still keeping an eye on Mary's blond head and shifting the shopping bag that held the presents they had already bought, she edged around to look at key rings. She grew absorbed in their variety. Some were decorated with the heads of animals, some divided in two, some simple circles. When she had chosen and paid for a gold metal ring with a wooden acorn dangling on a chain and a head that unscrewed to hold small change, she looked back for Mary, but her sister's blond head was no longer bobbing among the others. Bonita pushed her way up to the doll counter and examined every child, but Mary wasn't there.

Bonita inspected every counter that held toys, but there was no sign of Mary. She ran to the popcorn machine at the entrance to the store and looked for her there. She went out on the sidewalk and looked up and down. Third Street was crowded with Christmas shoppers. A man dressed as Santa Claus stood at a Salvation Army bucket at the corner, ringing his bell and wishing everyone a merry Christmas. Bonita asked him if he had seen a little girl running down the sidewalk, but he shook his head.

"Hi," Gerry said. "What's wrong?"

Bonita turned. "My sister's gone."

Gerry looked up and down the street. "When did you see her last?"

"Inside. She was at the doll counter. But when I went back for her, she wasn't there."

They looked all over the store, spending particular time at the doll counter and in the dollhouse furnishings because Bonita told Gerry that Mary liked tiny things.

"Laurel Landry probably did it," Bonita said.

"Who's Laurel Landry?" Gerry said.

"She lives down the street from me," Bonita said.

"Is she in here? We'll ask her," Gerry said.

"No," Bonita said. "But she probably came in while I wasn't looking and told Mary there was a new puppy somewhere and Mary went to look for it. She's done it before."

Gerry looked at his watch. "It's eleven-thirty. How long has she been gone?"

Bonita calculated. "Almost thirty minutes."

"I'm going to get my father," Gerry said.

Gerry's father was not far away. He was a big, blond, friendly man—Gerry grown up. He was a patrolman who had been assigned to the Third Street beat for the Christmas holidays. Lost children were his specialty. In two shakes, he had interviewed Bonita, organized a search of the nearby streets and stores, and summoned Dr. and Mrs. Gabriel from their tennis game at the country club.

When John and Lottie got there, Bonita and Gerry were waiting on the sidewalk in front of the dime store.

Lottie held her arms out to Bonita, who clung to her mother while her father conferred with Gerry and his father.

But Officer Winborn didn't find her. Mary was gone all afternoon. They had to extend the search, calling in the full force of the city police, and when Mary wasn't found by nightfall, the East Baton Rouge sheriff's department, and then later that night, the state police. Mary wasn't found until the early hours of Sunday morning.

Orlando Duplantis found her. Bonita had known he was looking for Mary because her father called him to help search. Orlando came to the house to talk to Bonita about what happened in the store.

"Why didn't you call me right away?" he said.

"I didn't know your number," she said.

"She's so little," Orlando muttered. He pressed the fingers of his left hand to his chest as if he had heartburn. "All by herself out there and she's such a little thing. What was the last thing you were doing?"

"Mary was looking at the dolls in Kress's." Bonita didn't tell him that she lost Mary because she was shopping for his Christmas present. Nor that she thought Laurel had come in while she wasn't looking and sent Mary out to look for a puppy or something.

Bonita found out later that he started at the Mississippi River near the state capitol building and, slowly moving east from the river, began driving up and down each street in a three-mile square. When he finished one square, he began another; when he had covered the city, he went back to the river and began again. He drove all night. At four o'clock in the morning, he found Mary behind the bakery where they had driven to get the cupcakes and ice cream for Bonita's birthday celebration.

Bonita was still up when Orlando brought Mary back. Every light in the house was on. Mary was tired from her adventure but cheerful. Bonita's father pressed two one-hundred-dollar bills upon the watchman, but Orlando brushed them away. He took Bonita into the living room, sat her down in a chair, knelt beside her, and gave her a card.

"This is my number at home. If she ever scoots off again, call me the minute it happens. Call me right away."

"I will," Bonita said.

"Memorize this number," he said.

"I will."

"Now." He drilled her until finally he was satisfied.

Orlando Duplantis accepted a cup of coffee and a piece of cake, but he wouldn't take any money, and the next day, the Gabriels couldn't say enough nice things about the security guard they had the wisdom to hire for their neighborhood. All of the neighbors agreed. Even though he hadn't caught the Peeping Tom who flickered through the Landrys' backyard, he had found Mary. A collection was taken for a Christmas bonus, and his salary for the next year was increased.

Traditionally, the December meeting of the Little Flowers was a Christmas party held at a student's house the day before school let out for the holidays. That year John and Lottie Gabriel offered to open their home for the celebration.

On the night before the party, Bonita waited until her parents were in their bedroom with the door closed, then went outside in the dark. She wore her navy blue school coat this time. She held the poinsettia-covered shopping bag she had carried the previous Saturday. Inside was Orlando's present, wrapped in blue paper with silver stars. It was a tiny present in a big bag.

"What are you doing up so late?" Orlando said when he stopped the car for her. "You should have been in bed hours ago. Come on. Get in with me. I'm just going to get my midnight coffee. You can come along for the ride."

Outside the Windmill Grill, Bonita plunged her hand down into the poinsettia-covered bag and withdrew his present. "This is for you.

Merry Christmas, Mr. Orlando. Thank you for finding Mary," she said.

"A present? You got me a Christmas present?" Orlando said. "When all I got you was this." He reached over and took a box from the backseat.

The present was wrapped in white paper. There was a green ribbon around it, but the bow had been tied by a man, Bonita could tell. It was pulled tight and squashed flat. Florette's hand was nowhere visible on it.

But Florette's spirit was in the present. Orlando had filled a box with makeup: face powder, two lipsticks, one red and one pink, mascara, and a little round pot of rouge. There was a set of silver-handled cosmetic brushes—fat ones for her cheeks, wedge-shaped ones for her eyebrows, tiny ones to outline her lips, and every size in between. Bonita looked at him, pleased.

"Thanks," she said.

"Do you really like it?"

"I love it."

"Good," he said. "The saleslady helped me pick it out. Everything there is exactly like Florette used to have in the dresser in our bedroom. I figured since you were so much like her that you would want to have the same kind of stuff she had. But you have to start out with the pink, like she told you before. Save the red lipstick until next year."

"I will. I promise." Again she looked at him with delight. "You really think I'm like Florette? I didn't know you thought I was like Florette."

"Oh, yeah. The way you look out for your sister. And the way you go after those other kids from your neighborhood. Florette never took nothing off nobody, neither."

"But I could never lead the telephone operators in a strike," Bonita said.

"Sure you could. You're just like Florette."

Bonita didn't know how to respond. She motioned awkwardly at his present. "All I got you was that little thing," she said.

He seemed happy with the key ring. Immediately he took his keys from the plain silver chain he had formerly carried and put them on the gold ring. When Bonita showed him how the acorn opened to hold change for a parking meter, he reached into his pocket and filled it with nickels and dimes. Then he went inside the Windmill Grill to get his coffee.

While he was gone, Bonita opened the glove compartment and studied the gun. She planned to borrow it so she could have it at the party the next day and put it back the next night. But the gift Orlando had given her made it seem somehow impolite to borrow his gun now. She hesitated.

The door to the restaurant opened. Bonita snatched the gun from its resting place in the pool of light, put it in the decorated bag, and shut the glove compartment.

"When's your big Christmas to-do?" Orlando said. He handed her a cup of vanilla ice cream and, after he had put his coffee on the dashboard, took a cellophane-wrapped wooden spoon from the breast pocket of his shirt and gave it to her.

"Tomorrow," Bonita said. She took the ice cream but didn't open it.

Bonita never did eat her ice cream. With the gun burning in the poinsettia-covered bag near her feet, she couldn't bring herself to put anything in her mouth. When Orlando finished his sandwich and got out, he came around to her side of the car, held out his hand for the uneaten ice cream, and dumped everything in the trash.

Before he let her out at the corner near her house, he said, "You'll have to hide all that stuff I gave you, you know."

"I know," Bonita said. "I'll hide it where nobody can find it. I'm glad you think I'm like Florette. But I thought you said I worried too much about Mary, that something bad might happen if I didn't stop."

"Now that I've had some time to think about it, and now that

I've seen how far off your sister ran, I might be wrong about that," Orlando said. "After all, you're the one up on the front. You need all the firepower you can get."

For a minute Bonita thought Orlando knew that she had stolen his gun. Her heart quickened. She prepared to defend herself. "What do you mean? What's 'up on the front'? What do you mean, 'firepower'?"

"I just mean that you're the one out there doing the fighting for her. Your folks and me—we're the generals back safe giving the orders. That sister of yours is different. There's no getting around that. And people start to squirm when somebody gets too different. You've found that out by now. Between the two of us, we look out for her pretty good, but we can't be with her every last minute. That's why I got these here tags to give out for Christmas." Orlando took a small box from his pocket and showed Bonita that it contained a heart-shaped tag on a chain. "I had little silver tags and chains made up for all the children under ten on my route. I put the name, address, and telephone number on it so they can wear it around their necks if their parents want them to. I'm going to deliver them tomorrow afternoon. Try and get your sister to wear it, and then, when she goes somewhere, if she gets lost, somebody'll know who she is."

"Okay," Bonita said. "I'll try."

When they got back to Bonita's house, she held the bag with the gun and the makeup in it carefully upright, got out of the car, slammed the door, and walked, instead of running, back along the shadows to the house.

The entire elementary school—over one hundred children—would be present for the Little Flowers Christmas party at the Gabriels' home. In the living room an enormous tree was put up to be decorated by the students with ornaments they would make during the party. If the weather was good, they would play games outside. Inside they would exchange gifts and have punch and cookies they had adorned themselves with red and green icing, silver sprinkles, and candy beads. Card tables covered with red cloths decorated with snowflakes and reindeer were to be set up all over the house by the mothers of the Little Flowers.

The day of the party, Bonita put the gun in her book bag. She didn't want to leave it where her mother might come across it while Bonita was at school. Carefully, she placed it between her books so that the gun's shape was not outlined against the smooth canvas back.

Bonita's navy blue book bag with the leather handle then took on a life of its own. Knowing that the gun glowed inside made the bag, for Bonita, a living thing. All day the bag sat flat on the shelf beneath her desk while she held the image of the gun in her head. Then she carefully carried it home again and put the gun in the bag, along with Orlando's Christmas presents, which she had put on the floor in the back of her closet.

After school, the atmosphere inside the Gabriel house sparkled with both the lights on the big Christmas tree and the excitement of a house full of children. Mrs. Matens, who had been baking for three days straight, brought tray after tray of cookies shaped as stars, snowmen, and angels. Bowls of silver and cinnamon sprinkles, of icing dyed red and green, were set about so each variety of Flower could have a turn decorating the cookies they would eat with the red punch.

Bonita, who acted like she was participating in the celebration, was actually following Laurel Landry. If possible, she eavesdropped.

When the Marigolds were almost finished decorating their cookies, Sister Alice called out to Laurel, who was passing by, "Gather the Roses, Laurel. You're next to have a turn to decorate."

Bonita looked around for Mary to tell her it was time to ice the cookies. She spotted her sister in the living room under the Christmas tree, holding first one and then another Christmas present to her ear and shaking it. Before she could unwrap one, Gracie's mother swooped down and plucked the gift from her hands, replaced it beneath the tree, and turned Mary in the direction of the cookie tables.

Bonita met her sister in the middle of the room. "Don't unwrap the Christmas presents, Mary."

"I want to!"

"It's not the polite thing to do. Only one of those presents is for you. Sister Veronica will call out your name and give it to you when it's time."

"But I want to."

"I don't care if you want to. You can't."

"But I want to anyway," Mary said, and her eyes began to glitter.

Bonita foresaw the antics this could lead to, so she said, "The Roses are decorating. All the silver sprinkles will be gone. I'll help you if you want me to."

The Roses took their places at the cookie tables. Laurel Landry looked at Mary as she sat down, rolled her eyes upward, gave a significant glance to her sister Flowers, and held her nose. All of the other Roses looked at Mary and did the same.

Mary dug a great glob of red icing from the bowl and plopped it down on the star cookie Mrs. Matens laid before her.

"She took too much!" Barbara Fontana cried. "Mary took all the red!"

Mrs. Matens patted Barbara on the shoulder. "We have plenty of icing to go around." Then she said to Mary, "Not quite so much icing, dear. Here, let me help you." And Mrs. Matens scooped the greater part of the red icing back into the bowl with a knife and then distracted Mary by saying, "Take this knife, dear, and spread, spread, spread." Mrs. Matens guided Mary's hand with her own in rhythm to her words, "Spread . . . the . . . icing . . . all . . . around. There. Isn't that a pretty cookie?" Mrs. Matens held it up for the rest of the Roses to admire.

"Stars aren't red," Laurel said.

"Stars can be red," Bonita said. "If Mary wants them to be."

Again Laurel rolled her eyes upward as if begging heavenly powers for patience.

When Mary dumped most of the bowl of silver sprinkles on her red star, Mrs. Matens began her patient process again. "Not quite so many silver sprinkles, dear."

Bonita turned away. She thought it must be getting harder and harder for everyone to ignore: Laurel's daddy was right; there was something wrong with Mary.

She saw Sandra Bonifanti burst through the door into the room and tear across the floor toward her. Sandra dragged Bonita out into the hall. "Guess who's here?" Sandra cried.

"Who?" Bonita said.

"PeeWee and Gerry!" Sandra squealed. Then she looked around and lowered her voice. "They rode up on their bicycles while the Daisies were out back playing Red Rover." Sandra put her hand over her mouth and came even closer. "Gerry wants you to come out. He said would I go find you. They've got presents!" On this last word Sandra bent double with joy. She took Bonita's arm. "They're waiting for us outside. Come on. We can sneak out the kitchen."

Gerry and PeeWee waited for them outside, astride their bicycles, feet touching the ground for balance. Each held a present of the same size.

"Hi," Bonita said. She felt awkward. She hadn't expected Gerry to give her a Christmas present, and she had nothing for him.

"Having a big party?" PeeWee said.

"Yeah, it's a big party," Sandra said. "All of those little babies in there are icing cookies and making red and green rings out of construction paper. Don't you wish you could come?"

"Not me," PeeWee said.

"It's not so bad," Bonita said. She smiled at Gerry. "If you like to decorate cookies, you could come help us." Then Bonita remembered that she had left Mary sitting at the table with Laurel. She should go back and watch out for her sister. Who knew what Laurel might do to Mary while she was gone. Or what Laurel might say about her mother.

Gerry thrust the present he carried at Bonita. "Here. Merry Christmas." PeeWee did the same with Sandra.

Bonita and Sandra opened the presents. They were identical white leather jewelry boxes. Each box had a tiny lock and key. When the lid was raised, two velvet-lined containers appeared on either side of a dancing ballerina. Bonita's ballerina had on a dress of pink. Sandra's wore a green tutu. Each boy had wound the key on the back of the box before giving it to them. Bonita's ballerina turned to "The Blue Danube Waltz," Sandra's to "Tales from the Vienna Woods."

"It's beautiful," Bonita said.

"Do you really like it?" Gerry said.

"I love it," Bonita said.

"I know exactly what I'm going to put in it," Sandra said. "I have tons of jewelry."

Bonita touched the soft pink velvet inside the box. She smiled at Gerry and he smiled back. She couldn't stop smiling at him; he had made her so happy. "Thank you," Bonita said. "Thank you. I'll keep it forever."

As the boys prepared to leave, Bonita heard the door to the back porch open, and she looked around. Laurel Landry was watching the four of them from behind the half-open door, a look of longing on her face. It crossed Bonita's mind to call out to Laurel, to say, as to a beloved younger sister, "Come and see what Gerry gave me," but before she could speak, Laurel let the door slam and disappeared into the house.

The boys rode away on their bicycles. Sandra and Bonita were still admiring their gifts when they heard a commotion behind them. Laurel Landry, trailed by all of the Roses, ran down the back steps holding a wrapped Christmas present high over her head. "I've got Mary's present," Laurel sang.

Mary ran down the steps behind her, reaching for the wrapped box that Laurel held over her head.

Without a word to anyone, Bonita put the white leather jewelry box on the step, in its bed of wrapping paper and ribbon, and ran inside. She went to the back of her closet and removed the gun from its hiding place. Ignoring the watchman's instructions to carry it pointing upward at her shoulder, she hid it in the folds of her navy blue pleated skirt and ran through the house and down the back steps.

In front of the garage, Laurel held the present high over her head. Mary jumped for it fruitlessly.

Bonita raised the gun. "Laurel," she said.

Laurel ignored her. "I've got Mary's present. You can't get your present."

Bonita pointed the gun straight at her. "Laurel," she said. "Give it back."

Finally, Laurel looked at Bonita. The ghosts of the fast friends they had once been materialized, but Bonita beat them back. Sisters were more important than friends; she knew her father would have told her that.

"You wouldn't dare," Laurel said. Her round face with its scattered freckles was tilted to one side.

Bonita put her other hand on the gun to steady it.

All of the chattering children grew silent.

With a cold edge to her voice, Bonita said, "Give Mary back her present."

"No, Bonita!" came a voice from behind her.

Bonita turned her head to look over her shoulder. Orlando, carrying the small box that contained the identification tag he had made for Mary, stood at the end of the driveway. Orlando walked forward along the grass between the two strips of raised concrete. He extended his hand. "Bonita, there's a bullet under the hammer. I've been carrying it that way ever since we had a prowler in the neighborhood," he said.

Orlando Duplantis wore a brown suit. Except for the one time with Florette on his day off, Bonita had never seen him out of his khaki uniform. For a moment she had to search her memory for who he was.

"The cylinder's full, Bonita," he repeated. "Because of the prowler. I put a sixth bullet in because Mrs. Landry saw somebody in her backyard. You've got a fully loaded gun in your hand. Raise the gun up to your shoulder like I showed you and don't touch the hammer."

Bonita hesitated. "Give Mary back her present, Laurel," she said.

Laurel handed over the Christmas gift. Mary grabbed it and immediately sat down on the grass and tore away the paper.

"Bonita!" Orlando said. "Bring the gun to me!"

Now that Bonita had succeeded in making Laurel give Mary the Christmas present that rightfully belonged to her, her arm began to tremble under the weight of the gun. Bonita began to shiver. She raised the gun so that it pointed skyward and turned toward Orlando.

"Just hold it steady, Bonita," Orlando said. "You can do it. Walk slowly and bring the gun to me."

As Bonita started forward, the toe of her shoe caught the concrete strip of the driveway and she stumbled. As she fell, the hammer of the revolver struck the cement and the gun discharged. The bullet struck Orlando Duplantis in the chest.

Sandra Bonifanti retrieved the musical jewelry box Bonita had left on the back step. It was Sandra who, after the ambulance had taken Orlando away and all of the other students clustered in tight knots, weeping, pulled Bonita's blue pea coat from a hanger in her closet and went to the police car where Bonita sat, trembling, waiting for her father to come home. Mrs. Moak had been summoned to take charge of Mary. Leona Fish and Mabel Davis were with Lottie inside the house. For once, Bonita was alone.

Bonita did not remember for a long time that the brazen Sandra had walked right up to the policeman who stood beside the car and, when he blocked her way, said, "She needs her coat. It's cold. And besides, she shouldn't be all by herself in there." Nor did Bonita recall right away that Sandra climbed into the backseat of the patrol car, put Bonita's coat around her shoulders, placed the jewelry box in her lap, and then sat beside her until Dr. Gabriel finally arrived.

Dr. Gabriel wanted his wife to remain at home, but the police were firm; they all had to go together in an official car. With her father's lawyer and both of her parents present, Bonita had to tell what had happened first to a police officer and then to a judge who, because she was so young, remanded her to her parents for the night.

Because there was a death involved, a police car would return to the Gabriel house the next morning, transport them to the courthouse again, and there, behind closed doors, Bonita would appear before another judge to be arraigned.

That night, after the Gabriel family returned home, Bonita's father gave her a pill to swallow so she could sleep, but all it did was cause strange thoughts. She sat on her bed in the dark with her eyes wide open all night. Near dawn she stood, turned on the light, and opened the jewelry box Gerry had given her. As the music sounded and the ballerina turned, Bonita filled the jewelry box. Into it she put the holy card with the picture of the good child kneeling in the folds of the Virgin Mary's white dress, the shriveled, clove-studded orange, and all of the makeup and silver-handled brushes Orlando had given her for Christmas. She closed the box and locked it with the tiny key. She pulled her dresser stool over to her closet and placed the jewelry box with its key on the very back of the top shelf. Then she took off all of her clothes, went to the hall closet, took the coat of the suit her father had worn to the police station from its hanger, went out into the driveway, and lay down on the grass where Orlando had fallen with only her father's coat for cover and waited for the sun to rise and warm her.

Chapter Seventeen

October 1995

After I went to the television station to see if Mary had shown up there looking for a message from Dan Rather—she hadn't—and checked the bus station and the airport to see if she had bought a ticket to New York with the money in my wallet—she hadn't done that, either—I returned to Daddy's house to wait for her call. I went out on the front porch and sat in one of the old white rockers. I left the front door open so I could hear the telephone.

I leaned my head against the back of the rocker and closed my eyes. Mary would come back soon. I would call the home and tell them that Mary had returned and promise to have her back bright and early in the morning. Everything would be fine. In a little while, all of this would be over and I could return to my normal life.

As I rocked there on the porch, I thought of *Evangeline*. With my eyes closed, I could imagine that no time at all had passed and that Adam Moak, Gracie Davis, Frankie St. Germain, and Adrienne Fish were sitting cross-legged on the floor around me while I read aloud to them.

I got up and went into the living room to the bookcase. My father's copy of *Evangeline* was there where she had always been, closed up between her red leather covers on the top shelf between *The Song of Hiawatha* and *Tales of a Wayside Inn*. I took the book out to the porch, sat down, and held it on my lap until the shadows of the oaks in the front yard began to encroach on the porch. When I checked the time, I discovered it was past five o'clock. Still no Mary. Then I heard the telephone. I left the book on the rocker and went inside.

"Hello," I said.

"Hey, Mary's sister."

"You said Mary would be here, Aura Lee. I did everything you said she wanted me to do. That was the deal, but she's not here. Where is she?"

"There is one more thing she wants," Aura Lee said.

I didn't say anything.

"Don't you want to hear what it is?" Aura Lee said.

"Not particularly," I said. "Do I have a choice?"

"You always have a choice," she said.

"I'm not so sure about that, Aura Lee," I said.

"Our Blessed Savior died so you could have a choice," Aura Lee said.

"Don't start with me about this saving-my-soul business, Aura Lee," I said.

Aura Lee didn't say anything. Neither did I.

Finally Aura Lee said, "Mary's sister, are you still there?"

I sighed. "Yes, Aura Lee. I'm still here."

"Mary won't come back until you confess your sins to me. She won't come back until I give you absolution," Aura Lee said.

"That's crazy, Aura Lee. Forget this absolution thing and tell Mary to get back here."

"I can't forget it, Mary's sister," Aura Lee said. "Your soul is in peril. Mary wants this. She wants your soul to be safe."

"No, Mary doesn't want that. You want it. This was your idea, wasn't it, Aura Lee? You put Mary up to this," I said. "I do have a choice, Aura Lee! And I choose not to confess to you!"

"But Mary wants you to," Aura Lee said.

"Where is Mary?" I said.

"You don't have to worry about Mary. She'll be safe. I have blessed her. She is protected," Aura Lee said.

"Aura Lee, this is really serious. You have to tell me where Mary went. It's dangerous for her to be out there by herself. You can't protect her. You don't have that kind of power. She could get hurt. Somebody could really hurt her. Don't you know what happened to her before?"

Orlando would have found Mary by now, I thought. Orlando would have divided the city into squares and driven over every one. He would never have stopped looking until he found Mary.

It's not true that after awhile you don't miss dead people anymore. I've missed Orlando Duplantis every single day of my life.

"Where is Mary, Aura Lee?" I said again.

"I promised her I wouldn't tell," Aura Lee said.

"Promises don't count when somebody's life is in danger, Aura Lee. You promised me that Mary would be back here at Daddy's house by five o'clock, and she isn't here. I did what she wanted me to do, and you made her break her promise."

"Promises don't count when somebody's immortal soul is in peril, Mary's sister," Aura Lee said. "Mary won't come back until your soul is safe."

I decided to try a different tack. "All right, Aura Lee," I said. "I give up. You win. I'm sorry. I'm sorry for my sins. Is that good enough for you?"

"You have to do it right, Mary's sister. You have to say, 'Bless me, Father, for I have sinned.' And you have to say how long it's been since your last confession. Then you have to tell me each sin. You have to tell me each and every one of them. And then you have to be really and truly sorry for them. I don't think you are sincerely sorry. You don't sound like you're sincerely sorry. You just sound like you want to get it over with so I'll tell you where Mary is."

"How can I confess to you, Aura Lee? You're not a priest. You're just a woman."

"It doesn't matter. Anybody can stand in for a priest. All you have to do is confess and be really, really sorry," Aura Lee said.

"Go to hell, Aura Lee!" I slammed the receiver down. Right away the telephone rang again. I ignored it.

I went to my room and closed the door. I sat down on the bed of my childhood. The room was just the way I had left it; not a pillow, not a quilt, not a doll had been moved. Sitting there in the living past, I didn't know which was worse: that the past was lost or that it still existed. I had no husband, no children, no friends; guilt had eaten up all my days. My life was almost over and I was right back where I had been in the beginning, chasing Mary down, and now I had to do it with my energy and youth exhausted.

I swept the flowered chintz pillows from the bed onto the floor. One by one I pitched the dolls that passed their peaceful days in my grandmother's old rocking chair into the far corner of the room.

I stood up. I went to my dresser and looked at myself in the mirror. I didn't even know who I was. I picked up the clock with the pink gingham dial and threw it right into my reflected face. A hole appeared in my forehead. Cracks radiated from it to my hairline, along my eyes, and down my cheeks.

I dragged the stool that stood before the dressing table over to my closet. I kicked off my shoes, got up on it, and felt around on the closet shelf until I put my hand on the jewelry box Gerry Winborn had given me for Christmas the afternoon I killed Orlando. Then, on my tiptoes, I reached to the far right-hand corner of the shelf, found the key to it, and, carrying both the leather jewel case and its key, I climbed down from the bench. I put the box on the dresser, unlocked it, and dumped the contents onto my bed. •

Out poured everything I had put away when I was eleven years old: the makeup Orlando had given me for Christmas, the silver-handled cosmetic brushes like Florette's; the things I had placed in the prie-dieu when I was in third grade and Sister Veronica had returned them to me transfigured—the blessed jump rope, the orange preserved with cloves, withered now to a black knot, its tatted cradle torn; and, loveliest of all, the holy card Sister Veronica had left for me with the picture of the Nativity in which a dark-haired child knelt in the white folds of the Virgin Mary's gown while the Blessed Mother sat holding the baby Jesus on her lap with a cobalt-blue sky filled with gold stars behind her haloed head. For an instant, I retrieved the memory of the night I had gone under the house to look for Mary when we were waiting to see Orlando and I had thought I was going to suffocate. Briefly, I saw again the glittering crystal sky waiting for me when I was finally able to pull my face up and away from the dirt and break out into the night.

The music box ground out a few strangled notes of "The Blue Danube." The ballerina was turning slowly when I walked away. I closed the door to my room, picked up my purse from the dining table, and walked out of the house. The telephone rang as I left. I could hear it all the way down the back steps. It rang and rang and rang and rang.

I headed for the only safe place I knew—the house on Bungalow Lane where I had lived for the last twenty-five years. As I drove west on Government Street, toward the Mississippi River, I was going the wrong way from progress and prosperity. All of the landmarks of my childhood—the dry cleaner, the bakery, the fish market, the Sinclair service station—were either boarded up or burned out. As I got closer to town, the landscape improved. Lawyers, title companies, loan offices, and mortgage holders had remodeled old houses and reclaimed derelict buildings. I cut over on Eighth Street to the oldest part of Baton Rouge, the neighborhood called Spanish Town. When I got out of my car in front of the white frame duplex, I could see the top of the capitol over the trees. I walked past the concrete birdbath in its ring of abundant chrysanthemums. The weathered sea horse had crumbled away fifteen years ago, and I had replaced it with a new one. I kept the azaleas around the house neatly trimmed and the grass carefully edged and mowed.

I walked up onto the screened porch. All of "Florette's mess"— the sagging red and yellow sling-back canvas chair, the black wrought-iron table, and the overflowing ashtray—were long gone. The broken tile floor was the same one where Mary and I had stood when Orlando brought us home with him to pick up the sandwiches for the picnic on the Amite River. Now the porch was orderly and beautiful. The floor was polished and waxed. I kept plants.

Gertrude and Abner Smith, my landords, had lived on the other side of the duplex. They were kind to me: left me alone but at the same time watched over me. When I had the Hong Kong flu in 1970 and couldn't understand words on the page or tell time from a clock, Gertrude fixed vegetable soup and brought me orange Popsicles that were the coolest, most welcome taste in my mouth since the time I lost Mary in City Park.

I never told them who I was, that I had visited the other side of their house when I was eleven or that I had murdered their former tenant. Sometimes I turned the conversation to the past. How long had they lived in the house? Since 1940. Had they gotten to know any of their renters well? Not too well—most of them had been men—you didn't get to know men as well as you got to know women, Gertrude said. How many people had lived on the other side of their duplex, my side, Orlando's side? Maybe half a dozen, Abner said.

Gertrude died in 1979. For almost ten years Abner got along fine without her. But in 1988 he fell and broke his hip, and that was the beginning of the end for him. As he got more and more infirm, it became apparent that somebody was going to have to take on the chore of looking after him. They had no children, so the task pretty much fell to me. It was either talk Abner into going to a nursing home, in which case he would probably have to sell the house to pay for it and I would have to move, or I could keep him there and take care of him myself. So that's what I did. I hired a sitter to stay with him during the day, and in the evenings I fixed us both something to eat. I cooked us breakfast in the morning before the sitter arrived and then left for my office. This was our routine for the three years that Abner lived after he fell. When he died in 1991, he left me the house. Everything in it was exactly as it had been the day he never woke up from his nap. I still lived in the side Orlando had rented.

My side of the duplex had always been rented furnished. The bed was draped with the same pink chenille spread that had probably covered it when Florette intermittently lived there. To the left of the bed near the dresser was a rocking chair, with an ancient floor lamp behind it, where I sat at night memorizing the poems of Longfellow. I could recite "The Song of Hiawatha" by heart. In addition to *Evangeline*, which was the first one I learned, I also knew from memory *The Courtship of Miles Standish*.

Immediately after I became a tenant of the house, I found two things that had been left in the drawers of the dresser in the bedroom. The first was a button in the shape of a poppy. I recognized it as belonging to Florette's flowered dress. In the bottom drawer, wedged into a crack, I found a yellowed postcard-sized reproduction of a picture called "Found," in which a sheepdog stands barking in the snow over a lost, crumpled lamb. On the back were four verses of a poem called "The Ninety and Nine." This postcard was addressed to Orlando, postmarked from Monroe, Louisiana, and dated December 19, 1954. He must have received it the day before I killed him. The message read: "Great bars up here in North LA. Everybody friendly as puppy dogs. Merry Xmas. Love, Florette."

I had looked for Florette for a long time. The first thing I had to do was discover her last name. In 1972 I went to Southern Bell's office and pretended to be her long-lost cousin. I told her former supervisor that I was from a Pentecostal family in rural North Louisiana and that we had been worrying about the lost sheep in our family, particularly Florette, who had come to South Louisiana and fallen in with a Catholic man. I said that no one knew the last name of the man she had married; nor did we have her address. I told her that I had been sent as a missionary by my family to find Florette and return her to the fold. I even showed her the picture of the languishing lamb in the snow and recited a few lines from the poem on the back about the ninety and nine that were found and didn't really count if there was so much as even one soul that was still lost. I really laid it on thick. I was so moved by my own words that I almost cried. The woman must have been, too, because she said she remembered Florette and told me that her last name was Campo. She even remembered that when Florette had left in 1954, she was going to live in Bunkie.

I never found Florette in Bunkie. Someone in a service station told me that she had moved on to Coushatta. But the trail died there. I don't really know what I would have said to Florette if I had found her.

I took off my black suit and hung it in the bathroom so it would get some steam when I showered, got down a red purse from the top shelf of my closet, and dumped the contents of my walletless purse into it. I retrieved the two hundred dollars in cash I kept for emergencies in an old coffee tin in the pantry. Then I put on the red poppy-covered dress I had a seamstress sew years ago from my design.

I had searched high and low in the notions department of every five-and-dime store in Louisiana until I found five poppy-shaped buttons to match the one I had found in the dresser drawer. Now I slipped on the red strappy high heels that went with the dress and set out for the Riverside Tavern.

Chapter Eighteen

December 1954

When the sun rose the morning after Orlando Duplantis died, Bonita saw its first light fall on the grass where she lay curled up in the driveway beneath her father's coat. Without moving, she watched the rays slowly widen but felt no warmth from them. When all the grass was lit, she heard a car stop and saw dark shoes come close and move quickly away. She heard banging on a door, and her father's slippers were suddenly near her head. Soon she felt the hem of her mother's batiste nightgown brush her cheek, saw her mother's beautiful bare feet fly by. Motionless, Bonita watched as her father, on his knees, prepared a syringe.

Then there were voices in the air all around her. Later, Bonita would remember them.

"Larry, please, Bonita needs your help," her mother cried.

"No drugs, John," Dr. Landry said.

"Larry, I can handle this myself," her father said.

"*No* drugs, John!"

"John, let Larry help! He knows what he's doing. My God, the child is naked. It's freezing out here!" her mother said.

The black shoes were beside her again. "We're supposed to have all of you there at nine o'clock," Bonita heard a strange voice say. "When the judge says nine o'clock, he means nine o'clock."

"Don't move her yet, John," Dr. Landry said. "I need to know what's happening inside her. She needs to be in enough pain to tell me."

"She can't tell you if she's dead of pneumonia, Larry!" her father said.

"You shoot her full of drugs now, John, I swear to God you'll never get her back from where she's gone!" Dr. Landry shouted. "She has to come out now. Get him out of here, Lottie! Both of you go wait with the police on the porch. Tell those two damned thugs they will just have to fucking wait!"

It all seemed far away to Bonita. Far away and then too close because what she remembered next were Larry Landry's sandals next to her face and his huge bare toes. Then he was on his knees beside her, and his voice next to her ear was soft.

"Talk to me, sweetie. Come on, talk to me. Aren't you cold? If you can't say anything, just nod. Nod your head if you can hear my voice."

Bonita could hear his voice, and although she was accustomed to doing as she was told, she couldn't find the strength to do what he wanted. She stared straight at his knee. It seemed unnaturally large and bony.

"I know you're cold. Aren't you cold? Tell me. Tell me how cold you are," Dr. Landry said.

Was she cold, Bonita wondered. She didn't know if she could tell the difference between being cold and not being cold. Something terrible flashed by in her mind, something that this man had called up with the word "cold." No, she would not think of that.

"I know you're Laurel's little friend. I'm sorry, but I can't remember your name. Tell me your name again," Dr. Landry said.

If this man would just stop talking to her and go away, she wouldn't have to think about her name. The pill her father had given her the night before had left her with a dry mouth and a terrible headache. She hadn't felt these things until this man knelt down to talk to her. Why wouldn't he leave her alone?

"Laurel said you had a nice name. She said you played games where you pretended that you each had a different name. Tell me what your name is right now," Dr. Landry said.

Names came to Bonita. One name stayed. The name that remained was not her own. What was it? Whose name was it? Bonita blinked.

The man's brown beard was close to her face again. "Good, I saw your eyes open and close. That's it, sweetie. Come on. Come on. Tell me. Tell me what to call you."

Bonita moistened her lips. She swallowed. "Florette," she whispered.

"Florette," Dr. Landry said. "What a beautiful name. Where on earth did you get such a beautiful name? But it's a pretend name, isn't it?"

Bonita turned her head until the grass scraped her face. She pushed her head toward the ground.

Dr. Landry adjusted the suit coat to fit more snugly about her. "You are cold, aren't you?" he said. "Let's go inside so you can get warm. It's too cold out here."

The smell of the dirt beneath the grass was suffocating Bonita. Every time the man said the word "cold," that terrible thing streaked though her thoughts again. Stop it! She wanted to cry out, "STOP!"

He said it again. "You're cold. I know. You're so cold."

Bonita raised a hand to ward off the word. The beautiful name did not belong to her. She remembered now. Her name was Bonita.

"Cold," he said. He said it again and again.

This time Bonita could not hold off the awful thoughts; cold air, cold ground. Dead. She screamed.

Bonita flung the coat from her, struggled to rise, and screamed again.

Dr. Landry was too slow. Bonita was up on her feet. Bonita was screaming and running. She ran on the grass between the concrete strips of the driveway to the place where she had fallen with the gun the day before. She turned and ran back to the street, where her way was blocked by the police car. She turned again and ran back up the drive. Back and forth, back and forth, she ran with all of the adults trying to stop her.

Lottie ran faster than any of them. She caught her daughter up in her arms, and when she had her, she wrapped her own gown about her until Bonita's screaming turned to simple sobbing. John Gabriel covered them both with his coat.

"You were right, Larry. I was wrong," John Gabriel said.

"John," Lottie said. "Can't this hearing wait?"

"I can call Guy Robertson," John Gabriel said. "He has agreed to represent us. Maybe he can get this hearing postponed."

"I don't think that's such a good idea, John," Dr. Landry said. "In a situation like this, it's best to move quickly and get her to a safe haven."

"But Bonita's in no shape to go anywhere," Lottie said.

"Waiting could be dangerous," Dr. Landry said.

"Then would you come with us to the hearing, Larry, please?" Lottie said. She turned to her husband. "Do you agree that Bonita really needs Larry with her in this situation, John?"

"Yes, Lottie, I agree," John Gabriel said, but he didn't sound agreeable about it. "Come with us, please, Larry," he said stiffly, as if asking his old friend for help was costing him his dignity.

"I'll meet you down there. I have to get dressed and cancel some patients," Dr. Landry said.

"Thank you, Larry. Thank you for everything," Lottie said, and she led Bonita back to the house.

* * *

At the hearing before Judge Linden there were cross words between the two doctors. John Gabriel wanted to keep Bonita at home and have her treated by a psychologist, an elderly woman to whom he referred patients who had problems with their nerves. When they came into Judge Linden's chambers, they sat down in red leather chairs before the judge, who sat behind his desk. Lottie took her exhausted, cried-out, long-legged daughter onto her lap and held her head against her shoulder as the men argued. Bonita heard everything as if it were coming from a great distance. Once her eyelids closed but flew open again as she remembered why they were there and what she had done.

"Nerves?" Dr. Landry said the word as if it had quotes around it. Then he made "elderly woman psychologist" sound as if it also had quotes about it. Then he itemized the ways in which this psychologist had failed numerous patients he had encountered in his practice just since he had been in Baton Rouge. "May I remind you that it was my daughter she threatened with that gun," Dr. Landry said. "I have a vested interest in the outcome of this hearing."

"It was your daughter who tormented Bonita's sister to the point where Bonita felt she had to take up a gun to defend her," John Gabriel said.

"If you would get Mary properly evaluated, your household wouldn't be in such chaos, John," Larry Landry said.

"Chaos? My household is in chaos? Don't you talk to me about chaos," John Gabriel said.

"I don't think Bonita can be properly treated in Baton Rouge," Dr. Landry said.

"Are you questioning my professional competence, Larry?" John Gabriel asked.

"Not your competence, John. Just your ability to detach yourself.

This is your daughter. You're not exactly objective. I've called somebody I know well in New Orleans, a child psychiatrist, Dr. Daniel Chastain. He can see Bonita this afternoon at four o'clock and assess her condition. I think, and so does he, based on what I have told him, that she should be in a safe environment right now. If you are willing to take her, John, fine. If not, I think she should be ordered there by the coroner's office and transported by ambulance."

"You think my home is not safe?" John Gabriel said. Bonita's father, whose fair coloring always betrayed him with a flush when he was angry, was now almost the color of the strawberry on the cover of Bonita's workbook on Louisiana.

"I didn't say that," Dr. Landry said. "I just think that Bonita should be in a place where this tragedy will not be compounded. There is a family history to be considered."

Lottie Gabriel gasped.

"You researched my family?" Dr. Gabriel cried.

"It was common knowledge when I was at DePaul, John," Dr. Landry said.

"What are we talking about here, gentlemen?" Judge Linden said.

John Gabriel glanced helplessly at his wife. Dr. Landry leaned close to the judge and, although he spoke in a low voice, Bonita heard every word. "Bonita's aunt, Diana Dollier, committed suicide in 1939 when she was twenty-two years old."

Bonita pulled away from her mother and whispered, "I think I have to throw up."

Lottie interrupted the men. "Please wait! My child is sick!"

Everything came to a halt while Bonita was led into the judge's private bathroom, where she twice retched dryly into the commode. Dr. Gabriel wet his handkerchief beneath the tap in the lavatory and handed it to Lottie, who wiped Bonita's lips and forehead. Lottie and John led Bonita back into the judge's chambers. When they were again seated, Bonita felt her mother's tears falling on her own face.

This was hell, Bonita realized. This was why Sister Veronica didn't want her students to ever, ever commit a sin, because you went straight to hell and you took everyone else with you.

Dr. Gabriel's attorney, Guy Robertson, stood. "Your Honor, may I try to clarify matters?"

"Please do," Judge Linden said.

"I think this was a tragic accident. It was a misguided attempt by a child to protect a sister who has been the constant target of teasing both in the sanctity of her home and at school. I think Bonita is devastated by the consequences of her actions. I think she should be somewhere safe where she can get treatment, so that, as Dr. Landry said, this tragedy is not compounded. I would like to ask that this be a voluntary commitment and that she be transported privately and not under court order. In addition, I would suggest that, since Orlando Duplantis has no living relatives that we know of, Dr. Gabriel pay burial costs for interment in a private cemetery in Mr. Duplantis's birthplace. I would ask that a ruling of accidental death be made and that the record of this hearing be sealed so there will be no stain on this child's record."

The attorney sat down.

"So far, I see no malice in this act," Judge Linden said. "I see desperation, perhaps, but no intent to do real harm. But before I rule I will need a month to get more details. We need to make sure that the slain man had no survivors who might need support. Today is December twentieth. On January twentieth, the district attorney will present me with background on Orlando Duplantis, and you, Mr. Robertson, may present a succinct summary of the circumstances that led to what I do believe was a tragic accident. But I want a month to pass before I rule. Dr. Gabriel, are you willing to take your daughter, Bonita Jane Gabriel, to the office of Dr. Daniel Chastain in the Medical Plaza Building in New Orleans, Louisiana, at four P.M. this afternoon and, if it is his recommendation that she be hospitalized for treatment, until such time that he deem it prudent for her to be discharged, agree to that also?"

There was a long silence. For several moments, Bonita did not know whether her father would agree to this or not. And if he didn't, what would happen to her, she wondered.

"Yes, Your Honor," Bonita's father finally said.

They stopped by the Gabriel house after the hearing so that Lottie could pack a few clothes for Bonita and fix her something to eat. When Lottie opened the refrigerator, Bonita, leaning against her mother like a two-year-old, saw a gold-rimmed bowl filled with chicken salad and a plate of asparagus. A note taped to the food said "Love, Alma."

"Where's Mary?" Bonita said when she was dressed in the wine-colored velvet dress she wore when she went with her family to mass.

"She's over at Gracie's right now," Lottie said. "I told them I'd pick her up at one o'clock. I'm not going to be able to go with you to New Orleans to see the doctor, sweetheart, but I'll see you soon."

"Tell Mary I said good-bye," Bonita said.

Her mother helped Bonita into her white wool coat and pulled the hood of the coat up over her head.

"John, Bonita's getting a terrible cold. Be sure she keeps her coat on in the car and turn the heater on."

"I'm sorry, Mother," she said when Lottie embraced her.

"I'm sorry, Daddy," Bonita said when they had to stop at Roussell's in LaPlace so Bonita could throw up again.

"You don't have to apologize for being sick, Bonita," her father said.

These were the only words they exchanged during the two hours it took them to drive to New Orleans and find Dr. Chastain's office.

The waiting room was empty. There were four chairs of dark wood with bright pumpkin-colored cushions. Bonita and her father sat down to wait. Bonita sat on the edge of the chair, prepared to rise quickly. On the wall was a painting. A stream with a bridge over it ran through the right side of the picture. It bothered Bonita that the water didn't run through the middle of the picture. She kept trying to move the little river to the center of the painting. When the door opened, she stood up, anxious, ready to be accused of something, but the person who came out knew her father, shook his hand and then said, "Dan Chastain, Bonita." The doctor even extended his hand to her.

Bonita put out her hand and took his. It was warm, and she jumped. It startled her to touch live flesh.

"Larry Landry called me about you. Why don't you and your father come in my office so we can talk."

"Yes, sir," Bonita said.

Dr. Chastain put his hand on his door, pushed it open to make the passage to his office a little wider, and ushered Bonita and her father inside. It reminded her of when Sister Veronica had ushered her into one of the pews in the chapel after Bonita had pushed Laurel down in the dirt.

Dr. Chastain wore a pale yellow shirt and white shorts. He was very tanned. Bonita saw a tennis racket leaning against the wall in one corner. She glanced around. There was another picture of the same village in his office over his desk, but in this one there were people, and the bridge over the river was squarely in the middle. It made Bonita feel a little better to get that bridge moved over. All of these details she recalled later; for the moment, she was like her father's sixteen-millimeter camera left running while its owner attended to something else.

Bonita didn't know what she was supposed to do. There were two more chairs with orange cushions like the ones in the waiting room. There was a long sofa with a brown cushion, one end of which was slightly raised.

Although she had clung to her mother at the hearing before the judge, Bonita did not attempt to do the same with her father, since she could feel his fury and his humiliation at being forced to go into another doctor's office to ask for help. And Bonita was fully conscious that it was she who was responsible.

"Would you like to sit down?" Dr. Chastain said.

"Where should I sit, Daddy?" Bonita said.

"Sit anywhere you want, Bonita," her father said. But when Bonita chose a chair and tentatively sat down, her father crossed the room and sat in the chair farthest from her, with the ankle of one leg resting on the knee of the other, as if to say to his colleague, "You see, I'm not really a part of this. It is she and she alone who needs to be here." At least that was how Bonita perceived it; that was the way she remembered it.

"Would you like to take off your coat, Bonita?" Dr. Chastain said.

Bonita stood again. She still wore the hood of her coat over her head. The coat was fastened with loops that fit snugly over puffy, satin-covered buttons. When Bonita put her hands to them, she could not remember how to unhook them, so she shook her head. "No, thank you," she said and sat down again.

"For God's sake, Bonita, it's too warm in here for that coat. Take it off," her father said.

"I can't undo these buttons," Bonita said.

Her father came across the room. "That's because you still have on your gloves." Abruptly, Dr. Gabriel pulled her hood back and took the mittens from her hands. He put them in his pocket, turned her to face him, and unlocked the loops that held the coat in place. His touch was ungentle. He helped her out of the coat and then put it across the end of the brown couch and returned to his chair.

Bonita sat down again and stared at the lap of her dark red velvet dress. She covered it with her left hand. Then she placed her right hand flat next to it. When tears fell on the back of one hand, she carefully wiped the moisture away with the thumb of her other hand.

The room was totally silent, and Bonita did not know who was supposed to speak.

"Bonita," Dr. Chastain said. "I'm going to ask you a few questions. Answer them if you can, but if you can't, don't worry about it."

Bonita nodded.

"Do you know what day of the week it is?" Dr. Chastain said.

Bonita did not want the doctor to know that she was crying, so she shook her head without raising her eyes.

"It's Saturday, Bonita," Dr. Gabriel said. "Yesterday was Friday."

Dr. Chastain looked at Bonita's father but didn't say anything.

"Do you know what month it is?" Dr. Chastain said.

Bonita looked directly into darkness: December. Bonita had bought a key ring in the shape of an acorn for Mr. Orlando for Christmas. The top unscrewed so he could fill it with nickels. Bonita put both hands over her face.

Dr. Gabriel started to speak again, but Dr. Chastain put out his hand and her father remained silent.

"Bonita, I always like to start out talking to a prospective patient and her parent," Dr. Chastain said. "But I think you and I are ready to talk alone. Would it be all right with you if I asked your father to wait outside for a little while?"

Although Bonita knew Dr. Chastain had done everything he could to keep from hurting her father's feelings, she still felt that if she agreed to talk with him alone, her father would feel left out. She raised her head and gave her father a despairing glance. Her father would not meet her eyes. Although Bonita could not articulate it, she knew that if her father left the room, it was farewell. She was on her own.

"Is that okay with you, Daddy?" she said.

Her father stood. "Of course," he said. And he walked stiffly past them, still not looking at his elder daughter. The door closed behind him, just short of a slam.

"I'm sorry, Bonita. I think I've just made your life more difficult," Dr. Chastain said.

Surprised, Bonita looked at him. She was not accustomed to adults telling her the truth. It confirmed what she had suspected for a long time: that she lived in a household with people whose words were usually evasive; not outright lies, just words that skidded past the actual reality of a thing. There was something wrong with Mary—no matter what her parents said, no matter how much they wished it not to be, there was something wrong with her sister. "It's not your fault. He was mad at me anyway," Bonita said.

Again silence fell.

"That's a pretty dress," Dr. Chastain said.

"Thank you," Bonita said. She touched the smocking at the neckline. "My mother made it."

"It's very nice," Dr. Chastain said.

"It used to be my favorite dress, but I don't like it anymore," Bonita said.

"Is that why you wanted to keep your coat on?" Dr. Chastain said.

"I guess so," Bonita said. She got up from the chair, retrieved her white wool coat from the foot of the brown couch, returned to her chair, and laid the coat across her lap.

"Does that make you more comfortable?" Dr. Chastain said.

Bonita nodded.

"Can you tell me why?" Dr. Chastain said.

"This dress looks like blood," Bonita said. "It looks like I have blood all over me." She pulled at the sleeves of her red dress as if she would remove it if she could.

"Whose blood is it?" Dr. Chastain said.

Bonita took her coat in her arms and rocked back and forth. She didn't answer. Dr. Chastain waited. "My Aunt Diana killed herself," Bonita said. "Did you know that?"

"Yes," Dr. Chastain said.

"How did she do it?" Bonita said.

"How do you think she might have done it?" Dr. Chastain said.

"She probably cut herself with a razor blade until all her blood ran out," Bonita said.

"Where do you think she might have cut herself?" Dr. Chastain said.

Bonita put her coat down, turned her hands palm up, and examined the veins in her wrists. The thought of hurting her own unblemished skin made her shudder. Sister Veronica would be horrified if Bonita damaged her healthy, God-given body. That was what Sister Veronica said to them at the end of every first assembly: "And always respect the miracle of your healthy, God-given bodies." Bonita put both hands down by her side, palms flat against the cushion she sat on. "I don't know. Do you know?" she said. Again, she rocked back and forth.

"Yes," Dr. Chastain said.

"You don't have to tell me," Bonita said.

"Thank you," Dr. Chastain said. "I didn't really want to."

Bonita stopped rocking. "Maybe you can tell me someday," she said. She knew now that she had moved away from her father and gone toward this man she hardly knew.

"Yes," Dr. Chastain said. "I will tell you someday."

Bonita nodded.

"Actually, I think that there are a lot of things that you and I might talk about," Dr. Chastain said.

Bonita looked at the picture of the bridge that crossed the stream in the little town that looked as if it might be in a foreign country and nodded again.

"Larry Landry told me that something very sad has happened to you," Dr. Chastain said.

Bonita looked away. "I don't want to talk about that," she whispered.

"But you might want to talk about it someday," he said. "If you and your father agree, I would like for you to go and live for a little while in a safe place where, if you ever got to feeling too sad, you would always have somebody to talk to."

"So I wouldn't do what my Aunt Diana did," Bonita said.

"Yes. So you wouldn't ever have to feel so bad that you would do what your Aunt Diana did," Dr. Chastain said.

"Will this be in DePaul Hospital?" Bonita said.

"Yes," Dr. Chastain said.

"Will I be on Rosary?"

"Yes, you'll be in the building they call Rosary. You'll be on the third floor—Rosary Three," Dr. Chastain said. "How do you know about Rosary?"

"I heard my mother tell my daddy that's where Aunt Diana was. My mother hated Rosary. My daddy promised my mother she'd never have to hear the words 'DePaul Hospital' again if she would come home from New York and marry him. He's mad because I made him break his promise. If I go on Rosary Three, I'll never see my mother again."

Dr. Chastain was silent.

Bonita looked hard into the corner of every wall in the room to keep the tears from her eyes. "I love my mother," she whispered.

"I'm sorry, Bonita," Dr. Chastain said. "I'm sorry that I have to ask you to go and stay in a place that has so many unhappy memories for your family, but I think it is the best place for you to be right now. Shall we ask your father to come join us so we can discuss it with him?"

"Yes, sir," Bonita said.

"While you are in the hospital, we will have plenty of time to sort out your feelings about what happened to your mother and her sister in the past and the events of the last few days," Dr. Chastain said.

"I can't have any feelings," Bonita said. "I killed somebody."

* * *

Bonita sat on a wooden bench outside the admitting office of DePaul Hospital and waited for her father and Dr. Chastain to complete the paperwork for her admission. To Bonita, the long, dimly lit hall was remarkably similar to that of the Academy of the Holy Angels. Even the walls were lined with the same pictures of saints in various stages of torment. For just a moment Bonita imagined that she had never taken the gun from the glove compartment of Orlando Duplantis's car, pretended, briefly, that she was waiting outside Sister Veronica's office, but the illusion was broken when Dr. Chastain and her father came out and escorted Bonita to the elevator and they rode up to Rosary Three.

Dr. Chastain rang a bell, and someone came and unlocked the door and let them in. Dr. Chastain showed Bonita where her clothes would be hung and where she would take a bath. The nurse took Bonita's little suitcase and wrote "Gabriel" on a piece of white adhesive tape, tore it off, and pressed it to the little bag. She did the same with Bonita's toothbrush and toothpaste, her comb and brush and all of her clothes. Dr. Chastain told her that, for the time being, she would be in a room by herself, with a white gown to wear at night and one sheet to cover her, and she would have to sleep on a bare mattress on the floor. Then he told the nurse that Bonita had one heck of a cold and would she call down to the pharmacy right away and order a decongestant for Bonita to take after she ate something. Then he asked Bonita if she could think of anything she might be able to eat, and she said maybe a grilled-cheese sandwich. Dr. Chastain called down to the hospital kitchen himself and told them he had a patient who had just come in and would they fix a grilled-cheese sandwich and send it up with a Coca-Cola in a paper cup. Then Dr. Chastain told her how sorry he was about it, but he was going to have to lock her in. He said an orderly would be watching her sleep through the little window in the door all night. He said he hoped that Bonita understood that it was for her own protection and would find it in her heart to forgive him, and Bonita said she didn't hold it against him because it really didn't matter to her where she was or what she did because Mr. Orlando was dead and she would never see him again. And what? what? what?, Bonita said, what was her sister going to do now? Now that she had killed the one person who liked Mary. Now that the one person in the whole world who had really and truly liked Mary was gone.

Chapter Nineteen

October 1995

I love the bars in Baton Rouge. I like the bars all over Louisiana. Before I came back to live in Baton Rouge in 1970, I wandered all over the state. I spent a lot of time at night in small-town taverns and ramshackle road-houses by the sides of old highways. No one ever tried to harm me in any of these places. Not once. It is as if some invisible force protected me—I think of it as Florette's power.

Florette was right: the folks in the watering holes of North Louisiana were friendly. My brief marriage came from an encounter in a place called Bud's.

I make it a habit never to sit at the bar. I choose places with tables, and my favorite table is one in the corner, preferably in the near-dark.

"Hey, Miss Florette," Billy said when I came into the Riverside Tavern.

Billy is young enough to be my child. His hair is long, severely bleached, pulled back, and secured with a rubber band at the base of his neck. Tonight Billy wore three gold hoops of graduated sizes in his right ear. On occasion he wears a trio of diamond studs. Sometimes we discuss our jewelry. Billy wants me to pierce an additional hole or two in my left ear, the ear that is exposed when I pull my hair to one side and secure it with a comb. Billy has even volunteered to pierce it for me with an ice cube and a needle stuck through a cork, but I shudder at his suggestion and he always laughs.

"Hey, Billy," I said. "How's it going?"

"Can't complain. How about you? Anything new?"

"Nope. Nothing," I said.

Billy made my drink. I usually start with a gin and tonic and then switch to club soda around ten. If there's someone in the kitchen in back, he'll fix me a grilled-cheese sandwich about eleven o'clock. I'm always home by midnight. Sometimes I go home alone. Sometimes I don't. You get to talking to a stranger in a bar and feelings spring up, but you can always count on them not to last. If I get uncomfortable in one location, just like Florette, I'll move on. There are always plenty of nighttime places close to the river in Baton Rouge. None of them last long, so I don't get too attached to a place. The Brunswick closed years ago.

I picked up my glass and was turning to go to my favorite table when Billy said under his breath, "There's somebody over there waiting for you, Miss Florette. He came in a few minutes ago. Said he was looking for a dark-haired lady in a flowered dress who liked to hang out here. I didn't tell him nothing, but he sat down anyway."

I patted his hand. "It's okay, Billy. Thanks for warning me."

I sounded calm because I didn't want to alarm Billy, but my heart sank. Who in hell knew I might be here?

The stranger was sitting at my favorite table. He stood up as I approached. He wore a suit, but in the dim light, the only thing I could make out about him was that he was exactly the same height I was and that he wore glasses.

"Are you Dr. Gabriel's daughter?" he said.

I looked behind me at Billy, who was waiting to see if this encounter was acceptable to me. What if I denied it? As I considered his question, the man stuck out his hand. "Steve Scott," he said. "I talked to you yesterday afternoon about your dad."

I nodded. I put my drink on the table, turned to give Billy a little wave that said all was well, and sat down in the chair Dr. Scott pulled out for me. He sat down across from me and put both of his hands flat on the table. We sat in silence. Dr. Scott didn't look as young as he had sounded on the telephone. He poured beer from a bottle into a glass that was already full. He looked uncomfortable. I wanted it that way. It seemed only fair, because I could feel a deep flush rising from my neck up to my cheeks. Somehow this man had found me. I thought of all the papers he had seen in my father's desk and of what he must know about me. The blood beat in my head, and worse, my nose started to run. I had to open my red bag, feel around for a handkerchief, and wipe the top of my lip. Still, I refused to speak.

"Gerry Winborn called me this afternoon," Dr. Scott said. "He wanted to know how you had taken the news of your father's death."

I held my tongue.

"I told him that you seemed ... unnaturally calm," Dr. Scott said.

"Unnaturally calm," I said, then repeated, "Unnaturally calm." I sipped from my drink after first taking several moments to squeeze juice from the lime slice into it. "You'll be happy to know that I am no longer unnaturally calm. I am no longer calm at all. My sister has taken off for parts unknown because I refused to have a proper funeral for my father; I have shed more tears today than I did in thirty years, and a madwoman keeps calling me about the condition of my soul. Would you be calm?"

Dr. Scott ignored my ill-tempered question and said, "Jim Singleton thought I might be able to give you a little help."

"What kind of help?" I said.

"You're going to need some pallbearers. I told him I would contact some of the members of the medical community. When I talked to the young doctor who was in practice with your father, he said he had already heard from several of your father's old friends. They want to do this. Will you let me organize it?"

"Why would you do that?" I said. "Did you know my father?"

"I know who he was, but I've never met him. I feel bad about being so cross with you because I couldn't find you. I would feel better about that if you would let me help."

"I have to find my sister," I said.

Dr. Scott did not point out that retreating to a dream world where everyone thought my name was Florette wasn't the way to find Mary. He said instead, "Winborn said they had received a call from someone at the home in Livingston Parish that she was missing. The Baton Rouge police department is looking for her. So is the Livingston Parish sheriff's office. Outside of getting in your car and driving all over two parishes and wearing yourself out looking for her, I don't think there's much you can do. I think coming here and getting your mind off it was the best thing to do."

"You were right, you know," I said.

"Right about what?" he said.

"About grief being upon you and you don't even know it. About calling someone to be with me. The trouble is—I don't have anybody to call."

"You have more people who care about you than you know. How do you think I found you here?" he said.

"How did you find me here?" I said.

"Gerry Winborn. He wouldn't tell me anything in the beginning. I was really pissed when I found out he knew where you were all along, but as I've learned more about you, I began to understand why. He looks after you, you know," Dr. Scott said. "Once, he told me, when he was still a patrolman and you were unwise enough to walk back to Spanish Town after midnight, he saw you and followed you to make sure you got home okay. That's how he found out where you lived."

"What do you mean?" I said.

"He drives by your house sometimes at night. He knows exactly which bars you like to visit. When he sees your light on, he knows you've made it home safely. Then, he says, he can rest."

"He knows?" I said. "He knows everything?"

Steve Scott nodded. "Your secret's safe with us." He drank a little of his beer and stood up. "I'll be in touch tomorrow about the pall-bearers. I just don't know what name to call you."

"Bonita," I said. "Call me Bonita."

Chapter Twenty

1955-1965

The locked room Bonita lived in for the first six weeks she was at DePaul Hospital was called a control room. Although Dr. Chastain told her again and again it was to protect her, Bonita believed it was to keep everyone safe from her.

After she had been confined for several days, her mother came to see her. Bonita heard the key turn in the lock, and when she looked up, Lottie was standing there. As Bonita struggled to get up, her mother came into the room, knelt and gathered Bonita in her arms, and rocked her back and forth.

"Do you have to keep her in here like an animal," Lottie cried to the nurse. "Leave the door open, for God's sake."

"It's okay, Mimi. I don't mind. I want to be here," Bonita said.

"You shouldn't be locked up in a cage," her mother said.

"I have bathroom privileges," Bonita said.

"I hate all their hospital lingo," Lottie said. "Don't talk like they do. Diana talked like that all the time, and I don't want you to do it.

Keep your language pure. Say, 'I can go to the bathroom whenever I want.' If you have to be here, you have to fight to keep yourself from becoming one of them. Do you understand me? You are not a mental patient. You are a child who was involved in a terrible accident. I will not have you turned into a zombie like Diana. Oh, God, how I hate this place."

"It's not so bad, Mimi. Everybody is really nice to me. All I have to do is tell Dr. Chastain what I want to eat and they fix it for me in the kitchen."

"Thank goodness for that. I was afraid you were going to stop eating."

"How's Mary?"

Her mother was silent long enough for Bonita to know that when she answered, it was not quite the truth. "She's fine. She and your father went to the zoo."

"So did you, Mimi," Bonita said quickly and laughed. It was the first time she had laughed since Orlando died, so she quickly smothered it, but she had seen her mother's eyes light up the way they always did when she or Mary said something clever.

Lottie held Bonita close to her. "What a brave girl you are—to make jokes in a place like this."

Bonita's mother had brought her a new flannel gown, pink fluffy slippers, and a matching robe patterned all over with roses. "We've got to get permission to get you out of this horrid ugly hospital gown. And your Christmas stocking is at the nurse's station. They wouldn't let me bring it in, but they promised me they would let you have some of the things tomorrow after your doctor looked at everything in it."

"I don't want any presents, Mimi," Bonita said.

"We are going to open the presents you wrapped and put them under the tree tomorrow. You shall have presents, too. I can't bear for you to spend Christmas in this place by yourself, but your father is on call. Today was the only day we could come."

Lottie began to cry silently. Bonita put her arms around her mother.

"It's so hard for me to come here, sweetheart. I don't know how often I'll be able to do it," her mother said.

"Don't come anymore, Mimi," Bonita said, but what she really meant was: I love you. I miss you. Come every day.

Bonita saw her mother again when, accompanied by both her father and Dr. Chastain, she attended the hearing the judge had set for January 20, 1955. By this time Bonita had told Dr. Chastain more about the events that led up to her theft of the gun, and the psychiatrist was able to provide the judge with a coherent account of the event. Judge Linden ruled that the death of Orlando Duplantis was an accident, and Bonita's records were sealed. Legally, Dr. Gabriel's lawyer said, it was as if it had never happened.

But, of course, it had. It then became Bonita's responsibility, she reasoned, to turn herself back into a person who could be trusted not to hurt anyone again. She began this transformation with the only things over which she had power: what she ate, how she moved, and what she thought. She set aside a portion of each meal that was brought, even when it was something she liked. Then she ate only what she had allotted to herself. In the beginning, she paced about her room incessantly. After the hearing she gave herself a daily allowance of five hundred steps; she deducted twenty-five steps for each supervised trip to the bathroom and spent the rest walking the perimeter of her room. After her admission into the hospital, she thought constantly of Orlando Duplantis lying on the grass; of her sister and mother and father. Over time she forced herself to think only of what she could see from her barred window: the grounds behind the hospital, the small white building that housed the occupational therapy department, the huge oaks that shaded the wooden pavilion and the volleyball court, the nuns who walked along the paths among the trees, and the infinite variety of the colors of the old weathered bricks in the high wall that enclosed the institution. When Bonita was finally well enough to come out of the control room and share a suite with three other young patients, she had in place a steely authority over her feelings that she lost only once.

After her Christmas Eve visit, Lottie didn't come to the hospital again. All Bonita had from her mother were her daily letters. In the early spring, when her father came for his weekly visit, he brought Lottie's red crystal bracelet with the message that her mother sent her love but, again, could not come to see her because she had to stay with Mary. Bonita threw the bracelet against the wall of her room and cried, "I don't want this jewelry! I want to see my mother!"

Her father summoned the nurse to calm her. "I don't approve of displays of emotion, Bonita," he said coldly. "You are going to have to learn to control yourself if you ever hope to leave here."

The day after his visit, in the little occupational therapy building, Bonita modeled bookends in the shape of the state of Louisiana, broke the red bracelet, and pressed a bead into each piece of soft clay to mark Baton Rouge before it went into the kiln. Then she carried the rest of the crystals with her on her afternoon walk to the Mississippi River, climbed the levee with the young nun who accompanied her, and flung the remains of her mother's bracelet into the wide water.

Bonita asked for schoolbooks so she could keep up with her class, and Dr. Chastain borrowed sixth-grade texts from the nearby Catholic school that Lottie had attended while Diana was in DePaul. A senior girl volunteered to come and tutor Bonita twice a week. The following September, Dr. Chastain said that Bonita was well enough to enter the seventh grade at this school if she continued to live at the hospital, so Bonita began to ride a bicycle to and from the hospital to school.

Over time, Bonita described to Dr. Chastain what it had been like to live with Mary in the Gabriel home, how she had felt when Laurel left them out of the birthday party, and the weight of her worries when Mary entered first grade. She quoted her father's words to her as they had sat together in the white rockers on the front porch the day before Mary entered first grade: "Look after your sister at school for the next few days, Bonita. And try to keep a lid on that little Landry girl. I don't want your mother hearing anything that might hurt her feelings."

When Dr. Chastain heard this, he clenched his jaw, and his lips went white.

In spite of his feelings about the part her father had played in the tragedy, Dr. Chastain was careful to make sure that Bonita looked closely at the part her own imagination played in what she had believed to be Laurel's persecution of Mary. Bonita admitted that she never actually saw Laurel in Kress's the day in December when Mary disappeared for twenty-four hours and she hadn't really known for sure when Laurel had whispered to Adrienne in the backseat of the car on the way to the first day of school that she was saying Lottie ought to go to the doctor so Mary wouldn't be as disruptive. And Bonita finally admitted that taking a gun from someone who trusted her was the act of a desperate person.

Bonita accepted the theory that certain illnesses ran in her family—"frailties of spirit," Dr. Chastain called them—and that she would always be at risk. Mary's case he could not comment on, he said. But Bonita knew that Dr. Chastain was very angry with her father.

In many of her letters, Lottie revealed such anguish over Mary's condition that Bonita appealed to Dr. Chastain for help on her behalf. Four times Dr. Chastain made arrangements for a psychologist to evaluate Mary and then set aside an hour of his own time so that he could talk to the entire Gabriel family at once. Four times Dr. Chastain made these arrangements, and four times Dr. Gabriel canceled them. After this, although he continued to pay for her care, Bonita's father's visits to her at the hospital ceased altogether.

It was then that Dr. Chastain suggested Bonita might have to construct a life that did not include her mother and her father and Mary. So, at her doctor's advice, Bonita never returned home, not at Thanksgiving, not at Easter, and not even on Christmas.

On Bonita's sixteenth birthday, she received a card from her mother that contained a generous check—"Spend it on something completely frivolous, sweetheart"—and a sixth-grade school picture of Mary, who was eleven and looked very blond and chubby. Her sister wore a fragile smile for the camera that made Bonita's heart hurt. Her father sent a card also. When Bonita opened it, another picture fluttered out. It was a girl who looked exactly like her, but this girl, almost her twin and dressed in a parochial-school uniform, stood beneath a spreading moss-draped oak in a place Bonita had never been. When Bonita showed the picture to Dr. Chastain, he turned it over and together they read her father's message.

> *Dear Bonita,*
>
> *Happy sixteenth birthday. I am going against your mother's wishes and sending you this, but I think it's important for you to know who you are and where you came from. This is a picture of your Aunt Diana on a school picnic in Evangeline State Park, taken when she, too, was sixteen.*
>
> > *Love,*
> >
> > *Daddy*

"That son of a bitch," Dr. Chastain muttered.

Bonita, fascinated by the fact that she had her aunt's dark hair and pale skin, looked at her doctor, startled by his words, and thought immediately of the two times she had heard her father curse.

"Why?" Bonita said. "I want to know what she looked like. Tell me why this makes you mad."

"Under normal circumstances, I think it would be a thing of great value to know you had inherited this radiant beauty. But these are not normal circumstances. Your mother knew what she was doing when she kept this picture from you. You look exactly like her sister. That's why she can't come and see you here. Your father's acting against her wishes is very disturbing. This picture sends a very scary message, Bonita. There is the subtle suggestion that because you resemble your aunt so much in the face, that you might have also inherited her fate. I knew Diana when I was a young medical student, and trust me, she was a very unstable, disturbed young woman. You have many more internal resources than she had—much more ego strength. I expect you to recover and live a normal life. If we can protect you from your father's destructive impulses."

"Why would my own father hurt me?" Bonita said.

Dr. Chastain looked at Bonita and shook his head. "I can't answer that question. All I can tell you is that sometimes you can be at the greatest risk from the very people who say they love you the most." He leaned forward, put his elbows on his knees, and, gesturing with the picture of Bonita's Aunt Diana, said, "Just as I don't understand why your father sent you this picture. I wish he hadn't done it, but now that we've talked about it, I feel a little better."

"Me, too," Bonita said.

When Bonita entered her junior year of high school, Dr. Chastain permitted her to board at the nearby parochial school and ride her bicycle back and forth to see him three times a week.

It was then that Bonita met Sister Dorothy, the nun who was the author of the text and workbook on the geography and history of Louisiana that Bonita had so loved in sixth grade. Sister Dorothy arranged for Bonita to do volunteer work at the Orleans Parish office of the Louisiana Department of Agriculture and, when she was old enough, to go to work there. Sister Dorothy encouraged Bonita's love of her state's native fruit and wrote a glowing recommendation to the college Bonita wanted to attend in Ruston so that she could study horticulture.

Before Bonita left New Orleans, Dr. Chastain gave her a warning. "I think your sister's condition will worsen without treatment. I don't want you to ever let yourself be put in the position of becoming the person responsible for her care. You are not the solution to your parents' problem with her. Her illness is not your fault. Don't ever forget this."

When Bonita was twenty-two and doing work that she loved in Lincoln Parish, Dr. Chastain dropped dead on the tennis court, and Bonita received a summons from her father to return home.

Chapter
Twenty-one

October 1995

The morning after Dr. Steven Scott found me in the Riverside Tavern, I called Johnella to see if Mary had turned up at the home, and when I found out that they were still searching for her, I went up to my office in the capitol to open my mail and catch up on a little work.

My coworkers knew nothing of my father's death, but one of the women who worked in Fertilizer and Feed came to the door of my office and extended her hand. Her name was Dolores Christian, and although she had come to work in the capitol the year after I had and I had known her for almost twenty-five years, we had never exchanged more than several pleasant words about the weather.

"The maintenance crew found this in the rollers of their vacuum cleaner after they did your office last week. When they couldn't find you, they left it with me."

Glittering in Dolores's palm was the red crystal bead from my mother's bracelet. The bead I had searched for in vain while I was on the telephone with Dr. Scott.

Although I always discouraged intimacy, something in the pleasure with which I plucked the red crystal from her palm must have permitted her next question.

"Where have you been?" Dolores said. She never would have asked me such a question before. I would have frozen her out.

"My father died," I said. "I've been making arrangements for the funeral."

"I'm so sorry. Did you just drive back?" she said.

"Back from where?" I said, although I knew full well what she meant.

"Wherever it was you went to do it. Where are you from, by the way?" Dolores said.

"I grew up here. My father's funeral will be here," I said.

"You're kidding. In Baton Rouge? You're from Baton Rouge? What was your maiden name?" Dolores said.

"Gabriel," I said. "Jane is my middle name. And 'Mitchell' I stole from a very brief marriage. My first name is Bonita."

"John Gabriel is your father?" she said. She looked astonished.

I nodded. "Yes," I said.

"Dr. Gabriel is my doctor. Was my doctor," she said. "I've gone to him all my life. He's taken care of my entire family. He's a wonderful doctor. I loved your dad. My whole family loved your dad. I just saw that he died in the paper this morning. I was planning to go straight from here to the funeral home after work. Do you want to go with me? Let me take you."

Dolores moved forward as if she might embrace me. That was really more than I was prepared for, so I turned away and moved back to my desk. But Dolores tried to take my hand. "Please, let me do something for you. You probably shouldn't even be driving right now. You're probably still in a state of shock. I'll drive you whenever you want to go. Let me take you. Please," she said with such feeling that tears came to my eyes.

I thanked her but said I had to do a few more things and wouldn't be able to stay at the office for more than a few minutes. If I hadn't needed to keep looking for Mary, I would have ridden with Dolores to the funeral home and been glad of the company.

As Dolores left, it seemed to me that she was the one in a state of shock. "I can't believe it," she said as she walked away. "Do you know who Jane Mitchell is?" she asked the man in the office next to mine.

Jim Singleton stood up when I appeared in the doorway of his office. "I'm glad you decided to have a service tomorrow and to have folks come by tonight." He came around his desk and took my arm. "Come and see," he said. "I want to show you something."

He led me down a silent hall to a long, rectangular room that looked exactly like a small church, except that there were no windows. It was lined on each side with oak pews. Oak paneling covered the walls, and the lights were shaded with opaque rose glass. On the floor was a maroon and gray carpet. There was an oak pulpit in the front of the room. To the right was a door that led outside, to the left were six pews that might have held a choir in a church, but here they formed a private place for the bereaved family to sit.

"The flowers are starting to come in," he said. "It's only been a few hours since the notice appeared in the paper, and look at what's arrived already." He swept his hand out and down as if this were some sort of cue for the flowers to step forward and be seen to be beautiful—and they were.

"Gerry Winborn called me at home early this morning after he saw the paper," Jim said. "With your permission, he would like to escort the procession to the cemetery."

"I would like that," I said.

"We usually hire several patrolmen to control traffic. Of course, it's been a long time since Gerry worked in that capacity, but he wants to volunteer his services. He wants to do this for you and your sister," Jim said. "In memory of your father."

"That's very kind of him," I said.

I didn't go to the casket and look at my father. I wasn't ready to do that yet. Jim seemed to sense this, because he said, "About tonight . . ."

I assumed he wanted some assurance that Mary would be muzzled and leashed, so I said, "I can't tell you anything about my sister. I don't know where she is. She never came back to the house. The bargain was that I would arrange a real funeral and she would come back, but she didn't. I just came by to see if she had showed up here. Obviously she hasn't."

"About tonight, Bonita," Jim said in the same gentle tone. "I realize that this is going to be very difficult for you—seeing so many people after all of these years. I'll be here, but I just want you to know that if you get overwhelmed and I'm not right handy to help, you have a place where you can retreat." He extended his hand. In his palm was a key. "This unlocks my office door. If you need to be by yourself for a while, just go in there and rest until you feel like coming back out."

It's always a shock when someone you knew as a kid turns out to have developed reserves of strength and kindness. I wished I had grown up as much as PeeWee Singleton.

I took the key from his hand. "Thank you," I said. "That's very kind of you. Can you tell me exactly what's going to happen tonight, Jim? Do I just sit here and wait?" I know he must have been amazed that I was ignorant of a social ritual that was so familiar to him, but he concealed it and gave me simple instructions for what I should do both tonight and the next day at the funeral.

"When your sister comes back," he said, "and I'm sure she will, I'll tell her the same things I'm telling you now."

I thanked him again and left.

In the dining room of the house on Oleander, ecru lace panels were caught up on each side of the wide windows. The few Haviland plates Mary had spared shimmered with a cold white light on the mahogany table. Behind the etched glass of the china cabinet, party dishes sat shaded, all excitement associated with them long ago exhausted. Mrs. Moak had left cinnamon rolls on the table with a note propped against the plate:

Dear Bonita,

I still have my key to your house. When no one answered this morning I let myself in and left you and Mary some lunch in the refrigerator. Mr. Moak and I saw the death notice in the paper this morning. We will see you tonight at the funeral home.

Love,

Alma

On the top shelf of the refrigerator, covered with clear plastic wrap, was chicken salad in a crystal bowl with a gilt lip so worn that only a few flecks of gold still adhered to its edge. A faded green majolica plate in the shape of a large curved leaf held lettuce, sliced tomatoes, dill pickles, deviled eggs, black olives, and two bundles of asparagus wrapped with red pimentos. I rested my head on the refrigerator door, stared at its shelves, and, just as the sound of saying my own name earlier that morning had evoked the distant past, so did Mrs. Moak's gift of food. It was probably made from the same recipes and brought over in the same dishes as the food she had brought over the morning of my hearing before the judge. For the first time, this confluence of the past and present was deeply comforting, and I closed the refrigerator door, turned around, and leaned against it for a long time.

I realized that I was starving. I went into the dining room, got one of the white china plates, filled it, and sat down at the table. As I was finishing my lunch of Mrs. Moak's chicken salad and asparagus, the telephone rang.

I knew exactly who it was before I answered. "Aura Lee," I said.

"Yes, it's me," Aura Lee said and laughed. "You knew it would be me because I prayed you would. I said, 'Blessed Baby Jesus, let Mary's sister answer this telephone and say "Aura Lee," ' and you did."

"What other miracles can you work, Aura Lee? Can you find Mary?" I said.

"Mary is safe. I told you I have blessed her. When Mary goes to the graveyard, she will be under my protection. Her soul will live, live, live. It's you who's in deepest, darkest danger, Mary's sister."

"I am not in deepest, darkest danger, Aura Lee. And you cannot protect Mary with anything you've got; not words, not prayers, not blessings, nothing. Nothing, Aura Lee!"

"Yes, I can, Mary's sister. When you go to the graveyard, your soul will be dead, dead, dead, if you don't confess to me."

The graveyard. When Mary goes to the graveyard. I knew where my sister was.

"Thank you, Aura Lee. Bless you, Aura Lee. I have to go now," I said.

I went out to my car and drove to the cemetery in East Feliciana Parish. I found Mary there, sitting next to Orlando's grave, plaiting a wreath of plastic jasmine.

"Where did you get those flowers?" I said.

"From over there." Mary pointed to an empty urn on a grave nearby. The cemetery was dotted with hard bright bouquets of artificial flowers designed to be everlasting, although some had lasted longer than others.

"I've been looking for you everywhere," I said.

"I know," Mary said. She didn't raise her head from her task.

"Why don't we go get some real flowers for Mr. Orlando's grave," I said. "Put those back and let's go get some that are alive. Maybe some chrysanthemums. All of these fake flowers give me the creeps."

The artificial lilies, tulips, and daffodils did give a curious air of unreality to the little cemetery. It was autumn. The earth, the trees, the grass, and the gravestones—all were wasting away. Only the plastic flowers would never wither.

Mary tossed aside the circle of jasmine and stood up. "Okay," she said.

I replaced the flowers in the pillaged urn and then put my arm around her waist as we walked to the car. "How did you get all the way out here?" I asked.

"The nicest man came along and gave me a ride," my sister said.

Chapter
Twenty-two

June 1965

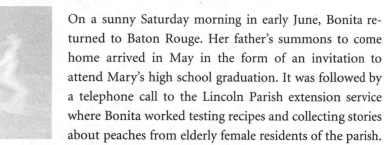

On a sunny Saturday morning in early June, Bonita returned to Baton Rouge. Her father's summons to come home arrived in May in the form of an invitation to attend Mary's high school graduation. It was followed by a telephone call to the Lincoln Parish extension service where Bonita worked testing recipes and collecting stories about peaches from elderly female residents of the parish.

"Bonita, this is your father. How are you?"

"I'm fine, Daddy. How are you?"

"I'm keeping fit. Did you get the invitation Mary sent?"

"Yes, sir. I did."

"And are you planning to come?"

Bonita hesitated. Although Bonita and Lottie had corresponded often during the years Bonita had been away from home, she badly wanted to see her mother, so she said, "Yes, sir, I'm planning to come."

"Good," her father said. "There's something else we need to discuss while you're here."

When Bonita asked to know what, her father said only, "We'll talk about it when you get home."

Bonita had risen while it was still dark to get a bus that would arrive in Baton Rouge before noon. As the bus drove south in the dawn that moved through shades of red and yellow, calling to mind the beautiful fruit she had so reluctantly left, Bonita felt as if she were dropping down through Louisiana to Baton Rouge as a ripe peach falls to earth. She had spent a long day and part of one night on the bus two months earlier to attend Dr. Daniel Chastain's funeral in New Orleans. Then her only feelings had been grief and loss. Now she felt both excited and anxious as she undertook this journey home, her first since the hearing in 1955 that had exonerated her of Orlando Duplantis's death.

Her father had said he would pick her up at the Greyhound bus station just before noon. He was not there to meet her bus, so Bonita bought a *Morning Advocate,* took her small suitcase, and went out to the curb to wait.

Bonita wore white high-heeled linen shoes, short white gloves, and a white straw hat. Beneath the hat, her hair was short and straight and dark, and the ends headed toward her chin. Her trim blue dress was of a linenlike material that had pink and yellow flowers worked into the weave. In the center of the flower, where the vital organs of a real flower would have been, was a small bound hole.

Bonita was unprepared for the joy she felt when she saw the familiar streets of Baton Rouge. It was wonderful to be home again. Terror streaked through her delight from time to time; not too far away was the building where she had given her statement to the police and then gone before the judge. But the horrors of the past were far outweighed by her happiness when she looked toward the Mississippi River and saw the smokestacks of the freighters heading out for the Gulf and the great white tower of the state capitol building.

Bonita opened the paper and began to read. A car came to a stop next to her, crunching over a broken wine bottle that lay next to the curb. Bonita looked up, expecting to see her father.

"How ya doing?" A man driving a blue Chrysler was smiling at her. He wore a white dress shirt with the sleeves rolled. Thick, curly dark hair filled the open throat of the shirt. He rested one elbow on the open window. The same thick dark hair grew over his forearm. "Need a ride?"

"No, thank you," Bonita said. "Someone's coming to pick me up soon."

"Don't tell me. Let me guess. You're on your way to a wedding?" the man said.

Bonita shook her head.

"Then it must be one of those ladies' things where everybody stands around holding a little coffee cup like this." The man raised the arm that rested on the open window and crooked his little finger. He grinned at her. "Hop in, sweetie," he said. "I'm going all the way to Airline Highway. I can drop you off anywhere along the way. You look too pretty to get all sweaty waiting for a bus."

"No, thank you," Bonita said. "My father will be here in a minute." She opened the newspaper to the society section to see if there were any pictures of people she knew.

"Come on, honey. I'm harmless. You don't want to stand out here in this hot sun. It's no trouble."

"No, I don't want to get in the car with you," Bonita said. "Please leave me alone."

"For Christ's sake. All I'm doing is offering you a ride!" The man pulled his arm into the car, jerked the wheel to the right, and sped away. A piece of broken glass flew up behind him and hit Bonita on the cheek.

There were pictures of someone she knew in the paper. Bonita's mother, Mary, Gracie Davis, and Mabel Davis stood before the fireplace in the Gabriels' living room. The caption beneath the picture read, "Graduates to be honored at luncheon." She was shocked to see how old her mother looked. Quickly, she read the story about the party that was to take place at noon at the Gabriel home before the graduation ceremonies at three o'clock. Bonita closed the paper and folded it. She raised a gloved hand to her face and touched the struck place.

When Bonita's father arrived twenty minutes later, he pulled over to the curb, got out, embraced Bonita, and put her small bag in the backseat of the car. "Sorry I'm late," he said. "I got held up at the hospital." They drove away together.

Bonita thought he seemed much less robust than he had been the last time she had seen him. His fair hair was thinning rapidly, and he had a frown line between his eyes that she did not recall. In spite of the heat, he wore a brown suit, a white shirt, and a brown and gold tie.

"You're looking well," he said. "Your job keeps you busy, I trust."

"Yes, sir."

"There are a few things you need to know before you see anybody in your old neighborhood. The Moaks lost Adam last year," her father said.

"Adam's dead?" Bonita cried. "How did he die?"

"He drowned in the Amite River at a swimming party," Dr. Gabriel said.

Bonita remembered Orlando's admonishments to her and Mary about the dangers of the dark river.

"You might offer Mr. and Mrs. Moak your condolences when you see them," her father said.

"Yes, sir."

"The neighborhood has changed a little. The Landrys moved away this spring," Dr. Gabriel said.

"Where did they go? Did they move back to New Orleans?" Bonita said.

"Oh, no. The great doctor has moved on to bigger and better

things here in Baton Rouge. They built a grand house in one of the new subdivisions out on Jefferson Highway. Baton Rouge has changed a lot, Bonita. You will hardly recognize it."

"It all looks the same to me," Bonita said.

"That's because we're still in familiar territory. There is a lot of new growth to the east and south. A lot of strangers pouring in to work at the plants. Esso's brought in a lot of new people. And Kaiser Aluminum is growing like Topsy."

Bonita touched the newspaper. "You didn't tell me Mary was having a party," she said.

"It's just something your mother and Mabel Davis cooked up for Mary's graduating class. We're very proud of your sister, Bonita. School wasn't easy for her, like it always was for you. It took a lot of work on her part."

Plus a ton of tutoring and a miracle from the nuns, Bonita thought. But aloud she said, "I know." Again she glanced at her father. "What was it you wanted to talk to me about, Daddy?"

"We'll get to that later," Dr. Gabriel said. "I'm glad you're here. I hope you can stay awhile. Tomorrow will be a hard day for your mother—it's your Aunt Diana's birthday. Even after all this time, your mother still grieves about what happened. Especially on the anniversary of Diana's birth."

As they turned onto Oleander Avenue, Bonita glanced at her father. She wondered if he had any idea that it was cruel to tell her this as he was bringing her back to the place where the most painful event of her life had occurred. She would, Bonita thought, have been better off if she had gotten into the blue Chrysler with the smiling stranger.

"I know Mary's glad to have you here for her big day," her father said.

Mary stood in front of the Gabriel house under the oak trees. She wore a white dotted-swiss dress with layers and layers of net petticoats. Bonita knew the fashionable look had returned to slim and straight skirts. The high heels of Mary's white shoes sank into the dirt beneath the oak trees where the grass struggled to grow in the shade. In her arms Mary held a yellow plastic pail. A yellow shovel stood straight up in the pail. As Bonita approached the house, Mary took the shovel from the pail and scattered something into the air.

Bonita averted her eyes from the driveway. "What are you doing?" she called to her sister.

"I'm feeding these crumbs to the grass," Mary said. Mary's blond hair was curled for graduation. Her lipstick was bright red.

"That grass could use some food," Bonita said as she drew close. She looked in the pail. "What's in there?"

"Crackers," said Mary. She dipped into the pail and scattered another shovelful into the air. She stuck her thumb and finger in and put a pinch of crumbs into her mouth. She offered the pail to Bonita. "Want some?"

Bonita took a few and rolled them around between her fingers. "May I give you a hug?"

Mary dipped her shovel into the pail and scattered another shovelful of crackers over the thin pale sprigs of saint augustine grass. "No."

"Not even a little one?"

"No," Mary said.

"Then I guess you don't want any kisses, either," Bonita said.

"Where would it be?" Mary said.

"Just on the cheek."

"I'll think about it," Mary said. "You can say hello to the birds. Tell everything hello—every tree and flower."

Bonita looked up into the green canopy of branches overhead. "Hello, birds. Hello, trees."

"You left out those gardenias. Don't forget them," Mary said.

"Hello, flowers."

"That's better," Mary said. "Now you can tell me congratulations. I'm the high school graduate, and everybody has to tell me congratulations. The birds have told me. The trees and the flowers have told me. Now it's your turn."

Bonita opened her purse and took out a box wrapped in white paper and tied with white ribbon. Tucked under the ribbon was a card that said "Congrats to the grad." She handed it to Mary.

"Thanks," Mary said. "What is it?"

"Open it and see," Bonita said.

"I hope it's a boyfriend," Mary said. "I could use a boyfriend. Everybody who's coming to the luncheon has a boyfriend but me. Is it a boyfriend?"

"No," Bonita said.

Mary opened the present. It took several minutes, and Bonita resisted the impulse to try and help. The box contained a gold bracelet and a round disc charm engraved with "Mary Dollier Gabriel" and the date. Mary put the present in the pail. "I still wish it had been a boyfriend," she said.

"I could hardly get a boy in that little box," Bonita said.

"It could have been a name. It could have been a name of a boy who likes me. A boy who would call me up on the telephone."

"I'm sorry," Bonita said. "I'm sorry that I couldn't get you a boyfriend for graduation."

"That's okay," Mary said. "I forgive you." Her blue eyes sparkled when she talked, but when she fell silent, there was something vacant about her face, as if the spirit animating her had flown out of her mouth with her words.

"Mary?"

"What?"

"Have you made up your mind?"

"You can kiss me. But just a little one." Mary put a hand over her eyes and extended her cheek.

Bonita brushed her lips against her sister's hot face. When they were young and Bonita had occasion to touch her sister—which was seldom, for Mary was very strict about physical contact—Mary always felt flushed. Bonita had always imagined that Mary's body temperature was several degrees higher than her own; that there was some engine racing within her.

"Thanks for inviting me to your graduation," Bonita said.

"Are you coming to see me march to the music this afternoon?"

"Yes," Bonita said. She took the pail from Mary, scooped up some cracker crumbs with the shovel, and threw them into the air. Then she put her hand on Mary's back. The white dotted swiss felt harsh under her fingers. "I'm going in to see Mother," she said.

Bonita's father, who had taken her suitcase inside, met her at the front door. "Bonita," he said. "There's something I have to tell you before you go in."

"What is it, Daddy?"

"Your mother is not well."

"Mimi's sick?" Bonita cried. "Why didn't somebody tell me? What is it?"

"She'll tell you about it herself," her father said.

Bonita stood in the door of her parents' bedroom. The beautiful Lottie they had all adored was gone; in her place was a gaunt woman whose dark hair was heavily streaked with gray. Her mother was so thin that in the red and white dress she wore, she seemed like a child dressed in adult clothing.

"Mimi, what's wrong?" Bonita cried and ran to her mother.

As she moved across the floor to her daughter, Lottie put one hand to her side as if to hold pain at bay. "Bonita," she said. "Come, let me look at you. You're so lovely."

"I look just like Diana. When I look in the mirror, I see her face," Bonita said.

"But you are not like Diana at all, Bonita," her mother said.

Bonita touched Lottie carefully, putting her arms about her mother as if she were something that might be easily broken. How could she have stayed away so long, she wondered. Maybe Dr. Chastain's decision on her behalf had been flawed? "Oh, Mimi, I've missed you so much," Bonita said. Tears ran down her face.

Lottie put both hands on her daughter's cheeks. "I've missed you, too, sweetheart. You'll never know how much. Oh, Bonita, I failed you so badly. Please, please, forgive me."

"I'd forgive you anything, Mimi. You know that." Bonita helped her mother into the rocker next to the bed. "Sit down. Tell me what's wrong."

"I have cancer, Bonita. It started in my ovaries almost six years ago. They removed everything, but it came back. Now it's in my liver. But that's not the worst of it."

"What could be worse than that?" Bonita said. "And why are you having this party?"

"I'm not doing anything for this luncheon. Alma Moak and Mabel Davis have taken over everything. Mary wanted it here so much that I consented. That's not what's on my mind," her mother said. She leaned sideways and reached painfully for the drawer in the bedside table.

"Let me get it," Bonita said.

"There is something in there for you. We need to talk."

Bonita opened the drawer and withdrew a manila folder that had her name on it. "Is this what you want?"

"Yes," her mother said. "Your father has bought the Landrys' house. He wants you to come home now and live in it with Mary after I'm gone. You've seen your sister. This cannot happen, Bonita. Trust me. It will destroy your life. I know. When Diana was so sick and my parents wanted to bring her home from the hospital, they wanted me to come and take care of her. That's when I fled to New York. It was only after she died that I came home. I came back to marry your father because I loved him so much, but you must not come back. As soon as we are finished with our talk, I want you to go."

"I can't leave you, Mimi," Bonita said.

"You have to, Bonita. If you stay here even a day, your father will convince you it's your duty to look after your sister. It's what he believes—that the family has to be responsible for all of its members."

"But it is my duty, Mimi," Bonita said. "I've caused everybody so much trouble. And I know it cost a lot of money for me to be in the hospital and to go to private school. I owe him something."

"That's what he will tell you, Bonita, but you owe him nothing. Your hospitalization was covered by our insurance, and I paid for your schooling. Your father has brought this on himself. He would not listen to anybody. When Dr. Chastain predicted that Mary would grow worse, and tried to get him to bring us all down there and get some help, your father was livid. The last time I saw him that angry was when we were all together with Larry Landry in front of the judge. Bonita, I am so sorry I let that happen to you."

"It wasn't your fault. It was mine. I never should have taken that gun," Bonita said.

"Well, I can help you now," her mother said. "When you went into the hospital, I got in touch with an old friend. Remember when I used to tell you about my college production of *La Bohème*?"

Bonita nodded.

"Wesley Stafford was Rodolfo. He's been practicing law in Baton Rouge for years now, though God knows why he wasted that beautiful voice. I wanted someone your father didn't know. The minute you entered DePaul, I called Wes and we set up a trust fund for you. Your father has always insisted that I keep the money I brought to our marriage separate. He didn't want to be accused of having married me for my money. Your grandparents left me a substantial amount, Bonita. It's not part of our community property, so I can dispose of it as I wish. I've made a will dividing it between you and Mary. There's already enough interest accrued to support you without your having to work. You're going to have to disappear," her mother said. "Today."

"But Mary's counting on me coming to see her graduate," Bonita said.

"Here is Wesley's card. I've called him and told him what I want you to do. I want you to go see him now. He is waiting at his office for you. He will help you find a place to stay. Now open that white envelope," her mother said.

Bonita did as she was told and gasped.

"I've been accumulating cash for you so you will have plenty when you need it."

"There are hundreds of dollars here, Mimi," Bonita said.

"Two thousand dollars," Lottie said. "I had Wesley open a savings account for you. Here's the passbook. It has over ten thousand dollars in it. Bonita, your freedom is all I have to give you now. Your father is going to have to deal with the decisions he made about Mary himself. Now let me kiss you one last time."

Bonita put her arms about her mother's frail body and wept.

"Go, Bonita," her mother said. "Go, call a cab and don't look back."

When Bonita left her mother's room wiping her eyes, there was a gaggle of girls in fluffy pastel dresses gathered about the telephone, giggling. While Bonita waited for them to finish, she looked into the other part of the house at the preparations for the luncheon. The living room, and dining room were filled with eight card tables covered with starched and ironed white cutwork cloths. Each table was set for four with Bonita's grandmother's china and crystal.

Everything that was ornamental in the Gabriel living room curved. The corners of the mantel were rounded. The valances above the draped windows were carved with pairs of iris turning toward a stylized sun.

More girls were arriving for the luncheon. Mary met them at the door and handed each girl a small corsage composed of a white carnation and a miniature mortarboard. As Mary bent her head to pin the flower on each girl's shoulder, her slender, curved neck became part of the design of the room, and Bonita briefly imagined that the woodwork sprang to life and the house itself moved to camouflage Mary among her graceful classmates.

But soon Mary's voice rose above the rest. Her jerky movements interrupted the pattern. It became so painful for Bonita to watch that she turned away.

Bonita went to look for her father. In the kitchen she was embraced and welcomed home by Mabel Davis and Alma Moak. After offering her condolences on Adam's death, as her father had suggested, Bonita asked if anyone knew where her father was. Mrs. Moak said he was probably in the bedroom at the back of the house.

My bedroom, Bonita thought. The door was closed. She knocked.

Her father opened the door.

"Why didn't you tell me Mother was sick?" Bonita said.

"She didn't want you to know," he said.

"Someone should have told me," Bonita said.

"That's what I wanted to talk to you about. I think you should come home now, Bonita. I'm going to need some help. I've picked up the Landrys' old house at a pretty good price. I was thinking of renting it for the extra income, but you and Mary could live together in it right across the street," her father said. "It would be ideal."

"What about my work, Daddy?" Bonita said.

"Maybe you can get on at the state capitol. I know plenty of people in the Ag Department. But it will probably have to be part-time, because I'll need you to be at home with Mary most of the time. Particularly this summer, while I look after your mother."

Bonita looked over her shoulder.

"Maybe we should talk about this at a more appropriate time," her father said.

"Yes, sir," Bonita said.

Near the telephone, one girl, taller than the others and dressed in black, detached herself from the group, frowning. When she saw Bonita in the doorway, she came quickly to her, took her by the arm, led her into Mary's room, and closed the door. "I have to talk to you. Do you know who I am?"

The girl wore a linen sheath similar in cut to the blue dress Bonita wore. "You're Laurel," Bonita said.

"I had nothing to do with this. I want you to know that," Laurel said.

Laurel, whose hair Bonita remembered as ginger-colored, the color of her father's beard, had been highlighted with brighter blond strands and gathered in a knot on her crown so that the effect was of sun glinting on her head. Just as they had when she was a child, little tendrils of hair escaped about her ears and softened the still overly round face with the too thin lips.

A string of pearls followed the neckline of Laurel's dress, and the bun at the top of her head was secured with an elasticized double strand of pearls. She wore no other jewelry. Laurel didn't in the least resemble her mother, and Bonita could catch only glimpses of Dr. Landry in his daughter's coloring. It seemed to Bonita that Laurel had made a totally separate person of herself, one who was neither her mother nor her father, and in so doing had made a clean getway from her family, while she, Bonita, was doomed to be an authentic reproduction of her dead aunt.

"Anything to do with what?" Bonita said.

"Gracie and some of the other girls have talked Gracie's cousin into calling Mary and asking her out on a date. She's so desperate for a boyfriend she'll do anything. She's been talking about wanting a boyfriend the whole year."

"Is it a real date? Maybe she should go," Bonita said. "Is he a nice boy?"

"Of course it's not a real date. I don't know if he's nice or not. I've never laid eyes on him. He can't be too nice to participate in a mean joke like this," Laurel said. "I swear to you, Bonita. I had nothing to do with it. I've tried to stop them, but they won't listen."

"So it's a trick?" Bonita said. She turned away, opened Mary's door, and walked out.

Lottie was standing in the doorway of her room watching. "Bonita! Go!" her mother said.

Bonita glanced at her mother. The telephone rang, and the giggling girls scattered. Her mother closed the door of her bedroom. Mary ran from the living room to answer it, high heels thudding heavily on the old wood floor.

"This is Mary Gabriel," Bonita heard her sister say. "When? When did you see me? You did? You liked me?" There was silence while Mary listened. "I'm having a party right now. It's for my graduation. I'm a high school graduate." Silence. "I know where it is. Yes, I'll meet you there. No, I won't tell anybody." Bonita heard the click of the telephone being replaced.

"Mary," she called.

Mary turned around.

"Who was that?" Bonita said.

"It's a secret," said Mary.

"Mary, are you going somewhere?" Bonita said.

"In a little while," Mary said.

"But you have company. You can't go off. You have to stay here for the party."

"I know," Mary said.

"And the graduation rehearsal. You have to go to the graduation ceremony at three o'clock. You have to march to the music," Bonita said.

"I know," Mary said. But she looked past Bonita's head, and Bonita knew her sister's mind was elsewhere.

"Mary," Bonita said. She put her hand on her sister's arm. "Listen to me. It's a trick. Those girls are playing a trick on you."

"It wasn't a girl. It was a boy."

Mary shrugged away from Bonita's touch and went to the buffet in the dining room, where she scuffled through cocktail napkins, half-used boxes of birthday candles, and tarnished demitasse spoons until she found a bus token.

"I'm going to meet my new boyfriend," Mary said and walked out the door.

Bonita ran after her sister. "No, Mary," she cried. "Don't go."

When Mary reached the sidewalk, she took off her shoes and began to run. Bonita paused by one of the old oak trees near her house and, leaning against it, removed first one and then the other white linen shoe. She left them in the grass and ran down the sidewalk after her sister in her stocking feet.

The mimosa tree in the St. Germains' front yard was in full bloom. It had grown so large and its limbs so heavy that a bough loaded with the sweet spiny flowers blocked Bonita's path. Bonita ran around it onto the grass and saw Mary turn the corner. By the time Bonita got there, Mary was gone.

Bonita stood in the street panting. Then she turned, walked back the way she had come in her torn stockings, plucked her shoes from the grass beneath the tree, and, again braced by the oak, put them back on. She mounted the steps and went in the front door, passing through the party just as each girl was finding her place at the tables. She retrieved her small suitcase from outside her mother's closed bedroom door, went to the telephone, and called a cab.

Her father came from the kitchen. "Everything's ready. Alma and Mabel have the plates served and the iced tea in the glasses, but we can't find Mary. Bonita, where is your sister?"

Bonita thought of her father's persistent refusals to get help for Mary, of Dr. Chastain's warning, and she said, "I don't know, Daddy. I have no idea where Mary might be." She picked up her bag, walked out of the house, and left him there.

Chapter
Twenty-three

October 1995

Daddy had a furrow between his eyes that the embalmer had been unable to smooth away.

"He looks alive," Mary said.

"He does, doesn't he?" I said.

We stood together before Daddy's coffin. It was past six o'clock; past time for the evening calling to begin. Good, I thought. Maybe no one will come.

Mary was neatly dressed in a black skirt, white blouse, and a long black jacket with pockets on each side that I had taken from my own closet. I had tucked one of Mother's embroidered handkerchiefs into one pocket and a small comb and a lipstick into the other. Mary wore black shoes with small flat heels.

"He looks like he could just sit up and talk," she said.

"But he can't sit up and talk. He's gone, Mary."

I darted a look at Mary as I said this. Her face was composed, but I could feel that she wanted to say more. I watched her struggle with her need to deny his death. Finally, in an act of will that I had to admire, Mary said, "Tell Daddy good-bye."

"Bye, Daddy," I said.

Mary nodded.

"The casket is beautiful," I said. "You made a good choice."

Mary looked pleased. "I did, didn't I?"

In the persistent cherry light of the funeral home's chapel, the rose-colored coffin glowed. The flowers surrounding it absorbed any indignity that sprang from its unusual tint. Indeed, it seemed more at home in its bower than a darker, woodier coffin might have been. The entire tableau pleased the eye, struck the right balance between what was alive and what no longer lived.

Mary touched the bouquet of white lilies she had chosen for Daddy's coffin. "These are pretty," she said.

"They are beautiful. You have good taste," I said.

Mary was silent for a long time. I heard the door on our left open. It was a powerful door and covered with tufted leather just like the door to the chapel at the Academy of the Holy Angels: when it closed, it sounded less like a door closing than the lid to a chest coming down.

Mary began to sing softly to our father, "So long, it's been good to know you."

I heard footsteps. Someone was approaching us. My heart pounded. "Sshh. Someone's here," I said. "Behind us."

Mary whirled to face Mr. and Mrs. Moak. When they embraced her, she beamed with pleasure. I had seen Mrs. Moak earlier, so I was not surprised by her dignified descent into old age, but Mr. Moak's appearance surprised me. He looked exactly like his son had looked when Adam and I were five years old and riding our tricycles along the sidewalk in front of our house. I wanted to tell them I was sorry that Adam had drowned so young and that I missed him, but I didn't.

Soon all of the neighbors who lived on Oleander Avenue in our childhood began to arrive. Mary and I stood together in the alcove for the family as they came to speak to us. Jim Singleton hovered nearby. Occasionally, when someone seemed to agitate Mary, he led him or her gently away with a remark on the weather or on the finer points of the race for governor.

Earlier, I had suggested to Mary a few sentences she might say: "It's nice to see you after so many years." Or "I'm sorry we have to meet again on such a sad occasion." Mary was not long content with such simple sentiments. Soon I heard her embellishing them. "Thank you for coming to this sad occasion. I wish we could meet again and again and again," she said to Mrs. Fish.

She told Gracie Davis's father that he looked as peaceful as Daddy did and maybe it wouldn't be too long before he was dead and in a coffin, too, and did he like that color because she had picked it out herself and she would be happy to pick one out for him if he wanted her to. At this point I put my hand on her arm to stem the flow of words and gave Mr. Davis an apologetic smile. He moved away quickly.

I dutifully asked after all of the children we had known. Frankie St. Germain was no longer known as Frankie, of course, but my calling him that made Mrs. St. Germain smile.

"Frank is an attorney in Atlanta. He married a beautiful girl from Marietta, and we have six lovely grandchildren."

Mrs. St. Germain told us that she was very lonely because she had lost her husband the year before. "You are fortunate to have your sister so close," she said. I looked at her to see if these words were ironic, because Mary had just told her that she wished Frankie lived in Baton Rouge so he could be her boyfriend; that she needed a new boyfriend because her old one had died.

Adrienne Fish was married to an architect and lived in New Orleans. Gracie Davis was married to a dermatologist and lived in Shreveport. No one mentioned Laurel Landry.

Finally, there was a lull, and Mrs. Moak whispered to me that she would take Mary out for a little air if I wanted to go and get a cup of coffee. I was grateful to her and went to the kitchen, prepared a plate with a few of the sandwiches Mrs. Moak and Mrs. St. Germain had brought, and let myself into Jim Singleton's office with the key he had given me.

I sat down at Jim's desk and slowly sipped my coffee. It felt good to be by myself for a little while. I hadn't been there too long when there was a knock at the door. I opened it. A tall man with blue eyes and thinning light-colored hair, wearing a dark suit that emphasized his heavy, slightly stooped shoulders, stood there. It was someone I knew, I just couldn't think who. But I recognized his voice the moment he said my name.

"Gerry Winborn," I said, and without a moment's hesitation, I stepped forward and hugged him hard. "I'm so glad to see you."

"How are you holding up?" he said.

"Better than I thought I would," I said. "Thank you for coming. And thank you for saying you would lead the way when we take Daddy to the cemetery."

"I guided cars for hundreds of funerals in my younger days, but this is the first time I ever felt I was the only one meant to do it. I would have done it for your mother, but I was at a law-enforcement seminar in California when she died. I'm sorry for your loss, Bonita," he said.

I looked in his face and saw the boy I had seen for the first time in the hall at the Academy of the Holy Angels. It is possible to fall in love when you are eleven years old and love that one person for your whole life. "I'm sorry for our loss, Gerry," I said.

"Where did you go?" he said. "I looked everywhere for you. Every lawman in the state of Louisiana was looking high and low for your sister that day, and I was scouring the countryside looking for you. I knew you had come home for Mary's graduation because I talked to your mother. She said you had come in on the bus a few hours earlier. And then, of course, we interviewed all of Mary's friends who were at the luncheon."

"Friends," I said. "That's a nice name for them."

"I know what they did to Mary was terrible, but my big worry was not for your sister. There were plenty of people worrying about her. You were my first concern. I didn't know how you were going to take it after all you'd been through. I wanted to find you so badly. So you wouldn't have to go through all that pain by yourself. But you just disappeared. It felt like you had vanished from the face of the earth," Gerry said.

"That was the worst day of my life," I said. "Worse even than the day I shot—"

Gerry shook his head. "Don't," he said. "Don't talk about that. I can't tell you how many hours I spent regretting that I didn't stay longer that day. While PeeWee and I were riding our bicycles away, laughing and talking about how excited you and Sandra were about those jewelry boxes, something terrible was happening to you. I've never forgiven myelf. If only I had stayed there longer. Maybe it wouldn't have happened."

"Maybe I would have shot you instead. Did you ever consider that?" I said. "Because you would have tried to take that gun away from me. You know you would have. Truly, Gerry, I was always glad you were safely gone. So it wouldn't have been you that I killed."

Gerry put his arm around my shoulder and held my head against his chest. Finally he said, "Tell me what happened when you came back home for Mary's graduation. Where did you go that day?"

"First I did what my mother told me to do—I went to see her lawyer, and then I went to the Alamo Plaza."

"I looked there," Gerry said. "I checked every motel in the city."

"I gave them a made-up name. I told them my name was Florette Duplantis," I said. "Actually, that was not the worst day of my life. The worst day was the next day, when I picked up the paper and there were those horrible headlines: LOCAL DOCTOR'S DAUGHTER AB-DUCTED. Abducted. That is the ugliest word in the whole language. You see, I didn't know what had happened until I saw the newspaper.

When Daddy asked me if I knew where my sister was and I told him I didn't know—that was a lie. I knew what those girls had done. Laurel told me. And I heard Mary on the telephone. I tried to keep her from leaving the party, but when Daddy asked me, as if it were my responsibility to know exactly where my sister was every minute of the day, I got so angry with him that I told him I didn't know and I walked out. I'm sure you don't know it, but he had bought the Landrys' house so I could move in with Mary and be her keeper. And then when they found her in that sugarcane field, and they put that picture in the paper of her lying there naked and bloody, it was more than I could handle. Who let that happen? Who would ever print a picture like that?"

"I was there when they found her, Bonita. I did my best to keep the newspaper people out, but one photographer got by us. I tried to get his camera. I promise you I did all I could to get the film. My dad had to pull me off of him."

"I don't remember much about what I did after that. I wanted to go see Mary in the hospital, but I couldn't face my father, so I just disappeared."

"Where did you go?" Gerry said.

"I wandered all over the state. I must have been totally out of my mind for months. My mother had provided enough money in trust so I didn't have to work. I got it into my head that I had to visit every parish in Louisiana. I wanted to walk on the ground. I started in Caddo and worked my way back and forth across the state. I would stop at some farmer's house and ask him if I could walk on his land for a while. I think word must have gotten out that there was some crazy woman saying she was from the State Department of Agriculture asking to walk around in their fields. People were amazingly gracious to me. The women almost always insisted that I stay for a meal. Mostly it was for lunch, the big meal of the day. All of the field hands would come in and we would eat the most delicious food. I would thank them and then set out for the next stop. I read the Baton Rouge paper every day that I could and only interrupted this routine when my mother died. I came to Baton Rouge just long enough for her funeral and then took off again.

"When I got to the southern parishes and I started to run into the sugarcane fields, I was in big trouble. I started looking for blood. And when I got to Ascension Parish and found the actual plantation where that bastard took Mary and raped her and beat her and almost killed her, I freaked out." I stopped talking and sat down in the chair behind Jim's desk.

"Bonita, stop it," Gerry said. "You don't have to put yourself through this for me. I didn't mean for you to have to account for everything."

"I can't stop now," I said. "I saw the guy who kidnapped her, you know. I had seen him while I was waiting for my father to pick me up and take me home for the luncheon. This man stopped and tried to get me to get in the car with him, only I knew better. Mary didn't. He was still cruising, looking, and he found her. He was driving a blue Chrysler and he had these hairy, hairy arms."

"Yes," Gerry said. "That's how Mary identified him."

"I would have killed him if I could have gotten to him, but you all had him locked up tight by that time," I said. "So there was nothing I could do but wander until I eventually got to the place where he took her. I guess that was where I was headed all along." I put my head down on Jim Singleton's desk.

"You don't have to go on with this," Gerry said.

I raised my head. "I want to tell you what happened to me in Ascension Parish, Gerry," I said.

"What did happen to you in Ascension Parish?" Gerry said. He reached across the desk and took my right hand.

"I wouldn't get off the guy's land. I got down on my hands and knees in the place where I was convinced I had found Mary's blood and I started to talk to the Mother of God, I told her exactly how I felt about her letting something like that happen to Mary, who was named for her, for God's sake, and for letting it happen on a piece of ground in a place with a name that was supposed to give us all something to hope for. We, too, would ascend to heaven like her precious son did! And look what she had let happen there! I never forgave her. And that's when I think I died. I stayed on in my flesh, but for all practical purposes, I was dead."

"What did those people do?" Gerry said.

"The wife called the sheriff, and he came and got me and put me in the hospital in Donaldsonville. It wasn't all that far from where my mother had grown up. They all knew the Dollier family. And the doctor who took care of me knew my father. He wanted to call Daddy to come and get me, and I told him that if he called my father, I would kill myself. And he knew I wasn't kidding."

"Then what happened?"

"I pulled myself back together. Went back to work in Lincoln Parish. I was married briefly. Very briefly. And just let the rest of my life go by. I came back here in 1970. I don't really know why."

There was another knock on the door. I stood up.

Gerry opened the door and Steve Scott looked in. "Hello, Winborn. How's it going?"

The two men shook hands and Gerry said, "I'd better be going. I'll see you tomorrow, Bonita." He patted my shoulder. "Promise me you'll call if you need me."

"Thank you, Gerry," I said. "For everything."

"Don't run off on my account, Gerry" Steve said. "I just wanted to tell Bonita that the pallbearers are all lined up for tomorrow morning. Once word got out, Jim said he had doctors calling him from all over the state, wanting to know what they could do to help. We recruited six of the ones who seemed to know your dad best. Just wanted to let her know."

Gerry kissed my cheek and left. I sat down again.

As we talked, Steve Scott looked at me with such a compassionate, steady gaze that I was reminded of Daniel Chastain.

"You've really been such a help to us—to Mary and me both. I don't know how to thank you," I said.

"There are a lot of people out there," Steve Scott said. "Your father had a lot of friends."

"It's nice to have so many of his friends come by, but trying to keep a lid on everything that comes out of Mary's mouth is wearing me out," I said.

"I know," he said.

"She told one of our former neighbors that he might soon be dead, too, and she volunteered to pick out a coffin for him."

Steve Scott laughed. "I'll bet he didn't stick around long," he said.

I laughed, too. "No, he left pretty fast."

"I'm glad you decided to go through with plans for a funeral. And for letting people come by tonight. I think it's good for both you and your sister to see that people cared about your father. And about both of you, too." Dr. Scott opened the door and said, "Don't forget. You promised me one of those new fruit books," and then he left.

In the chapel Jim Singleton was talking to a short, stout woman in a black dress who wore a beautiful orange silk shawl covered with embroidered red flowers. When he saw me come back in, Jim raised his hand without interrupting his conversation and beckoned me with his forefinger.

When I joined Jim and the woman he was talking to, he said, "You remember Sandra Bonifanti, don't you?"

"Of course," I said immediately. I remembered Sandra, but I didn't recognize her. I could see no remnant of the girl who had twirled in her uniform down the hall of the Academy of the Holy Angels, excited because the eighth-grade boys were coming to set up the chairs for assembly. What I did see was an extremely sophisticated stranger who, instead of dressing to conceal her age and her weight, chose instead to emphasize it with a silver streak through her dark hair and an unearthly amount of beaded jewelry. In addition to the orange scarf with the embroidered red flowers, beads of every color hung down her ample chest and about her thick wrists. She looked at me with the most alert eyes I had ever seen, but still I didn't recognize the old Sandra until she looked around the chapel and said, "God, I love funerals. All kinds of people come out of the woodwork, and you find out the most interesting stuff. That's one of the reason I moved back to B.R. In New York, when I read the obituaries, I never knew any of the people who had died. Here at home somebody's dying all the time."

I smiled because there she was: the old Sandra, the girl who, like Florette, didn't give a damn what other people thought. Then I saw the slightly pocked cheeks under the heavy makeup. "These god-damned pimples," I remember her saying in the girls' bathroom, and how she had shocked me. I laughed out loud and hugged Sandra, I was so glad to see her. "You haven't changed a bit," I said.

Sandra laughed. "I know. Isn't it awful? We could go back this very minute to Sister Genevieve's class and be elected hall monitors and nothing would really be any different."

"Nothing," I said.

"And everything," Sandra said.

"I hear you're really good at what you do," I said. "Jim told me how much he and his wife like your work."

Sandra looked surprised but pleased. She punched Jim on the arm. "I didn't know you knew anything about art, PeeWee," she said.

"I knew enough to buy the most expensive thing in the show," Jim said.

Sandra patted his wrist. "I'm just teasing you. You and Suzanne bought my favorite thing."

"It's called *Blue Luncheon*," Jim said to me. "You'll have to come see it. It's huge. It takes up a whole wall in our living room. Suzanne adores it. The whole picture is done in different shades of blue. It's three little girls sitting at a table eating something."

"Four," Sandra said.

"Four what?" Jim said.

"There are four little girls. One of them is hidden in the shadows. You have to look really hard to see her," Sandra said. "It's like one of those pages from our activity books at school—'Hidden in this picture is a cloud, a star, and a child. Can you find them?' Remember those?"

I nodded.

"You never told me that," Jim said. "Are these real people?" I mean, are these children someone I'm supposed to know?"

"It's a memory picture," Sandra said. "So it's full of distortions. Actually, it's my impression of those luncheons Mrs. Matens used to have out on her screened porch when she wanted to try out her menu on us before her bridge parties. Remember, Bonita, everything was always blue and white? It's Denise and Darlene and Bonita and me. Bonita's the one in the shadows that you can't make out."

"I'll be a son of a bitch," Jim said. "Wait until I tell Suzanne. You should have told me this, Sandra."

"Would you still have wanted it?" Sandra said.

"Hell, yes. I'd have paid twice what you asked," Jim said. "Excuse me, ladies. I want to find my wife and tell her this."

"How come you never came to New York to see me?" Sandra said to me. "I kept waiting for you to come so I could show you all around."

"I wish I could have," I said. "I've never even been out of Louisiana."

"Where have you been all this time?" she said.

"In full retreat," I said. "How long have you been back in Baton Rouge?"

"Two years. I like it. I like going places and moving in and out of the past to get there," Sandra said.

"But not all memories are good ones," I said.

"I know," Sandra said kindly. "I've thought about you a million times. When I moved back here, I hoped we could get together. I tried to find you, but I figured you had married, and I didn't know your name. I even called up Gerry Winborn. I think he knew where you were, but he wouldn't tell me."

"I was only married for a little while," I said. "What about you? Did you ever get married?"

Sandra held up three fingers. "This many times," Sandra said.

"Any success?" I said.

"Not once!" Sandra said.

We both laughed, but then Sandra took my elbow and moved a step closer. "Listen," she said softly. "There's something I've been wanting to tell you for a long time. I'm glad to get the chance to do it. You remember Laurel Landry?"

I said, "She's not here, is she?"

"I seriously doubt she'll show her face," Sandra said. "Wait'll you hear what I'm going to tell you. I got this from my cousin in New Orleans. You remember I was born there and didn't move to Baton Rouge until we were in fifth grade."

"I remember that," I said.

"Well, I still have a lot of family out in Gentilly," Sandra said. "And this is what they told me. The first thing you have to know about is Laurel's mother. Did you ever meet Ellen Landry?"

"No. Daddy and Mother had a coffee the day after they moved into the neighborhood, but she didn't show up."

"That's no big surprise. She was a major loon," Sandra said.

"I saw her twice," I said.

"I didn't know anybody ever saw her," Sandra said.

"She didn't know I saw her. The first time, I snuck in their house while Laurel was upstairs looking for some games for us to play."

"What did you see?" Sandra said. Her eyes were alight with a kind of unholy interest. It occurred to me that I shouldn't be telling this story, but I ignored that and went on.

"She was sitting with her back to me in a corner of the downstairs bedroom, playing jacks. This was the day of our party, and Laurel and her father had told us that she was too tired from moving in to come. But it was really scary. She didn't have a stitch on. And not only was she naked, but all of the clocks in the kitchen were covered with black cloth. Those were the only ones I saw, but I'll bet every clock in that house was covered. I always wondered why. I guess that's one mystery that will never be solved. Anyway, I got the hell out of there, she scared me so bad."

"I don't blame you," Sandra said. "Did you tell?"

"Not until later. Laurel told me that her daddy said there was something wrong with Mary. She said he said she should be tested, and of course, he was right all along. And then he said that my mother should see a psychiatrist because she was the one who was making Mary sick."

"That's what they thought back then," Sandra said. "That it was all the parents' fault. Can you imagine how horrible that must have been for your parents: not only was your sister sick, everybody was going to tell them it was their fault. But being a psychiatrist and knowing stuff didn't do Laurel's daddy much good, from what my cousin told me."

"What did she tell you?" I said.

"While I was in New York, and you were God knows where, Ellen Landry stabbed him and went after Laurel, too."

"Jesus Christ! Dead?"

Laurel nodded. "Stabbed him twenty-two times. She got Laurel pretty good, too. Severed all of the tendons in her right arm. Laurel lost the use of her right hand."

I remembered Laurel's chubby hand holding the pencil as she laboriously wrote her name on the piece of paper I had torn from my spelling notebook so many years ago. Then I thought of how Dr. Landry had come to my rescue after I shot Orlando. "What happened to her mother?"

"Killed herself," Sandra said.

I felt sick. "This makes me feel terrible." I moved a few steps away and leaned against the wall.

"Shit," Sandra said. "I'm sorry, Bonita. I didn't mean to upset you. I just wanted you to know that you were right to react to Laurel the way you did. There was something wrong in that house. Something really wrong."

Mrs. Moak touched me on the arm. "Bonita, may I speak to you privately for just a minute?"

Mary, I thought. Where was Mary? "Sandra," I said. "Do you see Mary anywhere?"

"She's right over there talking to the twins. Don't worry so much about her. She's doing fine."

And to my relief, Mary did look fine. Perfectly composed, she was talking to Denise and Darlene as if she moved about in this world all the time.

"Would you mind keeping an eye on her while I go talk to Mrs. Moak?" I said.

Sandra said, "Sure."

Alma Moak and I walked to the last row of pews and sat down together on the red velvet cushion. Mrs. Moak put her hand on my arm. "After the funeral in the morning, I know that you'll probably want to invite people back to the house for something light to eat."

I knew Mrs. Moak was telling me what I was expected to do, and my first reaction was to say that I had no intention of inviting people to come back to Daddy's house, but I held my tongue.

"A ten o'clock funeral always breaks up at an awkward time—just in time for lunch. Leona Fish and Mabel Davis and I would like to take care of the food. With your permission, we would like to go back to the house early, not go to the cemetery after the service here, and get things set up. Would you mind if we did that?"

"Not a bit," I said, "I think that would be a nice thing to do. People have to eat."

"And they like to be together for a little while longer after they leave the cemetery," Alma Moak said.

I knew she spoke from experience, and I was grateful for her guidance.

"There's comfort in the crowd," she said.

We both looked at the people standing in the chapel talking while Daddy lay at the head of the room, waxen and quiet. It was as if we were having a party and completely ignoring him. But of course that was an illusion. His absence was the strongest presence in the room. No one could ignore that coffin; his silence and those banks of flowers.

"You'll find most of the crystal and china gone," I said. "Mary threw it in the trash can yesterday. She broke almost everything."

"Oh, we use paper plates now. And paper napkins," Alma Moak said. "We'll just need a few serving pieces and some silverware."

When two women dressed identically in black linen approached us, Alma Moak patted my arm and stood. "Don't worry about a thing, Bonita. We'll take care of it," she said and left me alone with Denise and Darlene Matens.

I stood also. The two women looked at me, one with her head cocked to the left, the other with her head bent to the right. Denise and Darlene were almost completely unchanged. Both of their faces were unlined, and the pair of them still retained the innocent enthusiasm they had radiated when I knew them at school.

"We're so sorry about your father," Denise said. "He was such a wonderful doctor."

"I know he missed your mother so much after she died," Darlene said. "We used to see him walking after dinner. He told me once he tried to get in three miles a day."

"I didn't know he was a walker," I said. "Thank you for telling me that."

"Oh, yes, he loved to walk," Darlene said.

"If you saw him often, you must live nearby," I said.

"Yes," Darlene said. "We live just around the corner on Lantana Street."

"We live next door to each other," Denise said. "Our children grew up practically in each other's pockets. Our husbands are in business together."

"They ship seafood all over the world," Darlene said.

"Do you play bridge?" Denise said.

"No," I said. "I don't know how."

"We'll teach you," Darlene said. "And then you can come to one of our bridge-club luncheons. Denise has a big family room and she can handle four tables. We meet once a month and we can always use a substitute."

I preferred to think of them playing bridge on a screened porch, but I guessed no one did that anymore.

"Would you like to learn to play?" Darlene said.

"Yes," I heard myself say. "Yes, I would. Do you still serve chicken Kiev and melon balls in ginger ale?"

"You remembered our mother's favorite menu," Denise said. She turned to her sister. "Imagine remembering that after all these years."

I didn't say that because of the way I had chosen to live my life, it seemed to me as though it had just been yesterday.

"That's exactly what we served last month," Denise said.

"Your mother was certainly a good cook," I said.

"She was, wasn't she?" Darlene said.

"Bonita," Denise said, "Darlene has a nice voice, and sometimes I play for her to sing at the weddings and funerals of people who are special to us. If it meets with your approval, we would like to do something for your father. Is there something he was particularly fond of?"

I was touched to think that my father was special to them, but said, "You'll have to talk to Mary about that. She's the one who knows music."

I called Mary over and the twins repeated their request.

Looking absolutely normal, Mary gave their idea some thought. " 'Crossing the Bar,' " she said. "He liked 'Crossing the Bar.' "

"Yes, we could do that," Denise said. She turned to her sister. "Shall we give it a try?"

The Matens twins nodded, and Mary walked away singing in a strong voice, "Sunset and evening star, and one clear call for me."

I was getting tired. After the Matens twins—or whatever their names were now—moved away, I looked around to see if I could decently call it quits and go home. Then I remembered I had told Mary she could spend the night in the house on Oleander and I had to look after her until the funeral was over tomorrow. There were still hours and hours to go before I could relax and let go of her.

Sandra came through the door that led to the kitchen. Again I had the odd sensation of watching an eleven-year-old girl in a fifty-two-year-old woman's body.

"Mrs. Rather is getting a little out of hand," she said. "I think it's time she said good night."

"What's she done now?" I said.

"She's hit the coffee urn about seven times in the last thirty minutes, and now she's plotting her trip to New York to join her husband. I've been trying to tell her that New York's not all it's cracked up to be, especially if you don't have any money. She doesn't have any money, does she?"

"Not now." I had retrieved my wallet from Mary's pocket and most of the money. When I called to tell Johnella I had Mary under my wing again, and to get permission to keep her out until after the funeral, I had assured her Mary was cash-free.

"Are you taking her back to a secure place for the night?" Sandra said.

I shook my head. "I told her she could sleep in her old room at home if she didn't tell people she was married to Dan Rather and that Daddy was still alive and talking to her."

"Well, you're going to need some help. She's way too wired to sleep. You look worn out. Why don't I come home with you and watch Mary while you sleep for a while? Then you can get up early and I'll get a few hours before the funeral. What time is the service?"

"Ten o'clock," I said.

"You sleep until five o'clock, and then I'll get you up so I can grab a few hours. I used to be able to go all night, but those days are long gone," Sandra said.

So Sandra and I took turns watching over Mary, and I slept a few hours in my childhood bed.

At ten o'clock the next morning, the priest from Daddy's parish said a few nice things about him and gave a brief homily. Mary and I sat together out of sight and listened as Darlene, accompanied by Denise on the small organ behind the podium, sang "Crossing the Bar," and Sandra, at my request, read Longfellow's poem "Curfew." We followed Daddy's body out to the circular driveway, watching while the pallbearers loaded his coffin into a silver hearse, and there, waiting for us at the head of the column of cars, was Gerry Winborn sitting astride a motorcycle. Unlike the black-uniformed deputy Mary and I had seen on our first day together, Gerry wore the blue of the Baton Rouge City Police; and where the other man's black glasses had given me back only my own gaze, Gerry held his helmet under his arm as he waited for us to assemble. His eyes were not hidden from me. We looked at each other as Mary got into the gray limousine behind the hearse. I continued to look back over my shoulder at him even after Jim touched my elbow and told me the time had come to go. Gerry put on his helmet, brought his foot down in a quick movement that brought his motorcycle to life, and slowly led us to the place where Daddy would be buried.

Jim had placed a green canopy over the burial plot and set up half a dozen folding chairs for the family within its shade. Daddy's casket rested on a bier over the waiting grave. I asked Sandra and the Matens twins to sit there with Mary and me. There was one chair unfilled.

Gerry Winborn stood apart, his helmet under his arm, in the shade of one of the old oaks. While the men who had driven the limousine and the hearse arranged the flowers around the foot of the grave, I walked over and said, "Could you help us through this last part? Would you come sit with us?"

Gerry sat down between Mary and me. We each took one of his hands and held fast to it as the priest conducted the rites that would take our father from us forever.

After the funeral, Mrs. Moak, Mrs. Davis, and Mrs. Fish had food ready for us at the house on Oleander. The dining table was pushed against the wall under the windows; at one end was the silver coffee service, at the other a punch bowl of warm, amber Russian tea surrounded by crystal punch cups. On the buffet were platters of sandwiches, raw cauliflower, carrots and broccoli, and peeled and sectioned satsumas surrounding a fluted bowl filled with sweet orange-flavored cream cheese and toasted almonds. It was such a grotesque parody of the party my parents had given to welcome the Landrys to the neighborhood that I left Mary to do whatever she might think up, went into my old room, and sat down on my bed. I could hear people talking outside my door, could hear footsteps banging across the metal grate of the floor furnace, and then a knock.

"There's someone here to see you," Mrs. Moak said when I opened it. I looked past Mrs. Moak's shoulder and saw an overweight, middle-aged woman in a black dress with dark smudges beneath her eyes and deep wrinkles about her mouth. She might have been pretty once, but now she looked tired and old. I caught a glimpse of a different but similar face in my memory; I recognized the particular set of those lips, those hazel eyes, and the plump cheeks. Laurel Landry.

What on earth did I have to say to her? I could have gone the rest of my life without ever laying my eyes on Laurel Landry again, but Mrs. Moak walked off and left me with her.

The woman I hardly recognized didn't smile but said, "Could we talk for a minute?" She gestured toward my room. "Someplace quiet. Away from all these people."

I glanced back at the dolls I had thrown to the floor the day before. The jewelry box Gerry had given me lay open at the foot of my bed, the ballerina frozen in a perpetual pirouette. Its contents—the holy card Sister Veronica had given me, the blessed jump rope, the shriveled clove-studded orange in its tatted cradle, and the makeup Orlando had given me—were piled in a heap beside it.

I stepped out of my room and closed the door behind me. "Let's go outside," I said.

It was warm on the porch. We were in that part of the day when the morning was crossing over into afternoon. There were more shadows than sunlight shifting on the warm boards. Laurel and I sat side by side in the big white wooden rockers, our elbows resting on their wide, flat arms. I leaned my head against the back of the chair and closed my eyes. Like my father and mother, I, too, would die. Laurel would die also. One day this porch would never see us again.

"I didn't mean to intrude on your privacy," Laurel said.

I raised my head and looked at her. I had to turn my head slightly to see her face because our chairs were so close together.

"Back there," she said. "In the house." Laurel lifted her left hand from the arm of the chair. Her fingers curved back toward the front door. It was such a beautiful movement that I looked away, unwilling to grant her even that much grace. "I thought it would be nice to talk in your room because I was so happy there."

My astonishment must have shown because Laurel said, "When we played that game you made up. The one where you put that sticky green florist's clay on the Popsicle sticks and we turned over little oranges made out of cardboard to get points. You called it 'Fruit in the Trees.' You had gone to so much trouble. I never forgot that game. I don't think I've ever been happier—before or since. We all sat in a circle on the floor in your room; your mother brought us hot gingerbread and glasses of milk. It was an idyllic time for me. I was so unhappy at home..." This time Laurel's hand went up and out in the direction of her childhood house across the street. "I was scared there all the time. Afraid my mother would hurt herself. Or me. My father and I never knew what she would do next. You know. You saw her."

Yes, I thought, I saw her.

"I used to wake up on the days we were going to play that game in your room and read a book before breakfast, just like you said you did. A child's book, granted. But it wasn't the book, it was the reading of it. I wanted to be like you. I was so envious of Mary."

"Envious of Mary!" I said. "Why would anyone ever be envious of Mary?"

"Because you were her sister," Laurel said. "I wanted you to be my sister."

And I wanted you to be my sister instead of Mary, I thought but did not say aloud. "And then I ruined it all," I said.

"It wasn't your fault," Laurel said. "It was mine. My and my father's fault. He should never have told my mother those things about your sister where I could overhear them. It was the day she hurt me so. I knew he was trying to make her feel better."

Laurel and I looked across the street at the house that had briefly been her childhood home; the house my father had bought and then sold. It looked beautiful and serene in its coat of pale purple. Beneath the new glassed-in porch, someone who loved gardening had planted banks of wine-colored chrysanthemums. There was not the slightest hint that anyone had ever been unhappy or frightened in that house.

"A child's logic makes no sense," Laurel continued. "I believe I felt that if I could discredit Mary in your eyes, you would want a new sister to replace her. A different sister. Me. I'll never forget your face when we had that quarrel under the ligustrums. Instead of opening your arms to me, you closed them against me. I had made a dreadful miscalculation. When I lost your friendship, my life at home with my mother was lonelier than ever."

It was just as I had suspected long ago—that by withdrawing my friendship from Laurel, I had damaged her.

"But then," Laurel continued with a little laugh, "I was only five years old. That's no excuse for what I did later, but I find it hard to get too upset with that child who believed she could magically trade places with another."

"It wasn't just you," I said. "I used to imagine that Mary got kidnapped. And then you would be my sister. I wasn't five years old when I imagined that. I was close to eleven."

Laurel looked at me with the clear, head-on gaze I had always found so appealing. "My life was never the same after we quarreled," she said. "I was such a little beast. It was as if I had set myself this role to play—obnoxious brat—and I couldn't break out of it. I just kept going and going down that terrible path."

We rocked awhile.

"There was no prowler in our backyard," Laurel said finally. "My father said my mother saw a prowler because she had put a knife to my face and threatened to cut me and the only thing he could think to do to stop her was to call the police. He thought the embarrassment of it would make her stop. But it didn't. She did it again, and he had to tell that lie twice."

I said nothing.

"I always felt it was my fault that you shot that man. I've regretted what happened at that Christmas party—running out of your house with Mary's present in my hand—every day of my life," Laurel said.

"So have I," I said.

We were both silent for a long time.

"But the most terrible thing," Laurel continued, "was what happened to Mary the day we graduated from Holy Angels."

Laurel didn't look at me now. She turned her head to gaze down Oleander toward the corner. "For years, I've looked for you to tell you how sorry I was about what happened to Mary that day."

The silence was not a comfortable one. "Did you ever get married?" I asked, not because I really cared but because I didn't trust myself to say anything else to this woman.

"Twice. I've made the same mistake twice," Laurel said. "I was a terrible failure as a wife. I live alone now."

"Do you have children?" I said.

"Two girls. Both grown. We don't get along too well, but that's no big surprise. I wanted sons. One of my daughters looks just like my mother."

"She must be a pretty girl," I said. "Your mother was a beautiful woman."

"She was a sick woman," Laurel said. She put her left hand over her eyes. I thought she was going to cry, but she merely said softly, "She murdered my father. He loved her so much. We both loved her so much. She could be so sweet. She was so much fun to be around when she wasn't sick. But after my grandfather died, she was sick all the time. She covered all of the clocks with black cloth. She said it was to stop time." Laurel gave a half-laugh that turned into a sob. "As if that would bring him back. That's why we left New Orleans. My father thought she would do better in a different environment. She didn't. She just got worse and worse."

"I'm sorry," I said.

"What about you," Laurel said. "Married? Children?"

"Married once, but not for long. I never had any children," I said.

"Sad lives," Laurel said. "And all because of things that happened before we were even born." She took a handkerchief from her purse and wiped her eyes.

We stood up. For the first time, I noticed that all of Laurel's motions were made with her left hand. She kept her right arm close to her side. We looked at each other without smiling. Nor did we embrace.

Laurel looked directly at me again. "I know this is no excuse," she said. "But when you closed me out, I just wanted to hurt you and your sister any way I could. Silly, isn't it? To say a five-year-old was capable of so much feeling?"

"Not so silly," I said.

"I'm so sorry about that birthday party—the one with the pony."

I was surprised when I realized it still hurt to remember that day. I shrugged. "It was a long time ago."

"Well, I've got to go. I'm sorry about your dad," Laurel said and went down the steps.

She walked along the sidewalk and crossed the street to her car. From the porch I watched her go, just as I had watched her arrive so many years ago. Ghost children surrounded me: I was reading "Evangeline" aloud to Adam, Gracie, Frankie, and Adrienne; Mary lurked at the side of the house with a fistful of sand. I turned my back on the past and went inside.

Almost everyone was gone. Mary was lying on the bed in her room, surrounded by stuffed animals and dolls. I went into the kitchen to help Mrs. Moak and Mrs. Fish clean up. Sandra, Jim Singleton, and Jim's wife were discussing Jim's wish to own a motorcycle: Jim's wife was against it; Sandra, of course, all for it. I dumped a stack of used paper plates into a plastic garbage bag Mrs. Moak had put next to the door. Then, after Mrs. Fish washed it and handed it to me, I dried the crystal punch bowl and put it away.

Finally, there was nothing left to do. I thanked my father's friends for everything they had done for us, and they left. Jim and his wife went home. Sandra hung around the front door until I promised that I would call her and we would get together for lunch. The house was empty. The sun had gone behind a cloud, and it seemed that with everyone who cared about my sister and me gone, all of the light had been sucked out of the rooms.

I went to Mary's door. "It's time to go," I said. "I'll be waiting for you on the porch."

I locked the back door, and as I went through the kitchen door, I met Mary coming from her room loaded down with old dolls and stuffed animals. "I want to take these back with me."

"Fine," I said. "You want a plastic bag?"

"No, I want to carry them," she said.

I held the doll she had named Mud Pie, a doll that was severely ragged, and a stuffed monkey while Mary arranged herself in the front seat of the car with the other creatures.

As we drove back the way we had come two days earlier, Mary said, "I want to take Aura Lee a present. And Rhonda. And Leonard."

"Good idea," I said. "We'll stop somewhere before we get back to . . ." I stopped because I did not know what to call the place where Mary lived.

"That terrible place," Mary said. "That terrible place I hate."

"I'm sorry," I said. "I know you hate it. But I'll come and get you and we can go some places."

"Go see some things," Mary said.

"Yes," I said. "Go see some things."

"And Johnella," Mary said. "I want to take Johnella something."

"What do you want to get for Johnella?" I said.

"Some bubble bath," Mary said.

"And Aura Lee and Rhonda?" I said.

"I want to get a doll for Rhonda. And a lock for Aura Lee's box," Mary said.

We came to the bridge that crossed the Amite River, and Mary leaned forward to look down the winding stream where we had gone with Orlando for our picnic. She looked but said nothing.

When we got to the shopping center that contained the Jumping Jack's where we had gotten our lunch and the King Dollar from which we had been banned, I slammed on the brakes and made a quick right-hand turn into the parking lot, a turn that threw Mary against the door. "We're going back in that store," I said and screeched to a halt in a slot right outside the front entrance.

Mary looked alarmed. "He said never come back," she said.

"I don't give a damn what he said. Some insignificant watchman can't tell us what we can and can't do. We're not going to let some common person boss us around," I said. I opened the car door, snatched up my purse, and said, "Come on."

I sounded braver than I felt. I kept a close eye out for the ill-tempered security guard as I dragged Mary along behind me.

"First we've got to get us a cart. Then we'll go find Johnella some bubble bath."

We had a good time. We picked out a giant plastic bottle of lily-of-the-valley foaming bath gel for Johnella. We got a lock and a key for Aura Lee's box, two big bags of M&M's—one for Leonard and one for Mary—and, for Rhonda, a large rag doll that looked remarkably like Mud Pie. We didn't even see the security guard who patrolled King Dollar until it was time to check out. And then there he was. Over by housewares and small appliances.

"Come on, Mary. Let's pay for these things and get out of here."

I pulled Mary along by the sleeve until I found an express checkout line, fifteen items or less. We had been rung up. I had my money out to pay. We were fine.

Then two things happened at once: Mary broke away from me, saying, "Wait a minute, I want to get some malted-milk balls." And the cash register locked.

I cried, "Mary, come back!"

We would have been gone without that man ever knowing we had been there if the cashier hadn't had to get on the loudspeaker and call, "Supervisor to the register, please. Supervisor to register seven-teen."

The security guard looked toward register seventeen from his out-post in housewares and saw Mary making for the mountain of malted-milk balls that marked the entrance to candy.

I threw down three twenty-dollar bills. "Don't worry about the change," I said. I snatched up a plastic bag and into it I stuffed the foaming bath gel, the lock and key, the candy, and the doll. Then I ran after Mary.

"But you need a receipt," the cashier called after me. I could see Mary turning the corner into ladies' apparel with a milk carton that I knew was filled with malted-milk balls. The next time I saw her, she was heading for the entrance to the store with a large Bible under her arm and a blue blouse with a large plastic antitheft device dangling from it.

I was running now. I cast a glance over my shoulder. The security guard was walking our way at a speedy clip. Mary stopped long enough to rip open the carton of candy and stuff a few pieces into her mouth before she went out the front door.

Every alarm in the store went off.

I transferred the bag of presents from my right hand to my left and ran for the door. The guard was gaining on me. "That alarm gets the police!" he hollered.

He had farther to go than we did. I caught up with Mary outside, grabbed her by the arm, and said, "Run!"

We lit out with the Bible and the blouse and the malted-milk balls flying everywhere. We jumped in the car and I backed all the way to the road so the security guard couldn't get the license number. The last we saw of him, he was standing in front of Jumping Jack's waving his gun.

"Got any more of that candy?" I said.

Mary rattled the carton and held it out to me. I took a handful. She reached in for some, too, and leaned forward to punch on the radio. Out poured "H.M.S. *Pinafore*." We sang along with the radio as we flew down the road:

> *"When I was a lad I served a term*
> *As office boy to an attorney's firm.*
> *I cleaned the windows and I swept the floor;*
> *And I polished up the handle of the big front door."*

Mary pointed to me and I sang:

> *"He polished up the handle of the big front door."*

I pointed to her and she sang:

> *"I polished up that handle so care-ful-lee*
> *That now I am the ruler of the Queen's Navee."*

And then we sang together:

> *"We polished up that handle so care-ful-lee*
> *That now we are the rulers of the Queen's Nav-ee."*

We sang all the way back to that terrible place.

At the home, Aura Lee was waiting for us in the room dressed as a nun. She stood next to her open box. Everything it had contained now adorned her. The sheet, wrapped about her head and body, was secured with the piece of rope, from which the rosary hung. When we came in, Aura Lee smiled serenely and held out her hand to show us the dried rind of the orange. "Hail Mary, full of grace, the Lord is with you," she said.

Mary went to the metal table by her bed and put her black purse in the drawer. She stood by the bed with her back to me. The television was dark, the hot-pink letters of the alphabet carrying black top hats and canes gone from the stage, the blue numbers with the yellow hands and feet no longer an audience.

I stood in the doorway. I thought of all the things Mary would never have: a husband, children, a secure home. Through no fault of her own, Mary was going to be a prisoner forever. There was nothing I could do. I put the presents we had brought on the bed, walked past Aura Lee, and embraced my sister's back. Mary stood stiffly and endured it. I dropped my arms. I stood next to my sister, resigned. Mary turned and looked at me sadly, but without reproach.

Aura Lee was close behind me when I walked out past the comatose man in the crib and the patients who sat in the lobby. The man who had called me Mama did so again, and the young man again asked me for a Coke. The woman who was bound to the chair motioned once more for me to come over, and pointed to her bonds. I waved good-bye to them, went out the front door, and, on the veranda, smiled at Leonard, the black man with no arms and no legs, and at Rhonda, the harelipped girl with the flat head. "Mary brought you some presents," I said. This time they smiled back.

With Aura Lee on my heels, I walked quickly past the persimmon tree. I unlocked my car and opened the door. Before I could get to safety, Aura Lee came to my side and stood so close to me I could taste her sour breath.

"Tell me everything while you still can," she said. "I will plead for you."

I took hold of the open car door for support and closed my eyes. I stood next to Aura Lee and lost my place in time. I could have been at the beginning of my life; I could have been at its end.

Aura Lee put her hand on my shoulder.

Finally, I bent my head to her ear. "Bless me," I whispered. I choked on the word "Father" and stopped.

"When was your last confession?" Aura Lee said.

"October 4, 1954," I said.

"Who was your confessor?"

"Father Michael."

"Tell him," Aura Lee said. "Through me."

Thinking, I can't do this, even as I did it, I said, "I committed a mortal sin, and I've never made my confession."

"Tell me what you did," Aura Lee said.

"I shot someone. I killed a man," I whispered.

"Go on," Aura Lee said.

"I wasted my life. I never had children. I let my mother die alone. I abandoned my father." I let go of the car door, leaned forward, and rested my forehead on Aura Lee's shoulder. Her yeasty smell overwhelmed me. Tears ran down my cheeks. "And I closed my heart to my sister."

Aura Lee raised the hand that held the dried orange peel. "Look at me," she said. "Say you're sorry."

I raised my head and looked right into her kind eyes. "For these and all the sins of my past life, I am truly sorry," I said to that foul-smelling old woman wrapped in her white sheet.

"In the name of the Father, and of the Son, and of the Holy Ghost," she said, and laying the desiccated fruit first to my forehead and then to my lips, Aura Lee absolved me.